May 26-1913

H Emerson M. Whitten

Isl.

D0553723

San Antonio

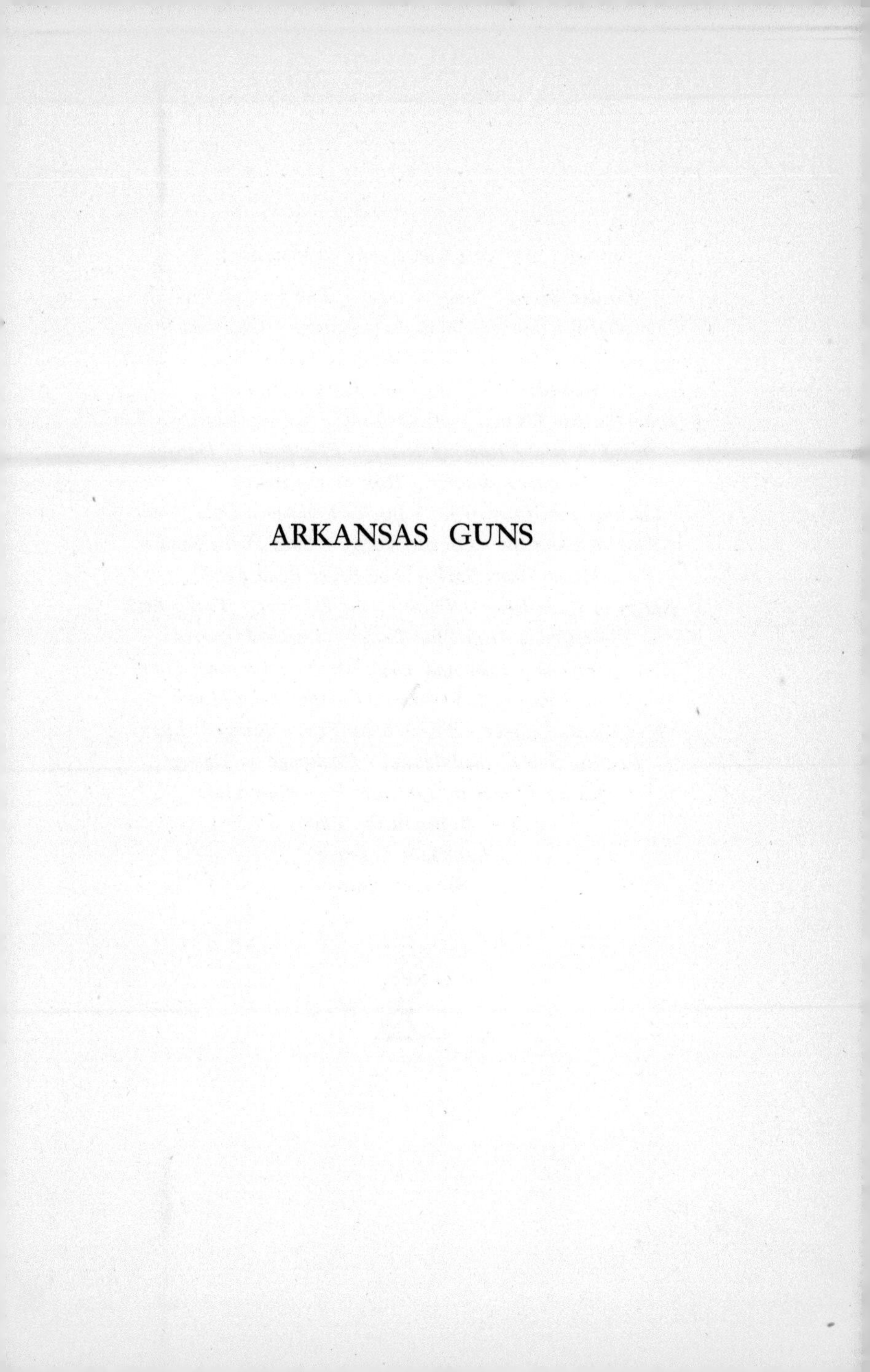

ARKANSAS GUNS

BOOKS BY WILLIAM MACLEOD RAINE

Border Breed · *Steve Yeager* · *The Yukon Trail*
The Sheriff's Son · *A Man Four-Square* · *Oh, You Tex!*
The Big-Town Round-Up · *Gunsight Pass* · *Tangled Trails*
Man-Size · *The Fighting Edge* · *Ironheart*
Beyond the Rio Grande · *Black Tolts* · *Under Northern Stars*
Broad Arrow · *Roaring River* · *The Trail of Danger*
Square Shooter · *Run of the Brush*
To Ride the River With · *Bucky Follows a Cold Trail*
King of the Bush · *On the Dodge* · *Sons of the Saddle*
Moran Beats Back · *The River Bend Feud*
Riders of Buck River · *Guns of the Frontier* · *Trail's End*
They Called Him Blue Blazes · *Justice Deferred*
The Damyank · *Hell and High Water* · *Courage Stout*
Who Wants to Live Forever? · *Clattering Hoofs*
This Nettle Danger · *The Bandit Trail* · *Ranger's Luck*
Jingling Spurs · *Saddlebum* · *Challenge to Danger*
Justice Comes to Tomahawk · *Glory Hole*
Dry Bones in the Valley
Reluctant Gunman
Arkansas Guns

WILLIAM MacLEOD RAINE

ARKANSAS GUNS

HOUGHTON MIFFLIN COMPANY BOSTON
19 The Riverside Press Cambridge 54

Library of Congress catalogue card number: 54-5696

Published in England as *Plantation Guns*

The Riverside Press
CAMBRIDGE • MASSACHUSETTS
PRINTED IN THE U.S.A.

To Charles Brackin,
my college classmate and friend for sixty years,
who lived in the mining camps of
Mexico and Arizona when
they were wild and rugged

ARKANSAS GUNS

1

A TALL RANGY MAN strode forward to meet Larry Harville as he stepped down from the train. The traveler was not instantly sure whether this was Andy or Tom. They were very much alike, and there was only a year's difference in their ages. He decided correctly that it was Andy.

The handshake of Andy was strong, his smile warm for the young fellow returning at last. Despite the difference in years and temperament, the tie between Larry and his half-brothers was close.

From the baggage car a trunk was being dropped to the platform of the depot. This the two Harvilles carried to a wagon behind the station, after they had tossed into the bed of the vehicle Larry's bags.

"Father and Tom all right?" the younger brother asked when he had taken the seat beside the driver.

"Tom is fine. Father is kinda laid up right now. That's why he didn't meet you himself."

"Is he very ill?" Larry asked.

"No, he's doing fine. Be up in a few days. Fact is, he got shot."

"Fooling with an unloaded gun," Larry suggested.

"No-o, the gun was loaded all right." Andy added, after a moment: "That blamed old feud between us and the Logans has broke loose again."

"Good heavens!" Larry cried. "One of the Logans shot Father?"

"The old major." There was a touch of pride in Andy's drawling answer. "But he's got nothing to brag about. It was even-steven. Father plugged him in the arm."

Larry understood now the reason why a Winchester rifle lay across the bed of the wagon at his brother's feet. He had assumed that Andy had brought it on the chance of jumping up game. This news was disturbing. His brothers and the sons of Logan, all of them hotheaded young men, would take up the quarrel. Almost certainly there would be more blood shed. The thought of it sickened him.

"What started the trouble?" he inquired.

"It was a fuss over the election. They were supporting different men for the county ticket. Our side won. Logan said something implying there had been fraud, and the remark was carried to Father by some interfering fool. When father demanded a retraction Logan stood pat. So they emptied their pistols at each other on the courthouse square."

"Will it go any further?"

Andy shook his head. "Cain't say. Father has sworn me and Tom over to keep the peace. We won't start anything, but no telling what they will do. Naturally we're not taking chances."

Compared with the trim, well-kept countryside of Surrey where Larry had been living for seven years, this land was rough and unkempt. Yet it had its own charm. They drove through a landscape pleasant with the young spring. There had been warm rains and the peach trees were pink with blossoms. Farmers were in the fields plowing. Behind the rail worm-fences they could see rows of cotton stalks from last season's planting, here and there puffs of white clinging to the bolls. By the roadside were occasional Negro shanties, in front of them black pickaninnies, their fat, almost naked bodies glistening in the sun. The houses of the farmers were one-story, an open-roofed gallery bisecting the building from front to rear. At each end was a fireplace of sticks and mud. If the chimney was decrepit with age, long poles propped it up.

About the country was an air of indolence, a hint of casual ease, that prevented the raggedness and the poverty from being distressing. The Negroes lounging near the wretched cabins or working in the fields looked happy and contented. They had enough to eat, and the future did not seem to worry them.

Brandon did not pretend to be anything but what it was, a small Southern town built of wood except for a few brick stores and the bank, with some comfortable homes set behind wide porches on streets shaded by maples and magnolias. In spite of its haphazard lack of planning, its dilapidated Negro quarter, and the general indifference to paint, Larry felt his heart warm to the old town which he had known as a boy. He was coming home again after many years of exile.

Apropos of nothing that had been said, Andy gave his brother information. "The Logans are up from the plantation this week."

Larry's nerves tightened as they drew in from the suburb toward the courthouse square. "You don't think they would . . . make us trouble?" he replied, after a silence.

"You never know," Andy answered evenly. "I reckon not. Likely the major has laid the law down to them. Anyhow, they won't shoot without giving us a chance for our white alleys. The Logans play fair."

This brought Larry scant comfort. He did not want to have a difficulty with the Logan boys on any terms. He remembered how wild and daring they were in schooldays, always ready to fight at the drop of a hat. They were probably just as uncurbed now.

In England the sanctity of law protected every citizen. It was a shock to be brought up so immediately against the turbulence of this young land where men reached so quickly for a pistol to settle trouble. He had always been a timid lad, with none of the rough-and-ready courage of his brothers.

Andy drew up in front of the house where he and Larry had been born. The place had run down a bit since Larry had seen it, owing no doubt to the absence of a mistress. Since the death of Larry's mother Colonel Harville had been a widower. The three cedars near the gate were still there, and so were the jonquils that lined the path, but dog-fennel ran wild over the yard and the roses along the fence had gone.

Colonel Maxwell Harville sat propped up on a sofa, his wounded leg stretched out in front of him. He looked older and grayer than when Larry had last seen him, but it was clear that the sap of life still ran strong in him. At sight of Larry the fine kindly face that reminded his son of Robert E. Lee's pictures lit up amazingly.

"Home at last, son," he said. "Thank God for that."

Their black cook Mandy waddled in, fat and smiling. She had been with the family for nearly twenty years. "Bress de Lawd, Marse Larry," she exclaimed, and folded him in her arms.

All through the evening memories of the past filled Larry's thoughts. The comfortable parlor was a little shabbier than it had been. From the time of his mother's death none of the furniture had been changed. Her portrait was on the wall, a slender, lovely English girl with a hint of something tragic in the eyes that watched her son whenever he was in the room. There were portraits, too, of Maxwell Harville's father and grandfather, the latter in the uniform of a captain in the Revolutionary War, both growing dark from the passage of the years. The only other pictures in the room were framed prints of Jefferson Davis and General Lee. All of these were a part of Larry's background.

His father could not keep out of his eyes the happiness that glowed in him. This best-loved youngest son was home again, a slim, graceful lad who had inherited his mother's charm. Neither the colonel nor Andy would have felt comfortable in the clothes Larry was wearing. They dressed carelessly, with attention only to cleanliness. But they approved of Larry's well-cut English tweeds, his custom-made shoes and fine Irish linen shirt. Though Andy had never been out of Arkansas except for one trip to St. Louis and another to New Orleans, he felt no jealousy toward this attractive blond youth who had been educated at Harrow and had traveled in France and Italy. Nor did he hold any resentment because Larry held a special place in his father's heart. He had been a frail child, the image of his mother, and Maxwell Harville had transferred to him the love he had felt for his dead wife. The boy became a victim of malaria. Afraid that he might lose him, the colonel had taken Larry back to an uncle in England. There he had lived till now, though it had wrenched his father's soul to be separated from him.

The colonel's older sons were replicas of himself, hot-tempered, fearless, occasionally a little wild, but at bottom dependable as steel. He understood them very well, these big, dark, handsome men. But Larry was like his mother, the English girl whose heart Maxwell Harville had won, then married and brought across the ocean to live at Brandon and on the plantation. To the day of her death she had loved her forceful husband, but she could never accustom herself to the violence of this war-torn land in Reconstruction days. Chills and fever had worn her down. When Larry was nine she had quietly slipped out of life from the husband and the son who had idolized her.

2

THE COLONEL WAS WORRIED and did not like to show it. His sons were just starting downtown.

"It's awkward, me being tied to this sofa," he said irritably. "You boys be mighty careful. If you meet any of the Logans pass them without saying a word. I don't want any more trouble started."

Andy smiled. He was twenty-six, a strong, deep-chested man with broad shoulders, and he felt competent to look after himself. "We'll be careful. I hope the Logans will be too, if we meet any." He added, "Larry isn't packing a gun."

"I don't want one," Larry said hastily.

The colonel deliberated. "Maybe you are right, son, since you are not used to handling one. In case anything comes up let them know you are unarmed."

Larry hoped devoutly that nothing would come up. Though he admired and loved his father, he could not help thinking that this business of two old gentlemen blazing away at each other with revolvers was both ridiculous and outrageous. They had opened up again a dormant feud, endangering half a dozen lives in addition to their own. Of course they felt their honor was involved and held the medieval idea that they must vindicate it on the field of battle. No doubt Andy and Tom shared the view of their father and considered his action entirely justified. It was about time, Larry thought, for them to come out of the dark ages.

They walked along the main business street to the courthouse square. Very few changes had taken place in the town, though it looked much smaller to Larry than it had as a small boy.

In front of the post office they met two young women coming out of the building. They were about eighteen, both very pretty. Larry thought there was a flicker of recognition on the face of the darker one, and after it, surprisingly, a flash of scornful anger. For a moment he blocked her way. When he stepped aside she passed with no acknowledgment of his "Sorry." His gaze followed her. There was music, he thought, in her rhythmic walk.

"One of the young ladies knew me," Larry said.

Andy's smile was a little grim. "She ought to know you. Both of them ought. You used to go to parties with them when you were a kid. The one with the red hat is Diane Logan. The other is Susan Travis."

His younger brother was astonished. He remembered Diane Logan as a dark, stormy little thing with black straight hair and long thin legs. "The ugly duckling has grown up into a swan," he said.

"She's considered the prettiest girl in this part of Arkansas," replied Andy. "The way things are, Tom and I are outside of her orbit, but she certainly has the other lads stepping."

The post office was a sort of informal club for the planters on the river who lived at Brandon to be out of the malaria belt. Nearly all of them had been officers in the Confederate Army, and they spent hours around the potbellied stove, in summer and in winter, discussing the tactics of Lee, Grant, Buell, Jackson, and Bragg with as much interest as if the Civil War had ended last month instead of fifteen years before.

Larry knew most of the bearded men present. Dr. Ordway, Captain Sanderson, Major Dever — they had been familiar figures when he was a small barefoot boy. While Andy posted a letter to his brother Tom, who was on the plantation fifty miles distant, Larry listened to the talk. They were arguing about the battle of Shiloh.

"No, seh," Major Dever insisted explosively, "we had them right plumb on the riverbank. If Beauregard hadn't ordered a halt Grant's army would have been driven in or cut to pieces." He hammered a fist on the arm of his chair. "The West would have been saved, Grant discredited, and the No'th set back on its heels. Right then the war was lost."

Andy introduced his brother. They had known him as the youngest of the Harville boys, a sallow, sickly lad, and they were surprised to see his tanned vigor. He was smaller boned than the other Harvilles, but the light ease of his movements suggested perfect health. They welcomed him home with the friendly warmth of the South. His clothes made him look a bit too English, but they reckoned he would get over that.

The brothers strolled through the business section and came to the old schoolhouse they had both attended at different times. Behind it still lay the grove of second growth where old Roberts used to send the boys to cut switches with which to whip offenders. In the center of it was a small clearing where the fights were held. Sid Hobson had once licked Larry there. The defeat still shamed Larry. He had not wanted to fight and had made a poor showing.

They tried the door, found it unlocked, and walked through a small entry into the schoolroom. There was no change, except that the room seemed not so large as they had remembered it. Larry went down the aisle and sat in the seat he and Sam Landon had once shared. Memories of the years he had spent here trooped through his mind. They were in sharp contrast with the life at Harrow. He wondered if his boyhood in England had influenced him so much that he would always be more of a Briton than an American.

Andy, too, had his memories. "I saw old Roberts give Tom an awful licking once on the platform here," he said. "Tom looked him in the eye and took all the old cuss could give without a yelp. His legs were black and blue for a month."

A fat florid man with a star on his vest met them on their way back. He looked at Larry accusingly. "You don't know me," he said.

"Oh yes, I do," Larry answered. "You're Gid Jennings."

"Right," the fat man admitted, and offered a hand to shake. "You young fellows sure grow up fast. Lemme see. I reckon you are about the same age as Hal Logan. Not five minutes ago I saw him and his brother Rod in Yandell's store."

From his carefully unstressed words one could not have guessed that the important thing he had to say was contained in the last sentence. But Andy understood it as a warning. Perhaps the Logan boys had been making threats.

"Did they ask you to tell us they were in Yandell's store?" Andy inquired lightly.

The marshall hurriedly disclaimed any intent of being a messenger. "Nothing like that. I just thought — " He cut his sentence off. "Hell, it's none of my business."

"You just thought — " Andy prompted gently.

"You could take the other side of the square, couldn't you?" the marshal blurted.

"Why, Gid, you wouldn't want us to take the sunny side on a hot day like this," Andy replied.

Larry spoke to his brother in a low voice. "Why not? Father said we were to avoid trouble. And I'm not armed."

"That's right. You're not." Andy frowned, trying to work the situation out. "Tell you what, Larry. I've got to buy a set of harness to take down to the plantation. We'll go into Tucker's and see what he has."

As they walked into the store Larry saw Jennings hurrying down the street. Andy laughed.

"Gid is sure earning his salary today keeping the peace," he said. "He has gone to tell the Logans you're not toting a pistol."

"Will that make any difference?" Larry asked unhappily.

"Yes. They won't call for a showdown when they know you haven't a gun."

There were more old acquaintances in the store. Larry had to smile and say the proper pleasant things, though the undercurrent of his mind was busy with the threatening danger. Nobody made any reference to the shooting affray that had occurred between their father and Major Logan, or to further impending trouble. Yet both the young men knew this was in the thought of everybody they met. It lent a pleasant excitement to the humdrum life of the drowsy little town.

Down Larry's spine there ran a chill, as if the wet feet of mice were pattering there. Nobody would interfere to prevent a tragedy. The law would not lift a hand to restrain these young hotheads from killing one another. In spite of himself he would be dragged into the feud, even though he knew it was all silly but calamitous folly.

Larry suggested again as they turned homeward that they take the west side of the square and miss passing Yandell's store.

"We cain't run away from this," Andy said. "I went far as I could when I fooled around at Tucker's to give Gid time to see the Logans. With you not armed, I don't think they will force a fight. You're on the inside. If they start crowding us, duck into a store."

"Leaving you alone. I can't do that."

"I'll tell them first off that you haven't a pistol. But what's the use of crossing bridges we haven't reached? We may not even meet them."

Before Andy had finished speaking he saw that a meeting was unavoidable. Rod and Hal Logan came out of Yandell's with the marshal and stood in front of the store talking. They were dark, black-haired men, lighter of build than Andy, lithe and lean of loin. Hal looked about twenty, his brother two or three years older.

Hal's glance picked up the Harvilles. "Look who's here, Rod," he said, an urgent note in his voice.

Rod turned at the warning. The smile went from his face as the light of a blown candle vanishes. His jaw tightened, the muscles standing out like a rope.

Since the sidewalk was blocked, Andy had either to stop or step down into the road. He stopped.

The hard eyes in Rod's reckless face fastened on Larry. "In this country men carry guns when there is trouble afoot," he said curtly.

"Where I have been living they don't," Larry answered. He hoped his voice was firm and steady.

"When you're in Rome, better do as the Romans do."

Rod did not wait for an answer. He turned sharply and walked away, Hal by his side, back flat and shoulders carried arrogantly.

Andy said to the marshal, a sardonic grin on his face, "Well, Gid, you staved it off that time. 'Blessed are the peacemakers,' the Bible says."

Jennings did not give the young man back his smile. He replied gravely, "Rod served notice on yore brother, Andy."

Larry did not need to be told that. The weight of the threat hung over him. When his father had been told what had occurred it disturbed him too. He knew that Larry, fresh from a sheltered life, untrained in the use of a pistol, was no match for either of the Logan boys. It would be plain murder to let him face them.

"We won't wait till Friday," he decided. "We'll leave for the plantation tomorrow. You stick around the house while we're here, Larry."

The colonel was a little surprised and disappointed that Larry did not protest at this injunction. He did not want the boy to run any risk, but he wanted him to be eager to face danger. No Harville ought to be afraid of a Logan or anybody else.

3

THE HARVILLES WERE GOING by train as far as Oldport. There Tom would meet them with a wagon and they would drive to the plantation. Larry was packing his father's personal belongings in a carpetbag when Major Dever came to the house.

From the sofa where he sat the colonel greeted his old friend warmly. "Hello, Bon. We're packing to pull out for the plantation. Glad you came. You met my boy Larry yesterday, I hear."

Bonville Dever was a short, slight man, gray-bearded, with quick, restless eyes. He was notably kindly but irritable. During the war he had been a ball of fire in battle. Though he had been persuaded to try to reconcile the Logans and the Harvilles, he found no pleasure in the task. Very likely he would be told that it was none of his business.

"We are pleased that he is back and looks so well," the major said. "Too bad he came home to find this trouble afoot."

The colonel purposely misunderstood him. "I'm doing fine," he replied cheerfully. "With a walking stick I can get around nicely. I had some business here, and we wanted to meet Larry. Just a flying visit. We have to get back to Rosemont."

Dever plunged. He might as well get it over with.

"The Logans will be going back to Hillcrest in a week

or two. You won't be any safer there than here."

"I reckon we can take care of ourselves," the colonel said stiffly. "We been doing it a right smart number of years."

"We've been talking this over, Maxwell — friends of you and Logan both. It seems to us you ought to patch up this feud. Both of you are fine men — fought in the war, helped us to get out of the reconstruction muddle, worked together to drive out that murdering Labreu gang. We hate to see this trouble go on to a finish."

"Hadn't you better talk to Major Logan about this instead of to me. After insulting me he refused to give an apology. What else could I do?"

Harville spoke quietly, but his eyes were stern.

"You fought it out face to face," Dever reminded the other. "That ought to end the matter."

"It ended the active trouble far as I am concerned. I have told my boys they are not to continue the difficulty. Am I responsible if the Logan boys serve notice they mean to fight?"

Dever knew that the sons of Major Logan always had been turbulent, unrestrained lads ready for a fight at any time. He realized that Colonel Harville had not been as much to blame as Perry Logan for the duel. For that reason he had come here first, in the hope of finding him the more reasonable of the two.

"Will you authorize me to tell Logan that none on your side will start trouble if they don't?" Dever asked.

"I won't send any message whatever to Major Logan," the wounded man answered curtly. "But I can't keep you from telling him that you have talked with me and have gathered my position to be as you have just said."

This was the greatest concession Maxwell Harville would make, Dever knew. It would be enough if the family of the major were as fair.

The peacemaker explained with some embarrassment why he had let himself be appointed spokesman of his group. "Ever since I had to kill Sawyer I have been unhappy when my friends have got into trouble of this sort. I can't blame myself for what I did, yet the feeling has always been with me that it was wrong — that there ought to have been some other way out."

He had fought a duel with pistols on a Little Rock street fifteen years earlier and had left his opponent dead on the sidewalk.

"You ought not to feel unhappy about it," the colonel said. "Sawyer was a particularly vile specimen of political rat, one who made it his business to stir up race trouble. We couldn't let the scoundrel continue to poison the minds of our friendly Negroes and incite them to violence. He was warned time and again. His own insolence destroyed him when he went out of his way to insult you."

"That is true. But I still have my bad moments about it. We ought not to take the law into our own hands."

"No," the colonel agreed. There was a thin, ironic smile on his lips. "If you get the Logans to accept that principle there won't be any more guns smoking."

Major Dever turned to Larry. "That the way you feel, young man?"

"Yes, sir." Larry tried to find words to express what was

in his mind without seeming to criticize his father. "I think the whole idea of private family feuds is medieval. It ought to pass away just as formal dueling has. There might have been some justification for this before laws functioned, or when justice could not be got in the courts, as in reconstruction days, but the leading men in the community should set a better example now."

Maxwell Harville flushed. "That is fine in theory, son, but no man can accuse me of corrupt practices and escape a settlement."

Andy was not at home. He had been sent to a farm three miles from Brandon, one owned by his father, to collect some money due from a renter. He was riding a young and skittish horse, but since he had a firm, sure seat in the saddle this did not trouble him. It was about eleven by the courthouse clock when he reached the square on his return.

At the post office he dismounted to pick up the mail and to leave the forwarding address. Under the pleasant spring sun the town seemed sleepy as an old man nodding in a rocking chair. There was no sign of life except a flop-eared hound stretched on the sidewalk industriously searching for fleas on its anatomy.

The town was still somnolent when he came out of the post office stuffing the mail into his pocket. Either satisfied or discouraged, the dog had given up the flea hunt and was sound asleep. A barefoot black boy had come round the corner carrying a paper sack of something he just bought at a store. As he approached, the boy showed white teeth in a wide grin and said, "Howdy, Marse Andy?"

The boy's father had been a slave of Colonel Harville

before the war. Andy gave the youngster his full name as he pulled himself to the saddle. "How are you, George Washington Daniel Clay?"

A moment later he had forgotten that the lad existed. Along the north side of the square a rider was coming. The horsemen would meet at the intersection. Andy paid no attention to anything except the erect, slim figure of Hal Logan, but out of the corner of an eye he saw Marshal Jennings come waddling out of a store and waving a newspaper at him. Gid shouted some words he did not take the trouble to hear. He had more important business on hand.

Hal flung a taunt at Harville. Already a revolver had jumped to his hand. "Don't tell me you're unarmed too," he cried.

The street that had been quiet a minute before was full of activity. The colored boy started to run and dropped his load. A cascade of sugar boiled over the sidewalk from the broken sack. The county clerk, leaning out of a courthouse window, yelled a warning to a man crossing the dusty road behind Andy. The man glanced hurriedly at one rider and the other, gulped frantically "Goddlemighty!" and bolted for the nearest store entrance.

Andy drew a revolver from the holster under his left arm. A bullet whizzed past his ear. His .45 roared an answer. The young bay he was riding flung up its head nervously and did an excited dance. Logan's horse also was restless. His second shot missed by four feet.

The sleeping dog awoke and dashed across the road, barking furiously, almost under the hoofs of Hal's mount. The horse went into the air, came down, and tried to bolt.

Its rider dragged in the animal's head and fired again. He rowelled the flanks of the gelding to drive it closer, and the horse gave a scream of terror and bucked.

Andy's bay was not still for an instant. The slugs from Harville's gun flew wild as those of his foe. The firing could not have lasted more than ten seconds, though the time seemed much longer to those watching from store windows and doors.

The hammer of Logan's gun fell without an explosion. His revolver was empty.

"See you later," he shouted to his enemy, then wheeled his horse and rode away.

Andy did not fire again. He examined his revolver and found two shells still loaded.

The marshal came to the edge of the sidewalk. "You hurt?" he asked.

"No." Andy drawled an apology. "We sure wasted a heap of good ammunition."

"I ought to arrest you both," Jennings said severely.

"That's right," Andy agreed. "The way we were firing one of us certainly might have hit an innocent bystander. We'll do better next time, Gid."

He gathered the reins and rode out of the square.

Major Dever was just leaving the parlor when Andy walked into the room.

"The major is trying to patch up a peace between us and the Logans," the colonel explained.

"Seems hardly necessary," Andy said. "Hal and I have just emptied our revolvers at each other. No damage to either of us."

"What!" his father demanded. "You're not joshing?"

"No, sir. We were both on horseback and our mounts went crazy. Nobody on the street was safe except Hal and me."

"Who started it?" the colonel asked.

"Hal had his gun out first. He didn't cut loose till mine was drawn."

"Where did it happen?" Larry asked. "Tell us all about it."

Andy told them what had occurred, not even forgetting the sack of sugar that had exploded all over the sidewalk.

Maxwell Harville turned to the major, anger in his face. "What have you got to say to that, Dever? Do you still think we can get anywhere with peace talk to the Logans."

"I think it is more necessary than ever now," Bonville Dever said. "Neither you nor Logan want yore sons killed. They escaped this time. If they meet again somebody will be killed."

"The major is right, Father," Larry said.

"You can't talk those Logans into sense," Maxwell Harville objected, slamming his fist down on the back of the sofa. "What they want is trouble."

"I can try," the major insisted.

"All right, Bon. Try. But make it clear I'm not sending you."

The Harvilles left for Rosemont before Major Dever reported the result of his attempt to make peace, but a letter followed them there a day or two later. It did not carry any promise from Perry Logan, but there was at least a hint of co-operation. He said he would try to keep his sons from looking for the Harvilles. If the colonel did not do as much he might expect trouble.

Since the plantations of Rosemont and Hillcrest were scarcely more than two miles apart it was inevitable that the young men must sometimes meet. The peace prospects did not look bright to Larry.

4

THE COUNTRY AROUND Rosemont and Hillcrest was very different from that which surrounded the town of Brandon. Except for the owners of the large plantations along the river bottom the inhabitants were for the most part poor whites and Negroes. It was a district of chills and fever. The dwellers in the small shacks dotted here and there showed in their sallow faces the effect of long years of malaria. In some of the two-room log cabins families of ten or twelve lived. Lank boys helped provide food for the hungry broods by hooking catfish on trotlines and shooting squirrels in the woods. Fields of poorly tended corn supplied meal for corn bread. Larry wondered how the indolent settlers found the money to buy the few store goods they needed — Arbuckle's coffee, a little flour, some clothes, quinine, snuff, and tobacco.

At Rosemont the house overlooked the plantation from a sycamore-shaded knoll some hundred yards back from the bayou. A porch ran along the front of it, and the building was bisected by an open-roofed hall extending from front to rear. This was called a gallery, and it was a catch-all for whatever any member of the family chanced to drop on his way inside. Saddles and spurs hung from wooden pegs driven into the walls. An axe, a broken bridle, and a boot jack had been swept to one side on top of a gunny sack. A cross-cut saw was propped against a buggy cushion. Mandy claimed the back part of the corridor as her domain. Strings of pepper were suspended from the ceiling. Between a barrel of flour and a large barrel of cider lay half a sack of potatoes.

Since Colonel Harville had become a widower the place had run down. Though Larry's mother had lived here only a few months in each year, the rest of the time being spent at Brandon, there had been a flower garden, vines on a trellis shading the porch, and a well-kept appearance about Rosemont quite missing now. The death of Maxwell's young second wife had been a blow from which he had never quite recovered. It might have been better for him to marry again, but he could not bring himself to put another woman in the place of Larry's mother.

The colonel sat on the porch in a big armchair, his wounded leg resting on the cane bottom of another chair. He looked around, not very well satisfied with what he saw. "I reckon, son, you remember how things looked when your mother was with us," he said to Larry. "There were ramblers and honeysuckle shading the porch. You couldn't see that fence for roses. And back of the house was an old-fashioned garden filled with colorful flowers. I've been mighty slack, looks like."

"Let me try my hand at fixing things up." Larry suggested. "You and the boys are busy, but I'm like a fifth wheel here. Some carpenter work and some paint would help the house a lot. It is too late to plant flowers now, but in the fall and next spring I could put in some perennials and a nice rose garden, if I'm still around."

"That's fine, boy." The colonel waved a hand to include house and garden. "I give you *carte blanche*. Make any improvements you like. It would be nice if you could get the garden to looking the way it used to in your mother's time."

Word came to them a few days later that the Logans were back at Hillcrest. At the nearest village, Big Hollow, Larry ran into Rodney at the store. He was buying some tenpenny nails and looked up to see young Logan swing into the building. Larry's stomach muscles tightened. It seemed to him that his heart held time suspended while the other man moved toward him. The dark eyes in Rodney's handsome face clung fast to his. They were cold and stern as those of a hanging judge.

Young Logan did not stop. He passed Larry as if he had not been there. The breath went out of Larry's body in a deep sigh of relief. At least for the moment the Logans had decided to suspend open hostilities. Larry paid for his purchase and got out of the store as fast as he could with dignity. Five minutes later he was on horseback headed for home.

At Rosemont the family discussed the incident, not at all sure how to interpret it. There might be a cessation of active warfare that applied only to Larry and not to his brothers. Even if the major had put his sons under a moral bond to keep the peace, the Harvilles knew that the least spark might start an explosion.

"Would it do any good for me to go over and have a talk with Major Logan?" Larry asked hesitantly. "I could explain to him that we are not for war but peace."

The color rose in the colonel's face. "We'll explain nothing to him," he exploded. "I'll make no more concessions to the stiff-backed old fire-eater. If he starts crowding us we'll crowd back."

Maxwell Harville was a little disturbed about Larry. It was right to want peace, but a man must not be afraid of war. As a small boy Larry had been timid, perhaps because of his physical frailty. He had outgrown his ill health, but he might not have escaped from the fears his imagination had conjured up when he was a child. The colonel did not for a moment harbor the thought that his son was a coward. No Harville could be that. But he might have lived too long in a land where a man did not need to have a fighting edge, one where law protected him at every turn. The father comforted himself with the knowledge that the alien half of Larry was English. No race hedged itself about with law so tightly, and none was braver when the call came to fight.

With his father's approval, Larry busied himself building a wing on the south end of the house. He brought two carpenters from Oldport and selected lumber at the nearest mill. Fortunately there was plenty of fine-grained white oak to be had cheap. Since the Negroes he employed for the rough work could be had for a dollar a day the job would not be too expensive. Larry had studied to be an architect, and had already spent a year in a London office. This was a good chance to pick up some knowledge of construction by actual practice. When he set up an office there would probably be a lean year or two but an English uncle had died recently and left him five thousand pounds.

Even though the heat of summer was not yet fully on them, the workmen liked to take it easy during the middle of the day. This suited Larry. He could be very energetic at times, but there was in him a streak of indolence. It was difficult to be hard on the shiftless black boys, who sometimes failed to show up but always had a plausible excuse next morning.

His father laughed at Larry's gentle, courteous treatment of them. "Call 'em lazy, black, good-for-nothing rascals," he advised. "They will think more of you if you do, and for heaven's sake don't make the mistake of ever calling one of them mister."

The colonel and his two older sons, Larry observed, knew how to handle these dependents much better than he did, at least as far as tangible results went. They praised, blamed, gave orders as if the help had the mentality of ten-year olds. There was still a touch of the feudal in the relationship between the Rosemont owners and employees. The tenants, men and women alike, brought their troubles to the colonel in sickness and in health. He was adviser, judge, and bank upon which they could draw if they made their cases good. Larry heard one big black field hand tell another, with a white-toothed grin: "The colonel sho' did gimme a cussin out for foolin' around with Jim's

Mandy. I got to lay off or git the stuffin' whanged outa me." What Maxwell Harville said was final. None of them seemed to resent his decisions. At times he was stern, but he was always just. The colonel was Authority, and their reliance on it was childlike. Before the Civil War there had been no need to make decisions for themselves. Few of them had escaped from the inability to rule their own lives.

5

WHILE LARRY WAS AT WORK supervising the building of the new wing and the painting of the house, he wore cheap jean trousers bought at the Big Hollow store and an old slouch hat discarded by his father. But before supper he always bathed and dressed in his English tweeds. Since his brothers had by this time established a casual give-and-take relationship with him, they sometimes teased him about his clothes nicety. They called him the belted earl. Larry took this good-naturedly, in the spirit it was meant, but he did not give up the habit. In a wrinkled suit and dusty boots he did not feel comfortable during the leisurely evening hours.

Until the job on the house was done Larry stuck pretty close to home, but as soon as this was off his hands he took time to ramble through the woods and hunt. He had never shot a revolver in his life, but he was a good marksman with a rifle. If he did not get any game he did not mind. It was a pleasure to stroll through the woods, which just now were brilliant with sun-splashed color. The white dogwood blossoms, the vivid young green of the gum trees' foliage, the lily pads in the marshes, and the glossy magnolia leaves, satisfied a sense of beauty in him and rested his soul.

One afternoon he walked through the big south cotton field and climbed over the stake-and-rider rail fence to reach the hickory slash beyond. He passed hogs rooting in the soft soil below the trees and knew they belonged to his father by the crop and underbit in their ears. From the hickory belt he emerged into more open country with a variety of vegetation. It was a colorful stretch, with yellow sassafras blossoms and scarlet buckeye bells aloft and clumps of flowering vines running along the ground. Occasionally he had to fight off mosquitoes, but he was used to the buzzing pests by this time. As a partial protection he smoked a pipe.

The country grew more brushy. Because he had a horror of rattlesnakes, he moved through the bushes slowly and carefully. He was just about to emerge from a clump of hackberries when he heard voices. The words he could not distinguish, but he knew that a man and a woman were speaking. There was a burst of laughter, gay and vibrant. He guessed the woman was young, probably still a girl.

Through the foliage he saw them come out of the brush, first the girl and then the man, Diane Logan and her brother Hal. She was wearing a dress of dark blue corduroy and carrying a straw hat in her hand. Her lovely young face was sparkling with life. Evidently Hal was ready for game, if not hunting. He had a rifle.

They started across the open toward the bushes on the other side of it. The girl looked back at her brother, to tease him.

"We're in Harville country," she called to him. "Aren't you scared?"

"Unfenced land is anybody's country," he answered, then flung back her taunt with a grin. "I'd be plumb worried if I didn't have you to protect me."

She said, a note of seriousness in the words, "You wouldn't need either me or a rifle, if you would just all of you put away your guns and behave."

Something was stirring the underbrush in front of the girl. She stopped, uncertain what it was. "Look, Hal!" she cried.

There was a savage grunt. From the thicket a big boar burst into the open, all its bristles up, plunging straight for Diane. She let out a cry and for a moment stood petrified, exactly between her brother and the furious animal. There was no time to run. She flung herself to the ground, to give Hal a chance for a shot. He fired — and missed.

An instant later Larry's rifle roared. The boar went down. Its body plowed along the ground and came to rest within five feet of the girl.

She rose, white and shaken, the shock of the experience in her terror-filled eyes. Her bloodless lips trembled. "If — if you hadn't been so quick, Hal — " She shuddered. The sentence died unfinished.

"God!" young Logan cried, still unnerved at his sister's danger. His gaze swept to the hackberry bushes through which Larry was pushing into the open. He said to Diane in a low voice, his eyes not shifting from the other man, "I missed."

"But — "

"Harville killed the brute," he explained. He took a look at the huge dead boar. "Right spang through the head."

Larry moved forward. Now that the danger to the girl was past he felt weakness running through him. He might so easily have missed or given the boar an infuriating flesh wound. Its tusks might have ripped the life out of her.

The girl spoke the thought in her mind. "I would have been killed if — "

" — if you hadn't done just the right thing, flung yourself down to give us a shot," Larry interrupted. He was amazed at the presence of mind and courage she had shown in taking so great a risk.

"Reckon I had buck fever," Hal said, with an embarrassed laugh. "You must be a better shot than yore brother or I."

"My shot was a lucky fluke. I hadn't time to get frightened." The strain showed in the gray face and bleak eyes of Larry. He kept thinking how horrible it would have been if he had not stopped the charging fury.

It was an awkward situation for Hal, one he did not know how to meet easily. This man was the enemy of his family, yet he had just done them the greatest possible service. He had put them under an obligation they could not escape. Hal was scarcely more than a boy, and he never would be a diplomat.

He said, stiffly, "For my sister and for all of us I thank you, sir."

The sickness of fear still filled Larry's mind. Just now the feud meant nothing to him. This fine, light-stepping girl had escaped so narrowly mutilation and perhaps death.

He said, unsteadily, "Thank God I was here to help."

Diane was recovering from the fright faster than Larry. She told him, her dark eyes fixed on his, "Maybe He sent you here. I shall always think so."

Disconcerted by the plight in which he found himself and unsure of where it was going to lead him, Hal took refuge in an escape to commonplace reality. He looked at the boar's ears and mentioned that it belonged to his father.

"The males get right wild sometimes," he commented. "I saw a big one charge Rod once. He sure lit out sudden for his horse."

"I didn't know they were dangerous," Larry said.

"Usually they're not." Hal turned to his sister. "I reckon we'd better be moving along. They say, all's well that ends well, like this did, thanks to Mr. Harville."

Diane looked at Larry for a long moment before she said in a low, husky voice, "I'll never forget."

She followed her brother into the brush.

6

LARRY TOLD THE ASSEMBLED FAMILY at supper the story of the afternoon's adventure. After several questions had been asked and answered Colonel Harville summed up dryly.

"Well, son, looks like you put a crimp in the Logan-Harville feud with one lucky shot. I don't reckon Perry will be very happy about one of us saving his daughter, but there isn't a thing he can do to change the fact that your quickness stopped that wild hawg's charge. He won't feel any more friendly to us, but none of them will go gunning for any of us now. We'll let them alone too. You did a good day's work. I don't like the Logans or any of their ways, but I'm pleased that this rarin' around the country shooting at neighbors will probably stop. We don't have to be friends with them, just act like we don't know them."

"I'm not sure Rod and Hal will see it that way," Tom differed. He was a tall dark man, with quick, cool eyes set in a face of strong bony structure. "They may 'low this lets Larry out of the feud, but not us."

"You'll find I'm right," his father replied. "The Logans have a strong sense of family obligation. They like to pay their debts in full. They won't annoy us any more — unless they get to drinking. If you meet them when they are that way, try to sidestep them."

The colonel was right. Larry received a stiff note of thanks from Major Logan. In it was no overture of friendship, but it was not hard to read between the lines that active hostilities would be abandoned, at least until some other occasion of quarrel arose.

Larry was tremendously relieved. He had not realized till now how much the feud had got him down, what a weight of worry he had carried ever since he had got home. It was pleasant to know that he was responsible for the changed condition. Though he could claim no merit in what he had done, none the less he could not think of it without a warm glow in his breast. There was a tie between him and Diane nothing could break. She knew it as well as he did. When she told him she would never forget, a message had flashed between them. It was not love. It was not even understanding. They did not know each other. It was a searching and a hope. Very likely they would never even be friends, but the memory of that moment would not pass away.

Larry saw Diane again next Sunday at church. The four Harvilles drove there in a surrey. It was the only church for whites in the neighborhood, a small one made of logs, Presbyterian in denomination. The minister was a white-bearded old gentleman who had been a chaplain in the Confederate army during the war. He preached long doctrinal sermons in the pulpit, and outside of it was a lively chipper little man full of reminiscences and anecdotes.

As the Harvilles filed into their pew Larry saw out of the tail of his eyes that Major Logan and his wife were already occupying the one opposite. Diane was seated at the organ on the right-hand side of the pulpit. Rod and Hal were not present. They did not often attend church.

The building was plain, almost primitive. It was plastered inside and lit by chandeliers suspended from the ceiling as well as light from the windows. The pulpit and the plain wooden pews had been shipped down the river from St. Louis to Memphis and freighted by mule teams across country a few years before the Civil War. The cost of building, equipping, and maintaining the church had been borne largely by the fathers of Perry Logan and Maxwell Harville. They were the principal planters in the Cache country. As young men they had been friends, but had become estranged before the present heads of the families were of school age. Both the Logans and the Harvilles had always been members and had attended regularly even when the feud was at its height.

The Reverend Jasper Campbell arose, stroked his long full beard, and announced that they would sing Number 83. He read the first two lines of the hymn aloud.

> "*Ring the bells of heaven! There is joy today*
> *For a soul returning from the wild!*"

The organ's volume rolled through the small building and the congregation rose to sing. It came in particularly strong on the chorus.

> "*Glory! Glory! how the angels sing;*
> *Glory! Glory! how the loud harps ring;*
> *'Tis the ransomed army, like a mighty sea,*
> *Pealing forth the anthem of the free!*"

Brother Campbell discussed in his sermon the doctrine of predestination. Larry paid little attention to the argument running through it, though the minister was a pulpit-thumper and occasionally brought back his wandering mind by sheer violence. His thoughts were on Diane, and so were his eyes when he felt he dared let them rest on her without attracting attention. This opportunity for a longer inspection confirmed his opinion that she was the loveliest girl he had seen. She was dark-eyed and spirited, clean of line as a young race horse. The cheek modeled by the firm jaw had the tint of a peach just beginning to find its bloom. There was a look of fineness about her. She had a clear soprano voice, and though she had not sung loudly the timbre of it had seemed to fill the church.

Even this early in summer the day was uncomfortably hot. A bluebottle buzzed at a window, trying to get out. Through the open door they could hear the humming of bees. The colonel dozed, his body propped against the end of the pew, and woke from time to time with a start, to look around indignantly as if to deny that he had been asleep.

The sermon wore to an end, and the services concluded with another hymn. Diane sang. Others sang too, but Larry heard only her voice.

> "*Just as I am, without one plea,*
> *But that Thy blood was shed for me,*
> *And that Thou bidd'st me come to Thee,*
> *O Lamb of God, I come, I come!*"

Larry thought it touching that this young girl, so innocent, so pure, her eyes lifted to God as she sang, should feel she needed any atonement. He did not know that at this moment her mind was full of the carnal reflection that this handsome youth just back from England, an enemy of her house, was the most romantic-looking man her eyes had ever seen, and that already between them a chord had been struck that vibrated in both their hearts.

She was remembering that even when as children they had been at parties together she had been very conscious of him. Her brothers had told her scornfully that he was a 'fraid-cat. He could not fight, and he was no good at baseball or marbles. In the water he was just as bad, no diver and a poor swimmer. He had been frail and sickly then. There was no evidence of ill health now. The excellent fit of his English clothes showed the graceful poise of the light figure. When he smiled at her once during the sermon she thought it charming, both shy and friendly.

As they were leaving the church they met in the aisle, and for an instant their eyes locked. Larry bowed and said good morning. She inclined her head, murmured something in acknowledgment, and followed her mother to the door. Her father's bow to Larry, meant to include no other member of the family, was stiff with embarrassment.

7

WITH THE AID OF A WALKING STICK Colonel Harville limped out to the front porch. His leg was doing nicely, though he still had, in his own words, to favor it. The plantation overseer, Thompson Burns, was tying a saddled mule to the fence. He came through the gate, bringing with him the mail he had stopped to pick up from the post office at Big Hollow.

Harville lowered himself into an easy chair and put the bad leg on a stool in front of him. He was smoking a corn-cob pipe and his clothes were unpressed, but the white shirt he wore was immaculate. Burns found another chair and sat down to report on the affairs of the plantation. Big Bill was getting slack about the weeds in his corn patch. He was having girl-trouble. Old Joe Smith's daughter was turning a cold shoulder to him and smiling at Buck Pettis. That was not so good, Burns thought. Buck was a bad nigger. He had been drunk at the gin yesterday and made some trouble there. Best get rid of him.

"Buck is not bad," the Colonel disagreed. "He's got off on the wrong foot lately. Send him to me. I'll straighten him out. And tell Dolly Smith I want to see her. Cain't have girls making trouble between our boys out of pure cussedness."

Joe Maginnis wanted to draw five dollars more on account. Said he needed to buy medicine for his little boy who had been sick.

"He's no manager," Harville said. "But I reckon his cotton crop will cover what we advance. Let him have two dollars in cash and a store credit of three dollars. What he probably needs is food in the house."

After Burns had gone the colonel settled himself to read his mail, one thigh flung across the padded arm of his chair so carelessly that the trouser leg was dragged almost to the top of the boot. He was a large man, deep-chested, strongly built. Though graying at the temples, he was still vigorous and forceful. In his kind eyes there was a deceptive indolence. Men who had followed him into battle twenty years before still told stories of his dash.

He opened a letter from his brother Horace, who owned a store at Fort Smith. What he read there and in the clipping enclosed from a paper of that town did not please him. He slammed a hand down on the arm of the chair.

Larry came out of the house, in his hands a rifle. At sight of him the sternness faded out of his father's eyes. Maxwell Harville loved his other stalwart sons, but he knew that this boy was his best beloved, the child of his lovely fragile second wife who had withered away in this miasmic land.

"Going hunting, son?" he asked.

"Thought I'd scout around the bottom, sir, and see if I could scare up a turkey."

"Fine. Might take an ear of corn in case you see any of our hawgs. They are wild as deer, and mighty hard to tole home."

Larry glanced at the letters and papers in his father's lap. "Anything for me?" he asked.

"Not a thing today. There's a letter from your Uncle Horace."

"The family well?"

"All feeling right peart." The colonel frowned. His eyes had fallen on the newspaper clipping. "But there is something here I don't like. You have read about that Labreu gang of outlaws. Four of them were to be hanged next Thursday. Well, there's been a prison break at Fort Smith. Six of the scoundrels got free and picked up guns in the town somewhere. They are maybe headed this way."

"You don't mean here?"

"If they stay in Arkansas they will come here. I hope they point for Texas."

"But why would they come here? I remember hearing about it when I was a little chap. You drove them away, after shooting and hanging several. That was soon after the war, wasn't it?"

"It's a long story, Larry." The colonel settled deeper into his chair to tell the tale. "Goes away back to the war. This scalawag Lige Labreu was in my regiment. He always had been a bad man. One night he and two-three other devils tortured a Yank farmer who lived down Powhatan way to make him tell where his money was hid. They killed him. Before I could get at them they deserted and became guerrillas. After the war they came back here and pestered the neighborhood. Those were wild days, what with the carpetbaggers and the Ku Klux projectin' around, and even we folks not having too much respect for law that was being run to take away our rights.

"Lige had two brothers most as bad as himself, and several no-account families here were kin of his. Two or three of his hangers-on are still around — the Moss and the Dull outfits are cousins of his. They did all kinds of deviltry — robbed folks and burned down houses and murdered a couple of men they thought were against them. Finally they went too far. Fellow named Flynn lived about three miles from here in that big house back from the Big Hollow road. Nobody with him except an old Negro woman to do the housework. He was a kind of a scamp — had thrown in with the carpetbaggers and made a lot of money after the war. One night they broke into his place and took him out in his nightshirt. The story is that he had been in with the Labreu gang and had held out on them. They hanged him to a walnut tree, letting him down two-three times to allow him to tell where the money was hidden. Flynn was stubborn. He wouldn't talk. They left him hanging there and shot the old woman. And from what I can hear, after searching the place they didn't find two bits. The upshot of it was that Perry Logan and I got together some of my old regiment and surprised the bushwhackers while they were trying to burn my gin."

"Major Logan?" Larry asked in surprise.

"The feud was dormant then. We had plenty of riffraff to fight together, and we hadn't fussed again yet. We shot three of the ornery scamps and hanged two. The rest skedaddled out of the country, Lige at their head. Later we heard they were in the Cherokee Nation. Lige went on raising hell there. About four years ago stories began to come out that he was at the head of a gang of ruffians robbing trains and stages. Judge Parker's deputies took after them.[1] There were several fights. Finally pretty nearly the whole caboodle were captured, taken to Fort Smith, tried, and sentenced to be hanged. Now a bunch of them have done bust loose, among them Lige and three of his sons."

"Won't they go back to the Nation?" Larry inquired.

[1] For twenty years Judge Parker's court at Fort Smith, Arkansas, was the fountainhead of justice to deal with the outlaws who flocked to the Five Nations. More than eighty murderers walked out of his courtroom to be hanged later for the crimes they had committed. United States deputy marshals scoured the brush to bring in the lawbreakers. During those decades many of them lost their lives in the performance of their duties.

"It's filled with bad men, the papers say. Just the country for them."

"The *Elevator* does not think so. Neither does your Uncle Horace. They have outworn their welcome there. Bad citizens dare not hide them any longer. The U.S. marshals and the Indian police would make it too hot for them. No, they will vamoose."

"But why not to Texas?"

The planter deliberated. "That would be one likely destination, but they seem to have started this way. Maybe that's a bluff. One point sticks out, though. We drove Lige out before he could find the money hidden on Flynn's place. He might come back and have another try for it. Lige knows the swamps as I do my north cornfield. He'd feel pretty safe hiding there."

"I should think he would remember how roughly you treated him and stay away," Larry said.

"He remembers," the colonel said grimly. "Lige never forgets an injury, he brags. He swore he would get even with us someday. In the sloughs and slashes of the Cache he might hide for months before we could rout him out. And he could do a heap of harm while he was there. He's a bold devil. Treacherous, too." The colonel slapped a mosquito on the back of his hand. "He would as soon destroy a human life as I would that skeeter. They tell a story about him. Whenever he kills a man he throws back his head and gobbles like a turkey, so folks got to calling him the Gobbler."

It was hard for Larry to believe that Labreu would lead his men back to a community where the lives of half a dozen of them had been snuffed out. His father might be right, but it was not likely.

"He can disappear into Texas and start there with a clean sheet to make trouble again," Larry reasoned. "That would be safer."

His father nodded. "In the long run, I reckon. But if he does show up here we'll probably have to stomp him out. Well, go get your turkey, son."

His gaze followed the young man's light figure as it moved toward the bridge that crossed the bayou, in his eyes a pride clouded by worry. He did not have to feel responsible for Andy and Tom. They were able to take care of themselves. But this blond boy was not accustomed to this rough environment, its strains and its slackness. It was unlikely he would stay here permanently. An architect had to live in a city. He felt that Larry would never quite be one of them.

8

LARRY CROSSED THE BRIDGE that spanned the bayou. Among the piles below he could see Shep Tolt baiting a trotline for catfish. He called a "How-d'you-do?" down to the fisherman.

Shep wore butternut jeans, a soft, cone-shaped hat with the original band and color lost, a patched cotton shirt, and boots so broken that the bare toes showed. He looked up with a friendly grin on his homely puckered face. "Jes' tolable," he replied. "Hit's a right nice day, Mr. Larry."

Young Harville agreed it was. He found Tolt interesting. Nowhere except in the South could such a character be found. He was an indolent, carefree ne'er-do-well who lived quite happily from hand to mouth. The man looked like a tramp, yet he had character. His word could be relied on absolutely and he would go a long way for a friend. During the war he had been a cool and daring sharpshooter, and later had been invaluable in helping Colonel Harville drive out the Labreus. He knew the Cache swamps as few did. His nickname was "Jes' Tolable," because of his invariable answer to greetings.

Larry crossed the bridge to the lower ground on the other side of the bayou. During the early spring this canebrake was covered by the overflow water from the bayou. One could travel through the water for miles on horseback or in a wagon, locating the road only by the three slashes on the oak and gum trees that marked its course.

He came out of the brake to a ridge of white oaks. This higher land was a riot of sun-splashed color. The shrubs were bright with tiny red berries that contrasted with the white dogwood blossoms and the scarlet bells of the buckeyes. Hogs were eating the mast. He noted that they were still thin from the winter they had roughed through. From the ear of corn he had brought with him he shelled grains and flung them to the razorbacks, who bolted down the slope like wild deer. Later they would return and eat the corn.

Beyond the ridge he could see the far-distant edge of

the cypress swamp. This slough was a miasmic horror. Its soft and spongy ground quaked beneath the feet. He had listened to grim stories of men caught in its quicksands, to vanish forever beneath the slimy green waters. Ugly moss-covered cypress knees rose out of the pool. Even on the ridge the mosquitoes were bad enough, but over the fetid surface of the morass the swarms were ten times as thick.

Larry caught a glimpse of a corduroy road that farther on wound its way into the quagmire. On a knoll beside this road was a ramshackle cabin with a sagging lath-and-dirt chimney. Several half-naked black children were playing in front of the house. Old Joe Smith lived here. He was one of the colonel's sharecroppers. Usually one or two of his daughters with their haphazard babies dwelt here temporarily with him and his wife.

A panting dog tore along the ridge after Larry and barked joyously when it caught up with him. The hound was one of several Colonel Harville owned. Spot had been asleep when Larry left, but had awakened in time to pick up the scent. It jumped up on him eagerly, but at his order, "Down, Spot," subsided to a decorous sniffing of the surrounding terrain.

Larry was making for a pecan grove farther along the ridge where he had shot a wild turkey a few days before. Through a tangle of muscadine vines he picked his way with a wary eye for rattlesnakes. Beyond this was a stretch of fine gums, the young foliage was a brilliant green.

His nostrils picked up the smoke of a fire. From a rise he presently looked down on its source. Two men were bending over a big iron kettle sousing something in hot water. They dragged out a hog and began to scrape off the bristles with hunting knives. Winchester rifles lay beside them within reach.

The young hunter had a prickling sense of danger. Except for an occasional intruder all the hogs in this run belonged to his father, and carried the crop and half underbit that showed ownership. Larry stopped, half minded to turn back before he was seen. But he was too late. Spot had trotted forward. One of the men glanced up. At sight of man and dog he cut off both ears of the hog and threw them into the fire.

Spot ran to the edge of the flame and picked up one of the ears where it had fallen, then hurried back and sat down at his master's feet to chew on his find. Larry did not look down on the gristly flap the hound had retrieved. It was important that he should not identify the earmarks. He had chanced upon thieves at their work. If he could not later swear the animal belonged to his father they would be more likely to let him go. The "poor white trash" of the neighborhood were not cruel. They would not bother him unless he was a menace to their safety. His feet moved forward reluctantly. He must not show he was afraid. He must be easy and friendly.

But as he drew closer the heart died under his ribs. Both of the men had picked up their rifles and were watching him intently, the black eyes in their evil faces unwinking. They were not dressed in the slovenly fashion of the small farmers of the bottomlands who cultivated ten acres of cotton in fields where girdled trees were still standing. They wore expensive embroidered high-heeled boots, low black felt hats, vests flung wide, and fancy bandannas knotted loosely around their leathery necks. Cartridge belts from which revolvers were suspended circled their waists.

The pit of Larry's stomach went icy. His palms sweated. He knew who these men must be, members of Lige Labreu's gang. Before words came he had to swallow twice. His throat was dry as a lime kiln.

"I . . . I came to get a turkey," he explained hoarsely.

One man said to the other, drawling the words with sinister irony, "He came to get a turkey." The long straight hair and the high cheekbones showed Indian blood, but the face held none of the silent dignity that distinguishes the tribes. The white in him, an inheritance of bad stock, gave the mean features a sly, cruel look.

"Who are you?" the second man demanded harshly. He was a bowlegged, barrel-chested fellow with the ugly lupine face of a dullard.

"Drop that gun," the first speaker ordered.

Larry knew that if he tried to raise his weapon he would be dead before he could pull the trigger. His slack fingers opened and the weapon fell to the ground. He wanted to cry out and beg them not to shoot.

Far back from over the ridge the voice of a Negro in song drifted to them.

> "*Way ober yondah in de harvest fields,*
> *Angels workin' on de chariot wheels,*
> *Tell all de membahs I'm new bawn,*
> *Tell all de membahs I'm new bawn.*"

Larry wanted to run, but he crushed down the rising panic. Before he could get ten feet bullets would crash into his back. He had to stay until they had decided what to do with him. He had to keep his chin up and pretend this was only a little misunderstanding of no importance.

"Traveling through the country, gentlemen?" he asked. "If you are short of anything drop in and let me know. Be glad to help you out." He wondered if his voice was shaky and if they knew how terror was clutching at his throat.

The bowlegged man laughed with no sound of friendly mirth. "You hain't answered my question," he said.

"My name is Lawrence Somerset," Harville replied. Somerset had been his mother's maiden name and was his own.

"I don't recollect any Somersets around here," the one with high cheekbones replied.

"We haven't been here but a little while."

"Where do you live at?"

"On the prairie, three miles above Rosemont."

"What are we a-waitin' for, Craw?" the big man asked brutally.

"No hurry, Fin," answered Craw, showing stained and broken teeth in a grin. "You might take a look at Mr. Somerset's pockets. We'll be wantin' his watch and his money anyhow."

The bandy-legged man took from Larry his pocketbook and a letter. He handed them to his companion. Craw read the address on the envelope letter by letter, his lips moving as he did so. Evidently his schooling had not taken him far beyond the second grade.

His gloating eyes lifted to Larry's white face. "So you're a Harville, you damned liar." The voice of Craw was a silkily cruel threat. "That's right interestin'. I been waitin' a considerable time to meet up with some Harville and git the dead wood on him. It was yore paw, I reckon, who ran us outa this neck of the woods when I was a kid. I shore hope he don't miss you too much."

The light breeze brought to them the chorus of old Joe Smith's song.

> *"Tell all de membahs I'm new bawn,*
> *New bawn, new bawn, new bawn baby,*
> *Bawn in de manjah.*
> *Tell all de membahs I'm new bawn."*

"Yes, suh, he'll feel mighty bad to have you killed off," the soft nasal voice of the ruffian continued. "Likely he sets the world an' all by you, Mr. Lawrence Somerset. Mebbe I'll write an' tell the old man after we've lit a shuck for Texas. Hit's a comfort to hear how our loved ones pass away. Onct yore paw had my brother Brad whopped to a frazzle with hickory saplings. Well, I shouldn't wonder but what we could find some pawpaws to tickle yore back when we git you back into the slough where *my* pappy is holed up."

Larry called on whatever reserve of courage he had. "You are Lige Labreu's son?" he asked.

"Got it fust roll outa the box, Mr. Somerset Harville. His youngest son Crawford. Good friends like you call me Craw. I 'low there's no harm in ownin' up, seeing as you hain't likely to tell." The malignity back of the man's grin was appalling.

Larry's memory carried back to a day when he had been

sent to the head of the school at Harrow for a thrashing. He had known it was due, and all the previous night — with the exception of brief troubled naps — he had lain awake in fear. He had been less afraid of the pain than the dread of playing the baby under it. When the time came he had steeled himself and suffered in writhing silence. But what he had to endure now was far more terrible than that. Always he had been a timid boy. From his mother he had inherited the almost visual imagination that lives in advance agony and danger. Lige Labreu was a devil, his father had said, and the man never forgave.

Some sure instinct told him it was no use to beg. It would only please the mean souls of these wretches. Better throw fear into them if he could. Perhaps, at the worst, by angering them he might get an easier and swifter death, the short sharp agony of a bullet in the heart.

"The gallows is waiting for you at Fort Smith," he told them. "If you kill me you will seal your doom. My father will never stop hunting you. He'll trap you like the rats you are." Larry flung scornful taunts at them, the panic in him driving him wild. He called them the scum of the earth, a bunch of scoundrels who ought to be sent to hell and would be as soon as his people had rounded them up.

On a dogwood twenty yards away a flaming oriole paused in flight. A buzzard slowly circled in the blue sky above. Neither Larry nor his tormentors saw them. Their whole attention was concentrated on one another.

A dull red of anger burned in the swarthy face of Labreu. He crashed the barrel of his rifle down on the head of his victim. Larry's hat was some protection, but the force of the blow staggered him. He weaved drunkenly. Labreu lashed out with his fist. Small blobs of blood came out on the bruised cheek. For Larry the world tilted up and down crazily. Hammers beat in his head.

"I'll learn you to blackname me, dad burn you," Labreu cried. "Hell ain't gonna be any hotter than the coals that char yore feet before we drap you in the slough, Mr. Harville."

A sickness churned in Larry's stomach. The hinges of his knees began to give. The outlaw drove another left at the tottering man's face. Larry collapsed. Craw kicked him in the ribs. The prostrate man groaned.

"He's afeared," the ruffian gloated. "The old colonel is mighty high and biggity. He wouldn't like for his whelp to be blubbering."

Though Larry's mind was not clear, he knew that what the fellow said was true. Either of his brothers would have known how to meet the situation. He would have taken command of it from the first or gone down fighting.

"Git up," Labreu ordered. "You got a li'l journey to take with us." He laughed triumphantly. "Hit shorely looks some smoky raound the edges for you."

With difficulty Larry got to his feet. He set them well apart to keep from swaying.

As his gaze traveled past the gleeful scoundrel he thought for a moment that his eyes were betraying him. They saw a man moving out of the dogwoods behind the outlaws into the open.

9

THE MAN WAS HAL LOGAN. He carried a dead turkey in one hand and a rifle in the other. The narrowed eyes in Craw Labreu's lowering face studied him — a dark young fellow, well dressed in a careless fashion, with a look on his reckless face that showed both pride and arrogance. Hard as an oak door, Craw decided, and quick on the trigger. No waste motion about him. He had already dropped the turkey and stood with the rifle in both hands, the barrel tilted upward.

Young Logan did not think any explanation of this situation necessary. The dead hog, the truculent strangers, Larry Harville battered and bleeding. The story was obvious. Harville had discovered them stealing one of his father's swine. There had been a fight, and he had had the worst of it. Now that he had unexpectedly come on the scene the thieves would depart as soon as they could.

"Hope I'm not intruding," he drawled. He was smiling, cool, undisturbed, apparently indifferent.

"Who are you?" demanded Labreu.

"Let me ask the questions," Logan suggested. "Who are *you?*"

Labreu had lived long enough in the brush, at odds with the law, to judge men accurately. The newcomer was no older than Harville, still almost a boy, but there was steel in his dark eyes and resolution in his manner. He had the fighting edge.

The outlaw's voice took on a wheedling note.

"Well, sir, I'm right glad you showed up. We're strangers travelin' through this country. A fellow sold us this shote, then along comes this man and claims it belongs to his pappy. We didn't want any fuss, but he starts to overcrow us and I had to kinda mess him up a little."

Larry had recovered his rifle. With the sleeve of his coat he brushed away the blood dripping from his eyes.

"That's a lie," he said. "They were going to take me into the slough to torture and murder me."

Hal did not like the appearance of the hog thieves. They were hard-looking specimens, too well armed and too well dressed to be renters or poor farmers hard up for food. But he was convinced Harville had become unduly frightened. Even if they were men on the dodge there would be no sense in torturing a man who got in their way.

"I reckon it's not as bad as that," he said.

The outlaws protested eagerly that they were tie contractors driving from Harrisburg to Texarkana. They had got a few miles off their road to do some hunting.

"Where is yore wagon?" Logan asked.

"Back there in the brush."

"How far away?"

"A right smart bit. We had to chase this shote before we got a shot at it."

"More lies," Larry put in. "The one who does the talking is Lige Labreu's son. He told me so himself."

Hal shook his head. "You're 'way off. I read only this mo'ning that the Labreus are all in jail at Fort Smith waiting to be hanged."

"That's right," Craw agreed quickly. "This young fellow has done gone crazy with the heat."

"Six of them broke jail three days ago," Larry explained. "My father got a letter from Uncle Horace, who lives at Fort Smith. There was a clipping from the paper there. Father thought likely they would strike for this country. Lige Labreu is camped back in the slough. This fellow told me so."

Craw denied vehemently that he had ever heard of the Labreus. They were peaceable citizens going about their business. His shifty eyes slid to Harville and back again to Logan. He had to talk or fight his way out of this. To let himself be taken prisoner would be fatal. His tricky mind ran over the chances. Both of these young fellows were armed. It did not matter so much about Harville. He was soft. But the one who had butted in was steel-hard. His gaze never shifted from Craw. The barrel of his rifle, held low in his hands, pointed straight at the heart and he could fire without moving it an inch.

"So you're a Labreu," Hal said gently. "I reckon we had better collect you. If you are what you say you are, I'll make all necessary apologies."

"We're in a sorta hurry," Craw mentioned.

The bowlegged man started to shift his position, to get at Hal from one side.

"Stay where you are," Hal ordered.

"Don't tell me what I'm to do," the wolf-faced man snarled. "Or by gum you'll wear a wooden overcoat."

"No need to git rambunctious, Fin," whined Labreu. "This young gentleman aims to be reasonable, same as we do. He prob'ly knows Harville has done got a crazy notion in his head."

"How do you know his name is Harville?" asked Hal.

"Why, he told us his name when he fust jumped us. Point is, we're decent folks, not lookin' for trouble. I'm willing to pay for the shote if the fellow who sold it tricked us. That's fair enough, ain't it?"

Logan's smile was politely skeptical. "Nobody could ask more. We'll call on Colonel Harville and let him fix a price."

"I ain't going nowhere to see nobody," the man called Fin said doggedly.

In the man's slitted eyes Larry read a danger signal. He had made his choice, and it was to fight. Below the boy's heart there was a tight, hard ball. His eyes shuttled a warning to Logan.

Hal did not need to be told. He knew what was coming unless he could forestall it. "I'll blast the first one that lifts a hand," he told Larry. "Step behind them and take their hardware."

Harville started to move behind Labreu, but he was too late. The butt of Fin's rifle rested on the ground. He jerked it up and his finger found the trigger. Before he could fire, Logan's gun crashed. The weapon dropped from Fin's hands. He clutched at his stomach, an agonized look on his face. His aimless feet brought him forward a step or two before the body slumped and toppled to the ground.

Labreu snatched a revolver from its holster. Larry came to life, and just as the man was firing jammed the stock of his rifle into the man's side. The bullet went wild. Before the outlaw could set himself for a second shot Larry drove the butt hard against his temple. The force of the impact flung him from his feet. He went down like a log.

Hal stared down at the man he had killed, a little frightened at what he had done. He had never before rubbed out a human life, and the shock of his action was disturbing. He had no sympathy for the ruffian lying at his feet. In no way was he to blame. But death is so final. He had made himself God for a moment and stricken the life out of a fellow man.

He said, his boyish face white but set, "I gave him his choice, and he wouldn't have it any other way."

Larry was even more shaken than his companion. He had all his life been sheltered from raw violence like this. If the break of the luck had been different he might have been lying there instead of the outlaw. His unhappy eyes swept the skirt of the distant slough to make sure the sound of the shot had not brought help to the escaped criminals, then shifted to meet those of Logan.

"We'd better get out of here," he said, almost in a whisper. "Somebody might come."

This palpable fear had the effect of restoring Hal's confidence. His gaze, curious and scornful, rested critically on the strange sight of a Harville who was afraid. The rest of the family were men fearless and strong. This blond lad apparently lacked the iron in the blood so abundant in the others.

"What's the hurry?" Hal asked. "We have guns enough here for half a dozen." He glanced at Labreu, who was beginning to show signs of life. "Better collect the guns.

He's coming to. I'll tie him up."

Hal bound the man's wrists behind his back with his own belt. While he was at work the prisoner became aware of what had occurred.

The man begged abjectly to be turned loose. "I'm a young fellow, like you-all. I ain't evah done either of you any harm. I been wild, sure enough, but I'll swear on a stack of Bibles to go right if you-all gimme another chanct. Lemme go, and I'll git the old man to burn the wind outa here, or if you'd ruther I'll holp you cotch him."

Logan was disgusted at the man's fawning cowardice. "Too late," he said bluntly. "Get up and travel."

The outlaw shuffled forward on his knees, the lank black hair falling over his face. " 'Fore God, genelmen, I'm through with my meanness. Cross my heart an' hope to die. You cain't turn yore backs on a repentant sinner. I— I ain't fitten to die yet."

Hal put a revolver to his head. "On your feet," he ordered.

Labreu got up. Beads of perspiration poured down his face. As he moved along the ridge he continued to plead for mercy. If they wouldn't turn him over to the law he would do anything in the world they asked.

"I'm turning you over to Colonel Harville," Hal told him. "Explain to him how you aim to join the church."

"Goddlemighty, not Harville," the wretch cried. "He hung my uncle and my cousin. Tha's what he'll do to me."

"It's what you deserve," Hal said. "I'm not in Colonel Harville's confidence, so I don't know what he'll do."

Larry's glance went often to the ground rising from

the swamp, half expecting to see armed men coming over the rise. But he saw no sign of others. They came to the corduroy road. Near the edge of the swamp old Joe Smith and his oldest boy Jim were cutting a bee tree. At sight of the small procession Joe stopped the saw and hurried toward them. He wanted to send word to Colonel Harville that he would return next day a borrowed mule. But as soon as he saw that one of the men was a prisoner he pulled up abruptly. Long ago Joe had learned from experience that when white men had difficulties with one another it was time for him to be absent.

"Have you seen anybody riding in or out of the swamp?" Larry asked.

"No, suh! I ain't seen nobody ceppen you genelmen."

Some time in the night Joe had heard horsemen on the corduroy road that led into the slough. This was so unusual, since the road was an old and rotting one, that he had got up to look out of his window. What he had seen disturbed him. Eight men, two abreast, had disappeared in the swamp. It brought to his mind the days of the Ku Klux and the months when guerrillas had lurked in the Cache bottoms to trouble honest men. But he made no mention of the night riders to Larry. It was better to know too little than too much.

When they reached the bridge Larry breathed easier. They were close enough to the house now for help to reach them if they were attacked. Shep Tolt was sitting beneath a gum tree with his back propped against the trunk. He could do nothing longer and with more enjoyment than anybody else in the community. At the sound of the men crossing the bridge he woke up from a nap and helped himself to a dip of snuff. His eyes opened wide at what he saw.

Hal flung a careless question at him. "Fish biting?"

"Jes' tolable," Tolt answered. "Been having a li'l trouble, Mr. Logan?" he inquired.

"Not a bit, Jes' Tolable," Hal answered cheerfully. "The other fellows had the trouble."

Colonel Harville was at the front gate talking with his overseer Burns when he caught sight of the advancing trio. He was so astonished that he stopped in the middle of a sentence. To see his son battered, bloodstained, and loaded with rifles and revolvers, was surprising enough, even if he had not been accompanied by a dragging prisoner who looked as though he too had been in the wars. But to find Hal Logan in the party was amazing. No Logan had set foot on the Harville plantation for many years.

Hal said, with a thin, sardonic grin: "Colonel Harville, meet Craw Labreu. He's expecting you to hang him."

"God bless my soul!" the colonel exclaimed. He turned to his son. "What happened?"

Young Logan was the hero of the story Larry told. He made it clear that Hal had saved his life and carried the burden of the fight. Maxwell Harville was shocked at the close call his son had had and deeply grateful to Hal for the help he had given. He was also much embarrassed.

His stammered thanks Logan waved aside. "Comes of not minding my own business," he said flippantly. "I reckon I ought to apologize for buttin' in. When I found this scoundrel was a Labreu I had to stay with it. But I'll promise to let you-all kill yore own snakes after this."

The prisoner fell on his knees before the colonel and

begged for his life. "I was jes' a-foolin' with yore boy, Colonel," he pleaded. "I wouldn't of hurt him. He got some excited an' jumped me, and o' course I had to defend myself. Colonel, I ain't bad, but I been brought up wrong. I been trying to break away from my pappy, but seems like it was hard to do. He kep' kinda toling me along. Save me, Colonel, an' I'll do anything you say — anything you say — anything. Tell you what, gimme yore word to turn me loose afterward and I'll lead you to the old man and let you take him. Honest, I wasn't 'lowing to do yore boy any harm."

As the fellow edged closer the owner of Rosemont stepped back to avoid being touched. "I cain't save you, and I wouldn't if I could. You've been condemned to death for murder. You'll be taken to Fort Smith and hanged."

"Hain't it wuth more for you to git the whole gang than jes' me?" Labreu whined. "I'll take you to the camp. Honest injun, I will. I'm the youngest of the lot. You kin let me go, and I'll never do another meanness long as I live."

"This fellow is bad as they come," Hal said. "But even so, there's something in what he says. Better make a gather of the rest of the bunch rather than just this one."

Maxwell Harville thought the suggestion over and came to a decision. "All I can do, if this man helps us to capture the rest of them, is to write a letter to Judge Parker and tell him the facts. He might commute the sentence to life imprisonment."

"It won't do any good, Colonel, not the leastest mite," Labreu whimpered, the sweat pouring down his mean face.

"The judge he loves to hang men. If you send me back there he won't pay no attention to what you write."

"It's the best I can offer," Harville said curtly. "Take it or leave it."

Craw took it, after a vain attempt to drive a better bargain.

The colonel turned to his foreman. "Burns, will you ride to Big Hollow and tell Sheriff Cantrell to get together three-four good men, arm them, and come here on the jump? My boys will join him. If he hurries he may be able to trap the Labreu gang before Lige learns what has happened."

"I'll go," Hal volunteered. "If you'll lend me a horse. And I'll bring back Rod with me. He would sure hate to miss this man-hunt even if he has to ride beside a Harville."

Five minutes later Hal was galloping down the road toward Big Hollow.

10

WHEN MAJOR LOGAN HEARD Hal's story his first thought was of the danger his son had escaped, and the second one of relief that his family had wiped out the obligation Larry had put it under in saving Diane from injury. Hal had paid the debt in full, for without his intervention Lige Labreu would undoubtedly have destroyed young Harville.

"Don't worry about the ruffian you had to kill," the

father told his boy. "It was your life or his. Far better he die than you."

"I'm proud of you," Rod said to his younger brother. "Wish I'd been there too."

"We'd best get going, or we won't be in time to join the posse," Hal mentioned. They had their rifles with them and their mounts were waiting outside.

"I don't like to have you riding alongside the Harvilles," Perry Logan said fretfully. "But I cain't tell you not to go. Wish this confounded arm would let me handle a gun. Is the colonel going?"

There was a faint twinkle in Hal's eyes. "No, sir, he isn't. It seems someone shot him up the other day."

The major rose from his chair and paced across the floor and back. He was a tall thin man dressed very neatly in a black Prince Albert coat, a boiled shirt, and a black string bow tie. He walked with such straight stiffness that Tom Harville had once suggested he must carry a ramrod down his back. The eyes above the Roman nose were keen and piercing as those of a hawk. At times they were cold as ice. He never laughed and rarely smiled. There were few friendships in his life, though he was a man of complete integrity.

"Well, get along with you," he told his sons sharply. "I cain't let my trouble with Harville keep you from helping to hunt down that devil Lige Labreu."

From the window he watched his lithe, dare-devil sons canter down the road. His wife joined him and slipped her hand into his. She was a gentle person, gracious and lovely. In her youth she had been a famous beauty, sought in marriage by half a dozen young men of good family and prospects. There had been surprise when she chose Perry Logan, a man without gaiety, small talk, or social graces. But she had never regretted her decision. To others he might appear stern and cold, but she knew the intensity of his devotion to her and their children. Sometimes she wondered that she had given birth to such reckless sons, but there was nothing she could do about it except pray for them. It seemed only yesterday that Hal had been a baby, and today he had killed a man.

Rodney and Hal Logan rode to the Harville cotton gin and sent word to the colonel by a colored boy that they would join the posse at the bridge. That suited Maxwell Harville. It saved embarrassment on both sides. He sent Larry to the bridge with word that the posse would start as soon as the sheriff arrived.

During the next half-hour the colonel pulled his watch out half a dozen times to look at the time. His sons were impatient to get going. A small farmer of the neighborhood, Mack Gillis, had joined them. He had been in Colonel Harville's regiment twenty years earlier. And Shep Tolt had ridden in on a mule with an old muzzle-loading rifle.

"I ought to have known we couldn't depend on Cantrell," the colonel sputtered. "He's a chair-sitting sheriff. Doesn't do anything but talk. He'll fool around until Labreu slips away."

"Why wait for him?" Tom asked. "There are seven of us. That's enough. He can deputize us when we come back."

If he could have led the party himself Maxwell Harville would have agreed to that quickly enough. But with his game leg he could not ride a horse. Lige Labreu was a wily old devil. He might prove too smart for his hunters and trap them. The Logan boys were hotheaded and his own sons, with the exception of Larry, were none too cautious. Mack Gillis was a good man, but no leader. As for Jes' Tolable, he would agree to anything the latest speaker suggested.

"I reckon we better wait for Cantrell," Maxwell said.

A few minutes later Larry returned to the house. He reported that the Logans were anxious to get started. They wanted to know what was holding up the party. Reluctantly his father gave consent for them to go. He felt no assurance that this was wise, but he knew that if there was further delay there would be small likelihood of surprising the Labreus.

In the presence of Craw Labreu, who rode with a rope around his neck, the other end of which was attached to the pommel of Andy's saddle, the colonel gave his sons instructions to shoot the prisoner if there was any sign that the posse was being led into an ambush.

Craw protested urgently that he had thrown in with the posse and they ought to trust him. He was a much frightened badman. When he showed up with the hunters one of the outlaws was very likely to shoot him for betraying the whereabouts of the camp. Looked like he was a gone goose any way it turned out, he thought dolefully.

Rod greeted their arrival at the bridge with flippant sarcasm. "Thought maybe you had decided to wait till tomorrow."

"Cantrell is sheriff," Andy answered coldly. "We were giving him a chance to join us."

They clattered over the bridge and trooped down into the canebrake. Hal was in the vanguard, presumably because he knew the spot where the fight had occurred. Andy was handicapped by the prisoner, but Tom hurried forward to come abreast of Hal. He was not going to let anybody get the impression that this was a posse led by the Logans. Rod quickened his pace. The three were fifty yards ahead of the others when they reached the place where the outlaw had been killed.

His body had been taken away and so had the hog. The iron pot still stood over the ashes of a dead fire.

Gillis said, "I'll be doggoned if that ain't my pot. Somebody stole it out of my yard last night."

They held a council as to what was best to do. Since the Labreus had found the dead body of their companion and did not know what had become of Craw, they would either move their camp at once or prepare an ambush for their enemies. Mack Gillis had been with Maxwell Harville when they had trapped the guerrillas at the cotton gin. He knew how tricky Lige was. The outlaws would have vanished, or if not would be lying in the brush waiting for them.

Craw worked himself into the debate and supported this view. "The old man is slick as a fox," he said. "Like as not he would git the whole caboodle of us. There are places in the slough where he could hold up a dozen of us and we wouldn't have a chance."

Larry suggested that they had at least better wait for the sheriff before going any further. Then they could work as a unit.

Scornfully Rod disagreed. "Who's afraid of a bunch of

cowardly murderers? Cut out the talk. You're either going on or you are not. Hal and I are, if we have to go alone. What did we come for, anyhow?"

To Tom and Andy this had the effect of a red flag in front of a bull. They announced at once that of course they were not going to turn back. That settled the argument. Jes' Tolable said that he 'lowed he had come to get a crack at Lige with Old Tried and True. Gillis fell in with the majority.

They moved through a stretch of blue gum woodland to the lower lands that bordered the slough. A narrow trail ran into the spongy bog, twisting like a snake as it followed the higher ground wherever possible.

Andy stopped the party. There were two ways to reach the camp from this side, their prisoner had told him. One would bring them by a wide detour to the rear of it. Craw had not traversed it since he had been here when a boy, but he thought he could find the old landmarks. The advantage of this route would be that the outlaws could not be expecting a posse to take it. They might be caught by surprise. Even if not, there would be less chance of the hunters falling into a trap.

Rod voiced the doubts of the rest of them. This would be fine if they could trust their guide. He was a Labreu, and the truth wasn't in him. Instead of avoiding an ambush, the fellow might be leading them into one. He might be, Andy agreed, but if so he was committing suicide. The colonel had given him an order to shoot the man at the first evidence of treachery, and he meant to do just that.

Craw pleaded for himself in his high nasal whine. All he

was trying to do was to fix it so none of them would be killed. He was honest to God through with the gang. Seemed like when a fellow tried to do right everyone was against him. He was a young man under thirty, and he never had been given a chance. There was no use for him to promise that nobody would be hurt. The men in the camp were most of them killers. They were desperate men and would not be taken alive if they could help it. He would do whatever they said, but it looked crazy to him for a posse to go butting in on a trail where they would be expected.

It did not look good to the others either. They decided on the detour. Craw led them along the winding trail for half a mile. The hoofs of the horses sunk into the soft earth and mud sucked at their fetlocks. As they moved deeper into the swamp the riders caught sight of sluggish miasmic waters through the cypress trees. Swarms of mosquitoes buzzed about them.

Craw cut away from the trail into boggy land over which it was difficult to travel. He stopped several times to make sure he was not lost. They were now in dismal, fetid swamp territory into which the sun could scarcely penetrate owing to the heavy foliage and the rank growth of moss depending from the huge trees. The horses splashed through water covered with a yellow-green scum out of which ugly cypress knees jutted. To Larry the atmosphere suggested horrible and ugly death. In spite of the dank heat he felt chilly.

After what seemed hours of travel Craw drew up on a small wooded knoll. They were a little farther north than he had expected, he said, but he was sure the camp was just beyond the next rise. If they wanted to leave him here while they made the attack, they would not have to bother watching him. They could tie him to a tree.

Rod laughed grimly. "Fellow, we're giving you the place of honor right in front," he jeered. "I'll side you and see no harm comes to you. We're off, boys."

He put his horse down the slope into the quagmire in front of him.

"No talking," Andy warned. "Get going, Labreu."

At the water's edge Craw dragged his mount to a stop. Rod was in trouble. His chestnut gelding could not find a footing and was sinking deeper into the water.

"Don't come in," Rod called to them. "There's no bottom to this sand." He was fighting to get his horse free, and the plunging of the animal was only sending it deeper.

On the summit of the rise beyond the water a man showed up. He gave a shout and disappeared.

Andy brought his horse up beside the prisoner and slipped the noose from his neck. "Watch Labreu," he shouted to Gillis.

The farmer ordered Craw to dismount and lie on the ground face down. Labreu did so. He would have liked to make a bolt, but since he could not, with a pistol at his head, he preferred to lie close to the earth where he was less exposed to the bullets already flying.

Several men could be seen on the ridge firing from behind trees they had chosen as cover. Two or three of them were using revolvers. Tom, Larry, and Jes' Tolable were answering the attack with their rifles.

Andy and Hal paid no attention to the drumming of the

guns. They were busy trying to save Rod. Andy flung him the looped end of the rope that was still attached to the horn of his saddle. Rod flung out a hand and caught it. He slipped the noose over his head and under his shoulders, then flung himself out of the saddle. As he went down into the water a bullet struck him in the back. Andy swung round his horse and urged it up the bank, while Hal dismounted and caught the arm of his brother when the rope dragged him near enough.

"They hit you," Hal cried.

"In the back. I'll be all right. I want a crack at these devils."

"Let's find cover first," Hal said.

Jes' Tolable's muzzle loader roared and a man on the ridge gave a yelp of pain.

Before Rod could get into action the firing had died down. The men on the ridge had withdrawn.

The members of the posse drew back to the shelter of the trees. An examination showed that a bullet had drilled into Rod's shoulder. He was bleeding a good deal. Hal and Gillis bound up the wound as best they could.

"We'll have to head for home," Hal said.

They all agreed to that. Rod was seriously hurt.

"Can you ride?" Larry asked the older Logan.

Rod looked at him angrily. "Of course I can ride. Think I'm going to walk?"

"I meant — " Larry started to explain gently.

"I know what you meant," Rod interrupted rudely. "What the hell are we waiting for?"

Freed from its burden in the saddle, the chestnut had

managed to drag itself out of the quicksand and was standing with drooping head on the bank. Hal exchanged horses with Rod and they started on the homeward journey.

Hal rode beside Rod, watching him closely. The wounded man made no complaint, but his lips were closed tightly and he clung with both hands to the horn of the saddle. The ride was for him a long grueling one. More than once his body swayed and Hal had to support it. But the wounded man would not let them stop. He counted milestones grimly — to the big gum tree, to the twisted oak, to the clump of pecans, to the bridge, and, last of all, to the Harville cotton gin. Here he collapsed and slid into his brother's arms. They carried him to the loading platform and sent for Dr. Watkins.

After the doctor had dressed the wound he was taken to Hillcrest in a wagon, the bed of which was filled with loose cotton. As soon as he reached home he was put to bed. There he stayed for a month.

Craw Labreu, the rope once more around his neck, was returned to Rosemont. The sheriff had just arrived with his posse. Cantrell was a plump, soft man. He was a politician, and he had talked himself into office. The task of running down desperate criminals was one he did not like at all. This Labreu gang did not live in his county. The ruffians were escaped prisoners of the United States marshal. It was his job to run them down, not that of the county authorities.

Harville tried to keep the contempt out of his voice. He pointed out that the desperadoes had attacked citizens of this county.

It was at this moment that the sons of the colonel arrived with the prisoner. They told the story of their failure.

"Cain't be helped, boys," their father consoled. "I reckon Logan and I muffed it half a dozen times before we did the job last time." He turned to Cantrell, politely sarcastic. "You won't mind taking this prisoner now he's laid down in your lap, will you, sheriff?"

Though he was annoyed at the planter's manner, the sheriff was careful not to show it. Harville was one of the influential men of the district. He promised to get Craw Labreu on his way to Fort Smith early tomorrow. That would get him there in time to keep his appointment with the hangman.

11

SUPPER WAS OVER at Rosemont and the family was in the big living room. Andy was mending a bridle, Tom lay on the sofa at indolent ease, and Larry had picked from a shelf at random a volume of Swift's essays. Their father had in his hand a copy of *Guy Mannering*, but was too full of the day's events to care about reading.

Though it was a warm night, the curtains were drawn. It would be like Lige Labreu to sneak up and try to pick off one of them from the outside darkness. There was no danger of an enemy getting close to the house without warning from the dogs, but even at a distance of several hundred yards a long shot might find its mark.

Larry was not very happy. Because he realized his own timidity, it was important to prove to himself that he was not a coward. During the march into the swamp he had been filled with an anxiety that had made him sick. While the guns were sounding he had not been at all afraid, but in the reaction from the strain nausea had overcome him. Probably his brothers despised him. Maxwell Harville would be ashamed of him if he ever found out. Why was he a poltroon, without that fine contempt for peril the other men in the family had?

The boy did his father's understanding less than justice. For to the planter his mother lived again in the son. He saw in him her sensitivity, her recoil from conditions harsh and raw, and he made allowances he would not have done for Larry's half-brothers.

Andy drove home a rivet in the leather and offered a comment. "I reckon it will be quite a job for us to comb those scoundrels out of the slough, sir. We didn't do so well this time."

The colonel closed the book he had been making a pretence of reading. "I hate to disappoint you boys," he said. "But it's not our business to clear out Labreu's gang. Either Cantrell or the United States marshals from Fort Smith must do it. When Lige was cavorting around here after the war there wasn't any law to speak of in these parts, so we had to kill our own snakes, as young Logan put it this evening. I don't expect much of Cantrell, but if he comes to life you boys can serve on his posse."

"Isn't it our business, sir, to protect ourselves?" Tom wanted to know. "These devils were going to take Larry into the slough and kill him. Must we sit still and take that?"

His father smiled. "Larry and Hal Logan settled that matter on the spot. They killed one ruffian and dragged the other out to be hanged. Doesn't that satisfy you?"

Larry flushed. He did not feel that he could let this go unchallenged. "Hal Logan did it. I hardly helped at all."

"Except for knocking Craw Labreu down," Andy differed. "I reckon that was some help, seeing he was about to shoot Hal."

"Larry did right well," his father agreed. "But I've been thinking this out. We'll let the law do its duty. You boys stay on this side of the bayou till that nest of cottonmouths is cleaned out."

"They'll think we are afraid of them," Andy objected.

"Doesn't matter what no-account trash like that thinks."

The dogs set up a loud chorus of barking. A voice from the outside shouted, "Hello the house!"

Andy got his rifle, opened the door into the gallery, and demanded who was there. The visitor gave his name.

"Are you alone?" Andy asked.

"That's right. I've brought a message for the colonel."

"Tell him to come in, but cover him all the way," Maxwell Harville ordered. "Chet Dull is full of tricks."

There was a mellow moonlight. Andy watched the man tie his white mule to the fence and come down the walk. He remained in the shadow himself, for fear an accomplice might be waiting in the background to shoot him.

"What do you reckon Dull wants?" Tom asked.

"We're going to find that out in a minute," his father replied grimly.

Chet was a cousin of Lige Labreu, and during the war had been one of his guerrillas. Later he had been a member of the gang that had terrorized the neighborhood. So it was generally believed. But there had not been sure proof, and at the day of reckoning he had been absent. The regulators had given him the benefit of the doubt. He and his family had remained in the neighborhood, though they had never been respected by honest men.

Dull wore butternut jeans thrust into the tops of dusty boots. His coat had faded to a mustard color. The hat above his carroty red hair, long since minus its band, was the shape of a cone. The sly meanness of the face was accented by the ingratiating smile with which he tried to placate the planter.

"Evenin', Colonel," he said, and mopped his cheeks with a dirty handkerchief. "Evenin', Mr. Tom and Mr. Larry and Mr. Andy. I don't recollect it evah being so hot at this time of the year."

Maxwell Harville did not invite him to sit down. He said coldly, "Did you come to tell me that?"

"No, seh." Dull swabbed his neck with the handkerchief. He found it difficult to come to the point. There was no telling how the fiery old ex-Confederate would take what he had to say. "Fact is, Lige asked me to drap in and see you, Colonel."

"Lige!" Angry color spread over Harville's face and ran down to his collar. "Why didn't he come himself? I'd like to see him."

Chet giggled nervously. "You got to have yore joke, Colonel. He kinda mistrusted his welcome, I expect. Thinks you don't feel friendly to him."

"What makes him think that — because I hanged his brother and shot two-three of his kin?" Harville exploded.

"Understand, Colonel, I don't hold with any meanness Lige may have done onct," Dull wheedled. "He's always been a mite rough. I'll say that if he is my own cousin."

"He's a murdering scoundrel, if that's what you mean." The stern eyes of the colonel fastened on the shifty ones of the messenger. "Best thing that could happen would be for him to be dragged back to Fort Smith and hanged by the neck."

"It will be hard for you-all to believe, but Lige has had a change of heart," Dull explained. "While he was lying in jail at Fort Smith. He talked with a preacher there and has repented of his sins. You know what the good book says, Colonel. While the lamp holds out to burn, the vilest sinner may return."

Maxwell looked so apoplectic that Larry offered a word to divert his mind. He quoted with a smile:

"*While the devil lay sick the devil a monk would be,*
When the devil got well the devil a monk was he."

"Was that son of his — the one who calls himself Craw — converted too before he threatened to burn my son's feet and throw him in the slough?" the planter roared.

"Craw talks a heap with his mouth," Dull said apologetically. "He was jes' devilin' the boy, I reckon."

The colonel glared at the envoy. "What did Lige send you to tell me?"

"Lige wants to live and let live. This very evenin' he could of killed two-three of yore friends, but he made his boys hold off, even if his son Sim was shot up. Lige says there's no use in him and you-all feudin'. Hit ain't neighborly."

The impudence of this choked the colonel's speech for a moment and the messenger continued, his unctuous voice pharisaical.

"Before he leaves he wants to git the money hid araound on Flynn's place. It belongs to him. Soon as he finds it he'll light out. He'll give you his word of honor cross his heart not to — "

"His what?" the colonel interrupted scornfully.

"One thing about Lige is he don't rue back on his word," Dull urged. "He's willing to let bygones be bygones."

"I'll bet he is," Tom ripped out.

"He says for you-all to send Craw back to him and he'll light a shuck outa here mighty fast, if you'll agree not to molest him while he's leaving. Seems to me that's fair." Dull tried again the friendly smile of a good-will ambassador.

The colonel slammed a fist down on the arm of his chair. "I ought to set the dogs on you," he said angrily. "Nevah in my life have I had a triflin' scoundrel like you talk that way to me. Now listen. Craw is in the hands of the sheriff. Tomorrow he is going to Fort Smith to be hanged. I wouldn't turn a hand to save him if I could — and I cain't. Tell Lige from me to stay the other side of the bayou. If he bothers any of the farmers or any of the black boys who work for me I won't wait for the law to drag him from his hole. I'll do it myself, as we did before."

"I wouldn't want for you to misjudge me, Colonel," Dull replied virtuously. "You know how Lige is when he thinks someone is doing him dirt. They say he shot up one of Major Logan's sons today. 'Course that's no skin off yore nose, but it might have been one of these here boys. I'd hate to have any of you-all git hurt, so I thought I'd holp git things fixed up. But I ain't throwin' in with Lige. Whatever he does, I ain't in on it."

"I won't misjudge you," the planter answered sternly. "You're trash — always have been and always will be. Now fork your mule and get out."

Dull looked at the planter reproachfully, gave a deep sigh of misunderstood virtue, and did as he had been ordered. Andy saw him out of the house and watched him ride away.

The Harvilles discussed the visit of Dull. Apparently Labreu wanted to make an agreement with the colonel to keep hands off in the hunt for him. The outlaw knew that without his help Sheriff Cantrell would make only a half-hearted attempt to arrest the desperadoes. They might shift around in the swamps of the Cache for weeks without being caught. At present all the roads to Texas were no doubt being watched carefully. It would be safer to lie hidden until the heat of the hunt had died down.

"Lige is smooth as a greased shote," the colonel said. "He'll work this out the way it looks best for him. But you can be sure of this. No deal I made with him would be worth a jackstraw. He's a revengeful devil, and before he leaves he is going to strike either at us or the Logans. The fellow is loaded with poison, and he hates us all."

"Why did Dull tell us about the money on Flynn's place?" Andy asked. "Looks like if they aim to go digging around there he would have kept his trap shut."

They could only guess at the answer. Larry thought maybe the outlaws had stopped on their way into the swamp and found the hidden cache of gold. There was a story current that Lige had forced Flynn to tell where it was concealed, and that in his haste the murderer had misread the instructions. Before he could return and search again his band had been broken up and he himself driven out of the country.

12

CHET DULL REPORTED to Lige Labreu the result of his talk with Colonel Harville as soon as his mule could take him to the appointed meeting at the old Peters cabin below the bayou ford. The decrepit log building was in a small clearing that had been abandoned twenty years earlier. The deadening [1] was covered with second-growth saplings. A corduroy road, rotten with age, twisted through the marsh to the remains of a worm fence. Until this night it is unlikely that anybody had been on the place for a half a dozen years.

Twice Dull repeated the hoot of an owl before he came

[1] A deadening was a field, often plowed and planted, in which the girdled trees were still standing.

out of the dense brush surrounding the abandoned homestead. After an answer came to him he moved forward to the broken-down rail fence surrounding the clearing. A man behind a girdled tree demanded who he was. Dull gave his name, and walked with the man to the house.

Behind it a small fire was burning. Three men squatted around it. One of them said, "Did you see the old mossback, Chet?"

"I saw him, Lige. He says he don't want any truck with you, and if you-all do a meanness to any of the folks around here he will drag you outa the Cache bottom himself."

Lige broke into savage curses. He was a big, powerful man, bowlegged and barrel-chested. His shoulders were deep and wide. Yet when he rose, in spite of his weight there was a pantherish litheness about his movements. The thin-lipped mouth was a straight gash in the leathery face, and the shallow, restless eyes were full of imprisoned fire. Tight trousers outlined the muscular thighs. From his hip a Colt's .45 dangled. It was as much a part of his costume as the custom-made boots and the low, black, wide-rimmed hat. He never traveled without it, nor without a Winchester rifle, if he was in the saddle.

"What did he say about Craw?"

The man who put the question was Brad Labreu, the oldest son of Lige. Except that he was more slenderly built he looked like his father. His face had the same wolfish look, a cruelty divorced from courage, and with it a sly meanness that weakened the bold front.

"Said Craw was in the hands of the sheriff, ready for

the scaffold at Fort Smith soon as they can git him there."
Dull added a bit of information he had picked up at Big Hollow. "Story folks are tellin' is that Craw made a deal with Harville to guide the posse to yore camp. I reckon Craw was to save his own neck. But the old colonel didn't talk like he was standing by Craw any."

Lige stared at him, his beefy face growing purple with anger. There was evidence to corroborate the treachery of his son. Somebody had brought the posse to the camp. Moreover, the enemy had crept up on it from the rear. Except the fugitives themselves, only Chet Dull and Curt Moss knew the location of the camp. It had to be one of these two or Craw who had betrayed the outlaws.

The man who had brought Dull to the cabin from the fence volunteered information. "When we was having that mix-up with these birds at the quicksands, I noticed something funny. One of 'em lay spraddled out on the ground and another one with a gun was squattin' beside him, like he might be a prisoner or something."

Brad said that he, too, had noticed that. It had puzzled him at the time.

Lige ripped loose again. If he was sure Craw had thrown them down he would let the law take and hang him. He could hardly believe it, after all he had done for the boy. Craw was worse than Judas Iscariot.

After his father had finished raving Brad asked whether this changed their plans. Did they go on with the jail-break? Or did they let Craw fry in his own fat?

"We'll go ahead." The voice of Lige had dropped to a purr more deadly than his former frenzy. "If he guided the posse I'll make him wish he had never been born."

"When do we start?" Brad asked.

"Right damn now. Git the horses, son."

"And we pick up the doc after bustin' into the jail. That the idea?"

"Correct. Doc Watkins batches it alone. We'll gather him in on our way back to camp."

The night riders clattered down the corduroy road and cut across toward the ferry. Before they reached the bayou Dull left them. It was better that he should not be seen riding with the fugitives. It would destroy his value as a spy on the movements of their enemies.

A cow horn hung on a gum tree at the edge of the bayou. Brad blew on it to summon the owner of the ford from the other side of the water. A man came out of a cabin and shouted across an inquiry. Grumbling at the late travelers, he brought the scow across the bayou by means of the wire ropes to which it was attached. When he discovered who his customers were he became at once humble and servile. Lige did not tell him they would be back in an hour or two to recross. The ferryman might get the idea of having a sheriff's posse there to ambush them.

They rode into the village of Bighorn by way of a lane used to drive cows back from pasture. Though the time was not yet ten-thirty scarcely a light was to be seen. In that country region people rose and retired early. The jail was on an isolated lot two hundred yards from the end of the business street. The outlaws left their horses with one they called Lem fifty yards from the building and went forward on foot. Brad had his hands tied loosely in front of him.

Standing close to the wall, Lige lifted his voice cautiously. "Hello, Tim, we got a prisoner for you."

He had to call three times before the tousled head of a man in a nightgown appeared at a window above. "What is it?" the jailer demanded. "Who wants me?"

Labreu gave the name of a neighboring farmer.

"We've cotched one of Lige's damned killers," he explained.

"Wait a minute." The head withdrew.

Presently Tim Fallon appeared at the door. He was barefoot, and the nightshirt was thrust into the top of his trousers. "Seems like I never get a prisoner except in the middle of the night," he complained.

Fright jumped to his face while he was still speaking. Lige had pushed a revolver into his belly. "Less talk," the badman growled.

"Jumping Jehoshaphat!" Fallon cried. "What is this?"

"We're emptying yore jail. Git yore keys. Look lively, or I'll plug a hole in you."

The jailer got his keys. He had only three prisoners. Two of them were Negroes in for chicken stealing. These petty thieves did not want to be released, especially by such notorious bandits as the Labreus. If they got out they would be hunted down, and very likely some excited posse man would pump a bullet into one of them on the assumption that they were connected with the outlaw band. But they found it not wise to labor the point with their rescuers. They slipped away into the night.

Craw was jubilant. "I knew you'd bust me loose, Pappy," he cried. "If you knew I was here."

His father did not respond to this enthusiasm. He was in a sour mood of ugly hate. "You never was wuth a hill of beans," he said with contemptuous anger. Savagely he turned on Fallon. "Didn't I say to keep yore hands in the air?"

"I have to hold up my pants with one hand," the jailer explained.

"Do like I say, damn you." The narrowed, shallow eyes of Lige fastened on Fallon and presently mirrored slow recognition. "You were in Harville's regiment during the war," he charged.

"That's right. I was in yore company."

"Yeah." There was a rising fury in the badman's voice. "And you were with him when he was huntin' me later."

A sudden fear flooded the jailer at the murderous malice he saw in the evil face. He lowered an arm in a gesture of goodwill. "Mr. Labreu, honest to God I got nothing in the world against you."

Rage boiled up in Lige and overflowed — at the world conspiring against him, the officers who had dragged him to Fort Smith, grim Judge Parker, Harville and his posse, most of all the weak-kneed son who had deserted him. All the bile of this concentrated hate broke loose on the unoffending jailer.

"Damn you, I told you to keep yore hands up."

The barrel of Labreu's revolver whipped up and pressed into Fallon's stomach. Twice a forefinger pressed against the trigger. The roar of the explosions filled the room.

The jailer stared at his murderer with open mouth, then sank to the floor, rolled over and lay still.

The younger Labreus and their companion outlaw stood for a moment shocked at the tragedy. They had seen Lige kill before, for no reason except that the lust to destroy had swept over him.

Lige flung back his head and gobbled loudly like a turkey. In the sound was something inhuman and feral, something that set him apart from ordinary murderers. To take human life filled him with a savage joy.

They left Fallon lying where he had fallen. Craw swung to the back of a horse behind his brother. Lige stopped at a small house in the outskirts of the village. He pounded on the door impatiently.

"A man has been hurt, Doc, and needs you to fix him up," he shouted.

"Be with you as soon as I have dressed," Dr. Watkins answered.

"Well, git a move on you," the outlaw said. "Them Labreus shot him up."

The light of a lamp showed through the window. Presently the door was opened by the doctor. He looked around, surprised at so large a group. It does not take five armed men to bring a doctor. Watkins had not been in the district more than a few years. All of these faces were strange to him, and he did not like any of them.

"What man is hurt?" he asked.

"Don't fool around with questions," Lige told him harshly. "Git yore bag and fork that horse with the gray stockings back of Lem."

A cold lump knotted itself in the doctor's stomach. He did not need to ask who these men were. They must be the Labreus. This gross ruffian must be the Gobbler.

Lige followed him into the house when he went to get his bag. It was not likely the doctor would be fool enough to come out shooting, but the Gobbler never took unnecessary chances.

They routed out the ferryman to take them across the bayou. It was like Lige to jeer at him when he mentioned the two-bit fare for the services. This mean streak in the outlaw had more than once turned into active enemies men who had been merely indifferent.

The night riders passed through a canebrake and drew up while Brad blindfolded the doctor.

Watkins was thoroughly alarmed. He was a fat little man unused to violence. "Is it far?" he asked, his voice quavering in spite of his wish not to show fear.

"Never mind how far it is," Brad answered. "You'll git there if you hang on to Lem's back."

After a quarter of an hour of travel, part of the time sloshing through water, Lem said over his shoulder, "Hang on tight, Doc, so you won't fall off in the slough when hit gits boggy." He added: "I don't 'low to go fishin' for you in the muck."

Watkins asked what Labreu would do with him after he had dressed the wound of the injured man.

"Why, you doggoned idjit, he wouldn't take the trouble to blindfold you if he was fixin' to harm you," Lem told the worried man.

The doctor found comfort in that. If they meant to

kill him there would be no need to blindfold him so that he would not be able to find the way to the camp again. It seemed to him hours later that he slid from the back of the horse stiff and sore.

Lige took the handkerchief from his prisoner's eyes and led him to a spot beneath a cypress tree where a man lay on a blanket.

"Fix him up good, Doc," the bandit ordered. "This yere is my boy Sim. I'm expectin' you to git him well in a hurry."

Sim growled, "Hit took you a hell of a long time to git back, Pappy."

"We had to bust Craw outa the calaboose, son," Lige replied mildly. "Has it been hurtin' you a heap?"

"Like blazes. Don't you let him hurt me more."

Watkins examined the wound. A bullet had struck the man in the side and been deflected by a rib, then plowed a way out through the flesh.

"You're in luck," the doctor said. "No vital organs have been injured. In a couple of weeks you ought to be good as new."

He dressed the wound and gave the man a sleeping powder, after which he made up several more and told Lige when they were to be taken, adding instructions as to nursing and feeding.

"Your boy will do fine," the doctor promised. "He won't need a doctor again. All he needs is rest, sleep, and good food."

Lige looked at him through narrowed, suspicious eyes. He did not trust anybody. The doctor might be lying to get away safely.

"So you say," he snarled. "How do I know you're tellin' me the truth?"

"You saw for yourself that it is only a flesh wound," the doctor said. "All he needs is to build up again the blood he has lost."

Lige was of that opinion himself. "I reckon," he agreed ungraciously. "But before you go I've got another job for you."

"Somebody else hurt?" Watkins asked.

"Not yet," answered the outlaw, grinning maliciously. "But he's going to be. A li'l matter of family discipline."

He led the way up a rise to the other side of the island that rose out of the slimy waters of the slough. Beneath a gum tree the rest of the gang were gathered. The doctor saw with surprise that one of them had been stripped to the waist and his outstretched arms tied around the tree by a rope attached to each wrist.

The man trussed up was Craw Labreu. He cried out to his father for mercy, that his idea in bringing the posse had been to let Lige ambush them.

"You always was a liar, Craw," Lige told him evenly. "You let Harville bullyrag you into guiding his men to our camp. On account of that yore brother Sim got shot up, and we had to move in a hurry to a new camp. You cain't do that to me. I 'low to tickle yore back so you'll remember it next time."

Craw tried to get down on his knees to beg, but he could not make it on account of a bulging knot below the rope. He sobbed promises of amendment if his pappy would only let him off this time.

Lige ignored his pleas. He nodded to Lem, who was

standing a little way back with two stout hickory branches in his hands. Lem dropped one of the limbs and stepped forward. He was a big, brawny, red-faced fellow. It was plain from his expression that he was going to enjoy settling this account.

"Give it to him good," Lige ordered. "I'll tell you when to quit."

The hickory whacked down on the bare back of the victim. A red welt leaped from the white skin. Drops of blood oozed out of the flesh. Craw let out an agonized shriek. The hickory whistled down a dozen times. The back of the howling man was a torn blotch of red weals and blood. Lem dropped his worn-out switch and picked the second.

Watkins turned his head aside to avoid looking at the tortured wretch. "Isn't that enough?" he asked the father in a low voice.

"I'll learn him to throw down on his pappy," Lige said with a pleased smile.

Six more lashes fell on the writhing back before Lige stopped the punishment. Brad released his brother's wrists and Craw collapsed. He lay moaning on the ground.

His father waved a hand cheerfully at Watkins. "Yore patient, Doc," he said, and turned on his heel to walk away.

The doctor did what he could for the moaning man. Brad brought Craw a glass half filled with whisky. He commented to Watkins, as the whipped man lay sobbing on the ground, "No sand in his craw."

Half an hour later Watkins was blindfolded again and put on a horse. Lem rode a mule and led the horse by a rope. The doctor hung on to the pommel of the saddle to keep from falling off. They twisted and turned a dozen times until the led man had not the least idea in what general direction they had been moving. About a quarter of a mile from the ferry the doctor's guard turned him loose.

13

COLONEL HARVILLE DECIDED that his boys had better ride in pairs when they left the plantation. He did not want one of them while riding alone to run into a bunch of Labreu's men.

Tom and Larry saddled to go to Big Hollow the morning after the fight in the slough. A broken singletree had to be replaced, and Maxwell was expecting an important letter in the mail.

"I don't reckon these scurvy scoundrels would attack two of you, unless they could fix up an ambush," the planter said. "When you get to the big oak tree you better cut through the woods so as not to be trapped if they're laying for some of us in the brush." He filled his corncob pipe, a frown on his face. "Keep your eyes skinned every minute. Lige is six feet of devil and a hundred eighty pounds of hell. And no Apache was ever trickier than he is. Stop at the gin on your way. Get word to everybody to stay at home nights and to keep doors barred. They better have their guns loaded and handy. No tellin' what these doggoned ruffians will do."

Tom said that Jes' Tolable would probably be hanging

around the gin. He would have him fork his mule and warn all the neighbors to be careful. He added that since he and Larry would be packing rifles there was no need to worry about them.

At Big Hollow they heard disquieting news. Lige and some of his men had somehow got into the jail, released Craw, and killed Tim Fallon. The village was buzzing with excitement and alarm. Tim had been found lying outside of a cell half dressed. Apparently he had been unarmed.

The storekeeper, Jud Holcomb, drew the Harvilles into his cubbyhole of an office to tell them something else. Yesterday morning, before Holcomb had heard that the Labreus were in the neighborhood, Curt Moss had been in and bought half a wagonload of supplies. He had paid for the food with a twenty-dollar gold piece. Since he was never known to have six bits in his pocket, this had surprised the storekeeper. Curt had later crossed the bayou on the ferry. The explanation of this small mystery was clear as soon as Holcomb learned that the outlaws were hidden in the swamp. Curt had bought the food for his Uncle Lige and had delivered the supplies to him. From the quantity purchased the inference could be drawn that Lige intended to stay in the slough at least one week and probably two.

The Harvilles dropped in to see Dr. Watkins. They wanted to find out how seriously Rod Logan was hurt. The doctor could not tell them definitely that Rod was in no danger. He had lost a great deal of blood. Fortunately the bullet had just missed penetrating his lung. But the wound was much more severe than the one received by Sim Labreu.

Tom opened his eyes wider at this. "You mean you have seen him?" he asked.

"Lige and his gang picked me up right after they killed poor Tim," Watkins explained. "They blindfolded me and took me to their camp." He told the story of what he had seen there, including an account of the terrible whipping Labreu had given his son Craw.

"I reckon Craw had it coming," Tom said.

"His brother Brad thought he was lucky to get off with a whipping," Watkins mentioned. "I heard him tell another man he called Lem that if his pappy hadn't already gobbled once that night he would likely have shot Craw. Until I heard of Tim's death I did not quite understand what he meant. Brad's idea was, I think, that the old man had satisfied for the time his urge to kill."

As they started back for the plantation Larry made a suggestion to his brother. "About that twenty-dollar gold piece Curt Moss gave Holcomb. Don't you think it odd that with the date of 1866 it looked so fresh and unworn?"

"What you getting at?" Tom inquired. "Someone may have had it tucked away and not had a call to use it."

"Or somebody who is dead may have had it hidden in a box in the ground until yesterday," Larry said.

Tom stared at him. "You mean — that this is part of Flynn's hidden cache?"

"Dug up by the Labreus the night they got here. Why not?"

"Might be." Tom's dark eyes quickened to a live interest. "What say we swing round past the Flynn place on our way home? If the Labreu gang were there digging night before last we might find signs of it."

Larry nodded. "Just what I was going to propose."

From Big Hollow they took a little-used road that cut across a prairie into a hickory slash. Beyond this the ground dipped and became spongy. The trail skirted a swamp until it reached a broken-down rail fence that enclosed a field of girdled gums long since dead. Turning sharply to the left, they rode up an incline from the summit of which the old Flynn house could be seen.

As they passed a walnut tree Tom hitched a thumb toward it. "Where the guerrillas hanged Flynn," he told his brother.

The house had been in its time a pretentious one, but now the piazza pillars were rotting, the windows were broken, and the front door hung suspended by one hinge. The live oaks were so thick that the sun scarcely penetrated the heavy foliage from the limbs of which moss and mistletoe pendants trailed almost to the ground.

The place gave Larry the shivers. There was something eerie and evil about its miasmic atmosphere. It seemed a fit scene for horrible and inhuman deeds. At night the field of girdled gum trees must look like a ghostly graveyard, and the house itself a spot haunted by echoes of a dreadful past.

Even Tom, whose imagination rarely troubled him, found it a gruesome locale. "Nice site to pick for a house," he muttered.

"The worst I've seen," Larry agreed, "unless he had chosen the slough. Flynn must have been a queer character."

"From what they tell me he must have been loony," Tom agreed. "He was a bad egg and had used Labreu's scoundrels in some of his meanness. The story is that he got away with the loot and left them holding the sack. If he had had any sense he would have known better than to try to use Lige as a cat's-paw and still stay in the country. But he was a stubborn old coot — told Lige to go climb a hickory. A fool never learns anything till it is too late."

They wandered through the house. No heirs had ever been found, and though the sheriff had in theory taken possession for the law, the furniture was regarded as anybody's property by the poor settlers in the neighborhood. A little at a time they had taken it. The large, high-ceilinged rooms still showed moldy traces of former stateliness, though the floors had been ripped up and the walls attacked with picks to discover any secret compartments that might be inside. Fragments of fine chandeliers still hung from the ceilings, and the slashed mantels were of walnut.

On the lowest tread of the broad stairway Larry pointed out tobacco juice not yet wholly dry. Somebody had been here within two or three days. Through the kitchen door they moved into the back yard. Beneath a persimmon tree there were signs of fresh digging. Dirt had been thrown up from an excavation, and on the loose soil was a round imprint that had probably been made by the base of a lantern. At the bottom of the hole was a mold about fifteen inches long by eight inches wide from which a box had evidently been lifted.

"Lige and his friends made a profitable visit here, looks

like," Tom guessed. "They must have found what they didn't have time to get before they were driven out of the country years ago."

"If they knew where the treasure was, why didn't they get it then?" Larry asked.

"The Ku-Kluxers came on them right after they killed Flynn and the old Negro woman, and they had to skedaddle in a hurry. After that this place was watched, to try and trap them. They made one attempt before they pulled their freight for Oklahoma and were driven off. Flynn must have weakened and told them where he had his money cached, or they wouldn't have known where to dig when they came back."

"I hope old Flynn's ghost haunts them," Larry said.

"They claim it walks here nights, but I don't reckon that would bother the Gobbler any. If all the poor devils he has killed off came back to scare him he would have a whole graveyard of haunts."

Until the past few days Larry had never met in his well-cushioned life anybody like the Labreus. They were beyond his understanding. In them there seemed to be no inborn sense of right and wrong. Tigers were as much moved by a moral code as these ruffians. On the way back to Rosemont, Larry mentioned this to Tom.

The older brother guessed at a partial explanation. Lige always had been bad, and the turbulent war days had given him a chance to indulge the evil without fear of punishment. His band of guerrillas had preyed alike on those favouring the North and the South. By the time peace came he was so used to violating the rights of others that he did not want to give up this lawless life of murder and pillage.

Always a fugitive from justice, he had come to hate everybody who stood for order and decency. Since his sons had been born and brought up in this atmosphere, they had become brutish as their father.

Soon after the riders struck the main road they pulled up at a farmhouse. Here Mack Gillis and his family lived. The house was small but had been recently whitewashed. There was a small flower garden. None of the slackness of a casual renter showed in the yard. Its neatness indicated self-respect in the owner.

Tom swung from the saddle and walked to the house. He had brought a message from his father to Mack. A pleasant-looking woman opened the door and invited Tom to come into the house. The door closed behind him.

Around a fence corner thick with blackberry bushes came a ramshackle wagon to which were hitched a bony mule and a swaybacked mare.

14

THE DRIVER OF THE WAGON pulled up to greet the horseman, "Howdy, Mr. Larry," he said with an oily smile. "I've seen you araound Big Hollow onct or twict, but I reckon you don't know me. My name is Curt Moss. I'm a friend of yore pappy."

Larry's glance traveled over the man humped up on the wagon seat. Moss was a big unkempt fellow with shifty eyes that looked out from drooping lids that half shuttered them. His shoulders were heavy and his body thick. Though he was running to fat, he still looked to be powerful. Young Harville guessed his age about thirty-five.

"I haven't heard my father mention it," Larry said coldly.

"Yes, sir, I've knowed the colonel a right smart time," Moss continued cheerfully. "Quite a man, he is. Set in his ways as this yere mule of mine. But I always got along with him fine. I remember you when you was a puny youngster before you went to England. Seemed funny for the colonel to send you away to that furrin country where all the folks is slaves to a queen, but, anyhow, you got back safe."

Larry said nothing, but there was contempt in his silence. He resented the impudence of the man. Even if he had not known that Moss was a hanger-on of the Labreus, he would have found him repellent. Something about him reminded Larry of a swollen toad, perhaps his manner of self-importance.

Moss gathered the reins closer. "Well, I reckon I'll be moseyin' along. I got to go down to the store for some provisions."

"Are you taking some more to Lige Labreu and his murderous scoundrels?" Larry asked. He flung the question out scornfully, to get it through the thick hide of the scamp that he was not deceived by his pretence of goodwill.

A change came over the man's face. The hypocritical friendliness went out of it as the light does when a candle is snuffed.

"Who told you I took food to Lige?" he demanded angrily.

"You told it yourself, when you paid Holcomb with a twenty-dollar gold piece dug up from Flynn's cache hidden beneath the persimmon tree in the back yard."

Moss was so taken by surprise that he did not even offer a denial. "All right. Say I did. That money belonged to Lige. Mebbe I took him grub. A man cain't throw daown his own kin. Lige is my uncle. I 'low you stand by yore folks. I got a right to help mine." The man's voice was sharp and challenging.

Rage boiled up in Larry and swept away his habitual caution. "My people aren't treacherous killers, murderers who ought to be stamped out like wolves," he retorted. "You can be sent to the penitentiary for what you did. I hope you are."

"You cain't talk thataway to me," Moss said thickly, wrapping the reins around the handle of the whip standing in its socket. "I'm an honest man, and by God, I won't stand it."

"There's not an honest hair in your head," Larry exploded. "You're a dirty scoundrel crooked as a dog's hind leg. Labreu is paying you well for everything you do to help him."

Moss jumped from the wagon and moved slowly toward the horseman. "I wouldn't take that from yore biggity old man, let alone his whelp," he snarled. "Git daown from that saddle, or I'll drag you off'n it."

He had not finished saying the words before Larry's feet hit the ground. The boy was very pale, but his eyes were blazing. They did not lift from the fat, furious face of his foe.

The big man stopped. His challenge had been accepted

too quickly to please him, and something in the youngster's expression was daunting. In his day Moss had been a notorious rough-and-tumble fighter. But he knew the reputation of the Harvilles. Perhaps he had made a mistake in believing that this one was not like the others.

"Don't you dass touch me," he yelped, and dragged a gun from his pocket.

Larry stepped toward the man, his gaze holding fast to the eyes of the bully.

A voice from the house shouted warning. "Look out, Larry." Tom was running down the walk, Larry knew, but he did not turn his head. His feet carried him closer to the man with the pistol.

"Keep back, you damn fool," Moss cried. The man felt trapped. He could not kill young Harville without forfeiting his own life. Tom would attend to that.

Larry discovered that the quirt still hung attached to his wrist. "Drop that gun," he ordered.

Moss tossed it into the wagon. "We don't have to fuss about nothing," he cried, and backed against the front wheel with his fists cocked protectively.

The quirt in Larry's hand whistled through the air and wound itself around the man's legs. It rose and fell again on the fat thighs of the big man. Moss crowded forward to get close. Larry's left fist drove him back, and again the quirt burned the flesh of the victim like a rope of fire. The strong fingers of Larry closed tightly on his opponent's throat. Moss was pinned against the wheel, his feet in a puddle of slippery mud. His feet slid forward, and he could find no secure footing to give force to the blows he flung at the face of his opponent. The whip swished down again and again.

Tom caught his brother's wrist. "That's enough, Larry," he said, and pulled Larry back.

"Goddlemighty, what's eatin' you?" Moss groaned. "I said I didn't want to fight. You 'most strangled me."

"Stay away from the Labreus, or you'll get worse next time," Tom warned.

Larry flung away the quirt, already sick of the rage that had swept him, then walked to his horse and swung to the saddle.

Tom took a look at Larry's bleeding, battered face. "He sure marked you up while you were whaling him."

The younger man put a hand to his face and looked with surprise at the blood. "I didn't know he was hitting me, to speak of," he said.

Tom chuckled. "A man cain't do but one thing well at a time. Curt was so busy hollerin' for you to quit skinning him that he couldn't give his mind to fighting, any more than you could get interested in how much he was spoilin' yore good looks."

The younger Harville was completely deflated. His plan of life did not include violent outbursts of anger. "I don't know what got into me," he said ruefully. "He gave me a chance to drop the thing when he flung his pistol into the wagon. What was the matter with me?"

"I thought you were doing all right," Tom said. "I kind of gathered that Curt wasn't very happy about it. He used bad judgment. Usually he picks a man he knows he can whop easy."

"The fellow's impudence annoyed me, but I had no business saying what I did to him. I lost my temper completely. After saying that I think we ought to leave the law to settle such things I act like a silly bully." Larry's voice was dejected, not in the least like that of a conqueror.

They turned into a short cut that took them through a hickory slash toward their home.

"You're not looking at this right," Tom said. "Curt has been asking for a whaling for a long time. A bully doesn't jump a husky fellow who weighs forty pounds more than he does. You're a peaceable chap. I don't suppose you've had a fight in years."

"Not ever. When I was a boy here, two or three boys licked me, but I didn't have spirit enough to fight back."

"It's time you had one then. I saw Mack Gillis watching you. He'll spread the news. Now that folks know you are ready to tackle a man big as Moss you will probably never have to fight another fellow."

Maxwell Harville was sitting on the porch when his sons rode up. His glance took in Larry's face. Though greatly surprised, he showed no sign of it. "I hope the other chap looks as bad," he said.

Tom was much pleased at what had occurred. Into his mind a furtive fear of which he was ashamed had more than once crept, the treacherous thought that his brother might be a milksop. On that subject he now felt quite easy.

"The other fellow *feels* a whole lot worse, sir," he said. "You'll have to watch this son of yours, or he'll get us into trouble beating up the neighbors. He's a regular fire-eater.

While Curt Moss had him covered with a six-shooter he walked up to him, made him throw the gun away, and flogged him good with his quirt."

"Where were you?" the colonel asked, somewhat skeptical of this version of the fracas.

"I was running down to the road from Mack Gillis' house yelling to Larry to look out for the gun. He didn't pay any more attention to it than if it had been a turkey-wing fan."

"You had better tell me all about it," Maxwell said.

"Ask Larry. I didn't see the beginning of it."

His father turned to his youngest son.

"Well, sir, I made a complete fool of myself," Larry confessed. "He was impudent, pretending he was a friend, and when I called him a hypocrite he was insolent. He tried to back out of it and I wouldn't let him. I can't tell you exactly why. The fact is I was too angry to think straight."

"What did you call him?"

"I said he was a dirty scoundrel and hadn't an honest hair in his head, and that he ought to go to the penitentiary."

"All of which is true," the colonel agreed. He, too, felt a foolish pride in the boy, because he also had not been sure of his spirit and was glad to have this evidence of pluck. "You did quite right, son. Don't worry about it. But you'll have to be careful. Curt will do you a meanness if he can. He might take a shot at you from the brush."

In spite of his father's approval Larry felt unhappy about what he had done.

15

JES' TOLABLE CAME to Rosemont with a strange story. He had got it from Bud Holly, a colored boy of about nineteen who worked at the cotton gin. Bud had been hunting for squirrels across the bayou, and after getting five or six had sat down beneath a gum and fallen asleep. Wakened by the sound of voices, he had crouched behind the big trunk of the tree. Two men were riding past and he had caught a snatch of their conversation. Though he did not know either of them, he felt sure they were two of the outlaws. One of them said they had to get more guns before they tried to make a break for Texas. The other answered that he did not like Lige's idea of snatching Logan's girl and swapping her back to her father for the needed rifles. It was too dangerous.

Bud was waiting outside, and the colonel listened to his tale first-hand. It seemed incredible, yet the owner of Rosemont believed the boy was telling the truth. Lige was a bold villain, and he probably thought he might as well be hanged for a sheep as a lamb. He would do anything that would help him escape.

The possibility of harm coming to Diane shocked Larry. "We'll have to warn Major Logan," he said. "His wife and daughter ought to leave at once for Brandon, where they will be safe."

"I could write a letter to him and send one of our black boys with it," the colonel suggested.

"One of us ought to go personally, sir," Larry urged. "This is too serious for a letter."

Maxwell Harville's finger tips drummed on the arm of the chair in which he sat. He thought Larry might be right, yet he did not like the idea of having one of his sons rebuffed by Logan.

"The major is a mighty stiff-necked old ramrod," he said, then smiled guiltily. "Maybe that's the pot calling the kettle black. But Logan might let you know that he did not need any help in protecting his womenfolks, especially any advice from us Harvilles."

"I'll have to risk that, sir," Larry answered. "All of us would be uneasy if we didn't warn him of the danger."

The colonel agreed. He would have been greatly distressed if any harm should come to Diane. Except for the confounded feud it would have been natural for one of his sons to pay court to Diane and possibly marry her, though he would have had competition to overcome. She had plenty of beaux, both at Brandon and in the plantation country. Young men buzzed around her as flies do about a lamp on a summer night. He had heard once that she was engaged to Melvin Darley. A few months later Ralph Philpott was rumored to be the lucky man. Just this past week he had gathered from something Andy said to Tom that Edward Travis was in favor now. She might have been engaged to each of them at one time or another. Southern girls moved in and out of betrothals lightly, though they took marriage very seriously.

Since his two older sons were not within reach at the moment Larry carried the warning to Hillcrest. His father's last admonition to him was to be just as stiff as the major.

Jes' Tolable rode with Larry. They took with them Bud Holly. The colored boy was not very happy at his part in this. If the Labreus heard of what he had done they might have it in for him.

Through a grove of splendid white oaks the riders came to a view of Hillcrest. The house was colonial in pattern and well proportioned. To reach it the graveled road circled a flower garden of roses, phlox, fuchsias, daffodils, and mignonettes. Larry had been told that Mrs. Logan spent many hours supervising the old Negro who took care of the garden. The whole place had a better kept look than Rosemont. The hedge in front was neatly trimmed, and recently the house had been repainted. Honeysuckle vines shaded one end of the wide porch. Throughout the wide doorway to the spacious hall a hanging stairway of charming design could be seen.

Diane came out of the house carrying a wicker basket and scissors. She wore a sprigged dimity dress, a wide-brimmed straw hat, and gloves to protect her hands from the thorns. Evidently she intended to cut a bouquet for the house.

At sight of the two armed men and the Negro following them she stopped in surprise. Larry swung from the saddle and came forward smiling.

"We come in peace and not in war," he said.

Diane blushed. The words reminded her of a line from Scott's poem "Lochinvar," in which the young gallant had invaded the hall of his enemy to carry away his love. She was filled with romantic dreams, as young Southern girls of the period were likely to be, but until this young man had come home none of the men who wooed her fitted the role of a Lochinvar. Most of them were sons of fathers who had fought well for a losing cause, but she had grown up among them and they were cut a little too much to pattern. This blond youth who had lived so long overseas was an unknown quantity, more appealing to her imagination because he was an enemy of her house.

"You want to see my father?" she asked.

"I'm glad to see his daughter too," he answered.

She flashed at him a look of pretended disapproval not meant to deceive. To the old colored man among the roses she called an order. "Uncle 'Lias, will you let my father know there is a gentleman to see him?"

While 'Lias was bringing the major Larry tried to keep the conversation going. Neither of them felt quite at ease. Both were aware that there was a tie which drew them together and a barrier holding them apart.

"It's a lovely garden," he said.

"My mother's," she told him. "It isn't at its best this month."

She asked him about English gardens, of which she had heard much. He told her of his aunt's garden in Surrey.

Major Logan came out to the porch, and Larry went to meet him. The major was in a light seersucker suit. He stood as stiff and erect as a grenadier at inspection, his cold, piercing eyes fixed on the young man.

"You wish to see me, sir?" he inquired.

"My father wants me to tell you something that this boy

Bud Holly overheard." Larry lowered his voice, so that the girl among the roses would not make out what they were saying. "It had to do with Miss Logan."

The major grew even more rigid. "How can anything this boy heard possibly have anything to do with my daughter?" he demanded sternly.

"Perhaps you had better let him tell his story, sir," Larry suggested. "There may be some danger for him in giving this information. I have promised that his name will be kept secret."

Logan listened to Bud's story. He did not want to believe it, but his reason told him it was true. Bud was a good boy, and anyhow he did not have imagination enough to cook up such a yarn. The major thanked Larry, quite formally, and the other two with more warmth. He said that he would take any precautions necessary to protect his family.

Larry's words had been for the planter and his attention upon him, but he had been deeply aware of the girl among the rosebushes, so still and hushed, her eyes soft and shining, her parted lips like a crimson flower. The swell of her small, firm breasts and the line of her fine throat enchanted him. She was in the immaturity of her late teens, had gone such a little way into life in spite of tentative excursions toward love. Yet he was sure there was in her an unawakened capacity for emotions that might some day be generous and perhaps violent.

The three men mounted and turned to go. Larry drew up beside the girl with a question. "How is your brother Rod doing?"

"Very well indeed, Dr. Watkins says. Already he is much better."

"I had heard so. I'm very glad." Larry was not entirely satisfied with the result of his visit. He was afraid the major did not take the Lebreus seriously enough. It had been in his mind to suggest that he send Mrs. Logan and Diane to Brandon, but he could not very well give him advice about looking after his own family. The major would probably think it presumptuous of him to warn the girl, but the fear in his mind was urgent. "Lige Labreu is a terrible man. He would stop at nothing. Don't leave the house unless you are well protected."

"I have already had an order from Father to stay at home," she said.

"Then be a good girl and do as you're told." Though he smiled, there was a serious warning in his voice.

Diane was full of curiosity about this call on her father. It was the first time in many years that a Harville had been at Hillcrest. She knew that Larry had not come for any trivial reason. Bud Holly had something to do with it. Of course the outlaws were involved. Larry had brought information of some sort to her father.

"You don't think the Labreus will attack Hillcrest, do you?"

"No. But I wish you and Mrs. Logan were at Brandon."

Perry Logan was still on the porch. He was watching the young people, a grim look on his face. His arm had been released only that day from the sling he had been wearing. Though he had no particular enmity toward this young fellow, he did not intend there should be any nonsense between his daughter and any son of Maxwell Harville.

Diane's glance shuttled to her father and back to the youth on horseback. "I think you had better leave, sir," she suggested.

He nodded, gave her a long look, bowed, and cantered down the winding road to join the others.

Jes' Tolable said, with a sly look at Larry, "I reckon Miss Diane is the purtiest gal in Arkansas."

Larry privately was willing to include more territory, but he kept his opinion to himself.

16

TWO MEN RODE OUT of the slash behind the Gillis place. They were Lige Labreu and his son Brad. At the stake-and-rider worm fence they drew up for a moment. A man was cultivating corn in the deadening.

"No two ways about it we got to git more rifles and ammunition," Lige said fretfully. "It was mighty bad luck losing two when Fin got killed off, and the one Curt got us was only a muzzle loader. If the boys had toted Winchesters instead of six-guns we would of got three-four of that damned posse instead of just woundin' one."

"We sure don't want to ride through Arkansas to Texas without all of us having rifles," Brad agreed.

"I hate to have womenfolks at the camp, account of it

stirring up the whole countryside, but looks like we got to play it thataway." Lige rasped his unshaven chin dubiously. " 'Course we don't aim to hurt her any if Mack don't act onreasonable."

"If it was the Logan gal I wouldn't mind being nice to her," Brad said, showing his teeth in a grin. "They say she's a humdinger with lots of jingle."

"One of the reasons I decided against her," his father answered sharply. "Like enough you boys would of gummed up the whole thing. She's a lady. If one of you-all had insulted her we'd never have got outa here alive. This place would be like a hornets' nest."

The man behind the mule caught sight of the riders and stopped thirty yards from the end of the row.

"Hello, Mack," Lige called. "Want to talk with you."

Gillis hesitated, then moved reluctantly toward the rail fence. A bell of warning rang in him. This meant trouble. If the ruffians knew he had been with the posse, as they very likely did, the chances were that they had come to kill him. It was a boast of Lige that he always paid his debts.

The outlaw showed his broken stained teeth in a grin. "You ain't scared to meet old friends again, are you, Mack?" he purred, a velvety deadliness in his voice. "This yere is my son, Brad. You'd ought to know him, seeing you've got a shooting acquaintance with him. Prob'ly I should thank you for takin' care of Craw so nice the other day."

The pit of Mack's stomach tied itself into a knot. He managed a weak grin. "I made Craw lie down so he wouldn't get hit," he explained. "Craw can tell you that I wasn't doing any shooting."

"That's nice," Lige murmured. "Last time I saw you before that was quite a while ago. You was lying back of a fence corner trying to plug a hole in me."

"I reckon you was returning the compliment, Lige. Like you say, it was a long time ago. Fellows kinda git dragged into things. I'd plumb forgot it."

"I got a fust-class memory," Labreu mentioned.

"We usta play together when we were kids, Lige," the farmer reminded the outlaw.

"So we did, and the other day you joined a posse to rub me out. But I reckon you kinda got dragged into that."

Gillis knew the fellow was playing with him, as a cat does with a mouse. At any moment he might get tired of this and shoot him down as he had poor Tim Fallon, against whom he had no personal grievance.

Tiny blobs of perspiration were breaking out on Mack's face. "I got no hard feeling against you, Lige," he pleaded.

"Fine. If I was sure you meant that, mebbe — " Lige let the sentence tail out.

Mack assured him eagerly that he did, but as he looked into the man's cruel, mocking eyes he knew that his words carried no weight. Nothing would move Labreu but self-interest and the anger simmering in him. His thin lips, lifted in a sneer that showed the crooked teeth, were a merciless gash in a beefy, red-veined face.

"I never did know what a good friend you are, Mack," jeered the outlaw. "Seems you been yearnin' all these years for me to come back." He turned to his son. "What you think, Brad? Seeing that Mack is on the mourner's bench for his sins against me, do you reckon I ought to forgive and forget like the good book says?"

Mack looked at Brad, hope and fear struggling in his face. He guessed that Brad was a weaker replica of his father. Crime and dissipation had stamped on his face the same shifty evil, but he lacked the arrogant assurance of the older man.

"Why don't we take him into the brush, slick him good with a hickory so he won't backslide, and learn him it don't pay to fight the Labreus," Brad proposed.

"You hadn't ought to talk thataway to our good friend Mack," Lige reproved. To Gillis he apologized blandly. "Brad is a drunken, swearin' devil when he gits started, but he's got a heart of gold and he'll cotton to you jest like I do when he knows how true you are."

Mack murmured something about a rough bark doing no harm.

The glittering eyes of the bandit stabbed into those of the farmer. "I'm takin' yore word for it that you are our friend, and I'm acceptin' yore offer to drive in to Oldport today to git us a few supplies we need. Nice of you to think of it, Mack."

"I sure would like to go, Lige, if — if I wasn't so dad-gummed busy right now. This corn needs cultivatin' before it rains." Mack dragged his excuses out hopelessly. He knew he had to consent.

"If you'd ruther not go jest say so," Lige said very gently.

"I — I 'low I can git off," the farmer replied. He knew

he was close to the danger line.

"I 'low you can." Lige apparently diverged from the subject. "I hear you're married, Mack, and I reckon you got a nice family."

"Yes, sir. We got two little girls — nine and ten."

"I expect you are mighty fond of them, like a good pappy had ought to be," Lige said, almost in a murmur.

Fear tightened in the chest of Gillis. He felt his heart pounding under his ribs. "That's right, Lige." Mack reverted to the trip he was to take. "Maybe I'd better get started right away."

"Good old Mack," the ruffian taunted. "You always was dependable. But I'm not aiming to rush you. Tell you what we'll do. You go git that mule you're cultivating with, and we'll all go up to the house. I'd like to meet the missus anyhow. We'll have a nice little talk, and then you'll hitch up and start for Oldport."

Gillis felt a heavy weight of despair in his stomach. This danger was going to involve his family as well as himself. He protested unhappily.

"Now looky here, Lige. We don't want to make a mistake. This has got to be kept quiet, or I'll be stopped before I git back. You know how kids talk. If my folks don't see you they won't have anything to gabble about. Let's jest keep this among us three."

"I won't make any mistake, Mack," answered Lige. He was still grinning, but there was a cruel bite to his voice. "And yore kids ain't a-going to talk. They'll be like clams. Don't worry about that. All you got to keep in mind is to do exactly like I tell you."

"What's the sense in letting them know anything about this, Lige? Hit ain't smart."

"Do like I say, Mack. Go git that mule." The eyes of the man blazed with savage malignity. "Onless you figure you don't want to oblige me."

The farmer's will to resist collapsed. He unhitched the mule and led it to the house, the riders flanking him. Two small girls were playing in the yard, but at sight of the approaching strangers they fled into the house to tell their mother company was coming. The outlaws tied their mounts to the fence and followed their unwilling host into the house.

17

MRS. GILLIS WAS a comely woman in her mid-thirties, ten years younger than her husband. She wore a patched dress from which the original color had long since faded. At the sight of Lige Labreu her brown eyes dilated. She opened her lips to speak, but no words came from them.

Labreu smiled, but there was no warmth in his gargoyle grin. "Why, we're sure enough old friends," he told her as he shook hands. "I didn't know Mack was so fortunate as to marry Fanny Trott. 'Member the time I took you to the dance at Big Hollow?"

She remembered it very well. Only because she was afraid he would do a meanness to her parents if she refused to go, had she consented to let him take her.

"It's certainly nice to meet you again, Fanny. And two pretty little gals jest like their mammy. Fanny, meet my boy Brad. Prob'ly you recollect him as a boy. He was a tough handful then. I sure had to wear him to a frazzle plenty of times, but he turned out good. Well, I'm sure pleased to see you and Mack so happy."

"We're poor folks, but we get along all right," she said.

"What might be the names of yore li'l gals? I'd like for to meet them."

He picked an open space on the clean bare floor to spatter it with tobacco juice.

The children hid behind their mother, clinging to her skirt and peeping at the strangers from this safe harbor. Without words they declined the invitation of Lige to make a closer acquaintance. They vanished behind the skirt.

Mrs. Gillis mentioned their names, Mollie and Sara Ann. "They're right shy," she said, to excuse them for not coming forward.

"Mack is going on a little errand for us to Oldport," Lige explained. "We need some store goods, and seeing as we are in sort of a hurry he's hitching up to start right away. 'Course we expect to pay Mack good for his time and trouble."

The frightened eyes of Fanny Gillis fluttered to her husband. She had felt sure there was something unpleasant and perhaps hazardous behind the man's false smiling geniality. Now she knew her fears were justified.

"Cain't you-all buy stuff at Holcomb's store?" she asked, crowding down the panic beginning to stir in her breast.

"Not the kind of goods we need, ma'am. Mack will tell you all about it when he gits back with a hundred dollars cold cash of his own for his trouble."

Mack said to his wife reluctantly, "Looks like I better go to Oldport for Lige, Fanny."

"Hit's right neighborly of you, Mack," the outlaw agreed heartily. "From now on we'll be good friends." His eyes rested on the children. "My boys are all grown up. I miss having little folks around. If you-all would loan me one of yores while her pappy is away it would sure give me comfort and the boys too. We would much [1] her plenty and take fust-class care of her at the camp."

The father and mother said "No" simultaneously. They understood what the invitation meant. The child was to be a hostage for the good faith of her father. Fanny saw the set of the Gobbler's mouth grow ugly and added hastily, "They are so shy, Mr. Labreu, that they would be turribly homesick."

"Think it over, and you-all will see it different," Lige suggested, intimidation in his soft voice. "She would be safe as if she was in God's pocket, cross my heart and hope to die. I give you-all Lige Labreu's word, and hit always has been good."

The children began to cry. The oldest one sobbed into the skirts a refusal. "I don't want to leave Mumsie. I want to stay here."

"We'll fix it so you won't have to leave yore mammy," the bandit told her, an offensive grin on his wolfish face.

[1] Vernacular, rural Arkansas: to pet or make much of.

"Fanny can come along and have a nice visit too. We 'uns have lots of nice things to eat, and yore pappy will bring you back some candy from Oldport."

Mack Gillis was a shambling, insignificant man, of small importance to anybody but his family. In these three his life centered. Fear dried his throat and choked the voice that came from it almost in a croak.

"Hit ain't convenient for Fanny and the girls to leave the place, Lige. They got the animals to look after. I'll do yore errand all right, I swear to God."

"I'm sure you will, Mack, you an' me always having been so friendly, but we got to remember there's a lot of durned scalawags projecting araound. We got to make certain they won't pester Fanny and the kids. I 'low to look after them while you are gone. Hit will be a pleasure." The ruffian's words were smooth as butter, but not for an instant did the threat leave his cold eyes.

"I'd ruther they stayed home," Mack answered doggedly. "A camp of men is no place for a woman and children. You know that, Lige. If I git a hump on me I can be back tomorrow night, or anyways before noon the day after."

Brad spoke up sourly. "I told you, Pappy, we'd ought to take him into the woods an' skin his back."

Lige waved his son into silence. He leaned forward, spacing his words to give them significance, eyes fixed on the farmer. "You got no say-so in this, Mack. Me, I give the orders. You're not going to run to Harville and sell me out, not if you have a lick of sense. Understand?"

"I wouldn't do that, Lige," protested Gillis. "I'll do yore errand good."

The badman's teeth showed again in an appalling grin. "Not when I'm taking nice care of yore family, you wouldn't throw me daown. You ain't lunkhead enough for that. I'm giving you a chance, fellow, which is more than I ought to do after you going gunnin' for us the other day. But if you are so dad-gummed dumb or stubborn as not to take it that's yore fault not mine."

Gillis looked the killer right in the eye. "I won't buy my life by turning my family over to you."

"Why, you crazy fool, I've told you I don't aim to hurt them any if you play fair," Lige cried. "And if I like I can take them, anyhow."

Fanny tried to hush the frightened children, both of whom were crying. She said, while her hands stroked their heads gently, "We'll go with Mr. Labreu, Mack."

"I won't have it," Gillis cried.

"We got to be reasonable, Mack," she said. "Mr. Labreu will look after us fine while you are away. We can leave enough feed for the critters."

"Tha's the way to talk," approved Lige suavely. "I'll treat you-all like you were my own folks, Fanny, an' like I said, I'll pay Mack big for what he does."

The harassed farmer made one last attempt to squirm out. "Looks like it would be better for you to send Curt Moss or Chet Dull to Oldport. They're kin of you folks and — "

Lige interrupted. "Tha's why I'm not sending them. We got enemies who air liable to be watchin' our friends, and we have to git goods through." He drew Mack into the next room. "Fact is, we got our tails in a crack. I kin tell you because it won't make any difference now. We left Fort Smith in a hell of a hurry and didn't have time to lay in enough weapons. Since we got here we have done lost two of the rifles we had. I need four more Winchester rifles and a lot of shells for them and our forty-fives. Take along plenty of straw and gunny sacks in yore wagon to cover the hardware. Thing to do is not buy all the guns at one store. Be smart about it, is all. You won't have any trouble. If anybody gits inquisitive, tell him you air buying for Colonel Harville to holp hunt us down. Nobody will suspect you."

"Soon as I tote the guns to yore camp I can bring my folks home?" Mack asked anxiously.

"Bet yore boots you kin. But you won't be at our camp. We'll meet you at the big bend of the old Polk corduroy road. 'Course I trust you-all, but I aim to protect Fanny and the children by blindfolding them before they reach our camp. I wouldn't want for Harville to torture them to find out where our camp is at."

Gillis said, distress in his voice, "If you do ary one of them a meanness — "

Lige broke in. "Use yore head, Mack. Why would I hurt them? Soon as you show up with the guns you'll git them back. Hit will be a nice change for them."

They returned to the other room. Mack looked so worried that his wife consoled him, her voice cheerful and confident. "We'll be all right. Mr. Labreu hasn't got anything against us and the children. We haven't done him any harm."

"I'm a father myself," Lige said smoothly. "They will

be safe as in a church. All is, I got to protect our crowd. Old Lige ain't so bad. And you can use that hundred dollars, I'll bet."

The amiability of the scoundrel did not deceive Mack. He was putting on an act to allay their fears. The fellow was treacherous as the devil. But there would be no point in his hurting Fanny or the children if he did the errand successfully, and there ought to be no trouble about that.

"Why don't you send somebody with me to Oldport?" the farmer urged. "Then you'll know I'm playing fair."

Labreu shook his head. "I don't want to draw any attention to yore trip. You're gonna do fine. I ain't scared you won't."

Gillis hitched the team and helped his family into the wagon. He was very unhappy, but he did not see what else he could do. Even outside of the peril to himself and his family he hated to buy the weapons. They were to be used to kill good citizens, very likely men he knew and respected. All his life he had lived decently, doing harm to nobody. How could he respect himself for making it possible for this evil crew to slay his neighbors? But he could make no other choice. To save himself and his family from Labreu he had to do as he was told.

It racked his heart to see the fictitious good cheer of his wife. She pretended to be pleased at the escape from her household duties for a day or two. She promised the children that it would be a lovely picnic.

As they drew out from the farmyard a turkey cock lifted its wattled neck and gobbled. The sound of it sent a chill down Mack's spine. He recalled the old story of Lige, that he had the shocking habit of flinging back his head and gobbling like a turkey after killing a man.

The wagon and escorting riders crossed the bayou at the ford, which was two miles below the ferry and around a bend from it. The more direct route Lige avoided, because he would be less likely to be seen the lower way. The trail took them through a canebrake to an old corduroy road rotten with age, one that was beginning to sink into the spongy ground of the swamp.

Lige called a halt. He shifted his weight in the saddle, called Mack to his side, and gave him final murmured instructions. The farmer was to take the short county road to Oldport, but after he had bought the guns was to return by a roundabout almost deserted road. A messenger would be waiting for him at this point when he returned. If he handled this slick he would have no trouble at all.

From his hip pocket Lige drew a small leather pouch. He shook out of the bag into his hand ten gold pieces. His eyes clung to them avidly. Money was the man's God, and he felt an almost physical pain at parting with this bright yellow gold. Two of the pieces he dropped back into the sack. The others he handed to Gillis, with detailed orders as to the guns and ammunition needed. He was to try to beat down the merchants, but in any case he was to get the goods.

"Hit will be the best day's work you ever did, Mack," he concluded. "When you turn over these rifles to me you git five twenty-dollar gold pieces. Keep yore trap shut afterward and old man Harville won't ever know you holped me."

Mack's worried eyes shifted to the fetid green water of the swamp. The air was thick with buzzing mosquitoes. He saw a moccasin slide from a log into the slimy stagnant pool below. No sun reached the spongy ground owing to the dense foliage of the cypress trees and the great streamers of moss trailing from the branches. A shudder of horror convulsed his slim body. There was death in this miasmic atmosphere.

"I cain't go through with it, Lige," he pleaded. "Hit wouldn't be right for me to leave Fanny and the young 'uns with you."

The outlaw's face appalled the farmer. His thin lips tightened, his shallow eyes mirrored a venomous cruelty. "Why, that's up to you, Mack," he said. "But when a man rues back on me he don't live to do it twice."

Mrs. Gillis was watching the two men closely. She knew by the outlaw's look that her husband was rebelling again. It was too late for that, she knew, even if there had been at any time a chance of refusing with safety. Fanny moved toward them, managing a smile. "Don't be scared about me and the children, Mack. I overheard a word or two. It's guns he wants. You go git them, and he'll turn us loose. He would be a plumb idjit not to, and I never heard Lige called that."

"You married a woman with horse sense, Mack," the fugitive killer said. "If you stick to yore part of the bargain I will to mine."

Fanny looked at the scoundrel, a spark of anger in her eyes. "But you can keep the money. We won't be needin' it."

"Take it or leave it, ma'am. Jest so I git my guns."

Brad Labreu ripped out a startled oath. He pointed to the canebrake from which they had emerged a few minutes before. "Look there, Pappy!" he cried.

A colored boy on a mule was watching them from the edge of the brake. Lige threw up his rifle, but Gillis caught it by the barrel. The bullet tore into the soft ground.

"Hit's only Jim Smith," Mack cried.

Lige was furious. He turned snarling on the farmer. Fanny stood frozen. She thought he would kill her husband, but he checked himself. The Gobbler had a use for Mack alive.

"You durn fool!" he exploded, the desire to destroy Gillis still burning in him. "I've a mind to blast a hole in you."

Fanny stepped in front of Mack. "That wouldn't be good judgment, Lige," she said.

Brad's rifle cracked. The bullet whistled past the colored boy. Jim Smith had wheeled and was plunging into the cane thicket. Brad gave his mount the spur and dashed in pursuit. He, too, vanished in the slash. Again they heard the roar of his gun. But when he returned a few minutes later he told his father that he had lost the boy in the thicket.

"I'd a got him if it hadn't been for this interferin' lunkhead," Lige stormed. "He had to grab my gun as I fired."

"I told you we'd ought to slick him," Brad reminded his father.

"You can't learn some fellows anything without beating it into their hides," Lige agreed sourly. "But fust off Mack has an errand to do. If he don't do it good — "

Labreu ground his teeth together, without finishing the sentence.

Mack watched his wife and children blindfolded, then helped to the saddles of the horses. The outlaws were going to lead the animals into the slough. Gillis started to speak, but the words choked in his throat. He climbed to the seat of the wagon and drove away. If there was a more unhappy man in the world it would have been hard to find him.

18

TOM HARVILLE was at the gin dickering with a farmer about an increased credit at the store against the next cotton crop when Jim Smith rode up on a mule and tied at a hitching post. The boy hung around in the background. He wanted to talk with Tom, but it was not his place to interfere in a conversation between white men. Jim was so fidgety that Tom guessed he wanted to see him.

"Be through in a minute," Harville called to him.

But presently Tom and the farmer went into the office to take a look at the books to find out how much credit had already been given the farmer. By that time Tom had forgotten young Smith.

Larry reached the mill on his way from the house and was at once accosted by the Negro boy.

"Mistah Larry, if you has time I would like to speak with you," Jim said.

Larry stopped to listen. Jim was a ragged, barefoot boy black as the ace of spades. A tuft of kinky hair had pushed through a hole in the old straw hat he wore. "I done been shot at," he gulped.

"What!" exclaimed Larry.

"Yassuh, Mistah Larry. On the yonder side of the bayou."

Larry thought instantly of the Labreus. "Who shot at you?" he asked.

"I dunno. Fur as I know I've nevah seed the genelman before."

"You must know why he was shooting at you."

"No, suh." To relieve his embarrassment Jim drew with his big toe two parallel lines in the dust. "Ceppen it was because I saw him with Mr. Gillis and his fambly. But with all this yere talk going on about the Labreus I 'lowed mebbe — "

He stuck there, and Larry eased him over the hump. "You did right to come to me, Jim. Tell me the whole story."

Jim told it. Larry called Tom out of the gin.

"The Labreus tried to kill this boy," he explained.

"Great jumpin' horned toad," Tom cried. "What for?"

"He saw too much. Tell my brother, Jim."

The boy whimpered a little. He drew a ragged sleeve across his eyes. "They liked to of scared the livin' daylights outa me, then one of them come a-chargin' at me, an' I lit a shuck like the heel flies was aftah me."

"You're all right now, Jim," Larry said. "We'll look after you. Now tell Mr. Tom about it."

"He come rip-snortin' on my tail an' shot at me again, but he lost me in the canebrake."

Jim repeated his story for Tom. They decided to take him to Rosemont to tell his experience to the colonel. On the way to the house the boy voiced his fear again.

"They might git me yet," he said.

"No," Larry reassured him. "They didn't want you to tell about seeing them with the Gillis family, but now you have told you aren't important to them any more."

Maxwell Harville was puzzled at this development. He could have understood it if Lige had shot Mack Gillis down for joining the posse, but the fellow must know that to include a woman and children in his vengeance would stir up a bitter resentment bound to destroy him in the end. There was, of course, always the chance that Lige had bought Mack to throw in with him. Labreu had been giving him money, the boy said. But even so, the colonel did not think it in Mack's character to join up with a bunch of murderers.

He put questions, to get at any point the boy might have missed.

"How did Mack and Lige act to each other? Were they nice and friendly?"

"Looked like they was havin' a fuss and Miz Gillis went ovah an' talked to them. Mistah Gillis knocked down the rifle of that fust one who shot at me. The li'l gals was crying, seemed to me."

Larry had a suggestion. "Perhaps Labreu means to use

the Gillis family as hostages to bargain with us."

"Sure. So we would hold off while he and his gang skedaddle," Tom guessed. "He would have the dead wood on us."

"Looks like he would have picked somebody more important than Mack and wouldn't bother with the children. According to Bud Holly he had Miss Logan in mind. And why was he giving Mack money if that was true?"

"Another point," Larry said. "They wouldn't have shot at Jim, but used him to send word to us that the Gillis family were being held to insure the gang's safety."

The colonel frowned. "Dad gum it, I've known Mack 'most all his life. He fought well in the war. He has been a good citizen. I let him have his farm cheap, and he has always acted as if he appreciated it. Yet this looks devilishly queer. I'll have to get word of this to Cantrell. I reckon we've been dragged into this all the way, boys. We cain't stand back and let this devil do a meanness to our women and children. They have laid it right on our laps."

From Sheriff Cantrell, when he reached Rosemont a few hours later, the colonel did not get much comfort. That officer said he had already led a posse into the slough and had not seen hide nor hair of any of the outlaws. Lige knew the big swamp as well as the sheriff knew the streets of Big Hollow. He no doubt kept guards posted, and could lead his men away from any danger spot as soon as his sentries notified him. Of course, Cantrell said, he would be glad to do his best. If the Harvilles and other good citizens wanted to be deputies that was fine. He would co-operate with them fully. Through the governor of the state he had been trying to arrange with the government to send a batch of United States marshals to handle this irruption of condemned criminals, and he had hopes that soon such a posse would run the desperadoes down. These were not local bad men. It was absurd to expect him to arrest such a gang escaped from a federal prison. This was not a county but a national job.

Harville commented dryly that it would probably be a great comfort to the Gillis family that the Washington authorities and not Cantrell would be to blame for not trying to save them.

" 'Course we got no proof Mrs. Gillis and the children aren't in the Labreu camp with their own consent," the sheriff said. "It looks thataway, with Labreu giving Mack money."

The colonel could not answer that convincingly. It was not evidence to say that he had known Mack more than thirty years and had never known him to walk any but a straight line.

A posse must be sent out at once. Jim Smith could guide it as far as the spot where he had seen the outlaws with the Gillis family. From there it might be possible to track the outlaws to their hiding place. The colonel was not very hopeful about this. Labreu was a past master at vanishing without leaving any trail behind him. Harville did not like to dicker with Lige. It hurt his pride and self-respect. But the safety of the captives was the first consideration. He sent two of his sons to talk with Dull. This was galling, after he had treated the man so contemptuously. His idea was that Chet should get in touch with Labreu and find out upon what terms the bandit would release his prisoners.

Andy and Larry stopped first at the Gillis farm. They found it deserted except for the chickens, the turkeys, a cow, and a pig in a sty with ten squealing young ones. After feeding the animals they took a look around the place. In the root house were Irish and sweet potatoes, some jars of apple butter, and a few glasses of blackberry jam. On the back porch was a dasher churn filled with cream. Blobs of butter sticking to the side showed that somebody had left the churn just before the task was completed.

"Mrs. Gillis wasn't expecting to leave," Andy said. "Something came up suddenly that made her change her mind."

"Lige changed it for her," Larry said.

"I reckon. But you don't know that."

"Does Mack Gillis chew tobacco?"

"No." Andy looked at a splatter of tobacco juice on the clean floor. "Lige chews, though."

"A neighbor dropping in wouldn't mess up a clean floor like that," Larry said. "Must have been someone who didn't care what she thought. Lige, I think."

"If she was scared to go with him why did he take her and the kids?" Andy ran a hand through his thick black hair to help thinking. "It doesn't make sense. He has to keep his camp ground hidden. Why take outsiders there?"

When they presently looked over the farm they discovered that the cultivator had been left in the middle of the cornfield instead of at the end of the row. Mack, too, had left in a hurry.

There had been, Larry was convinced, the pressure of

fear impelling this hasty departure.

The two brothers passed through Big Hollow to the clearing where Chet Dull and his family lived. The head of the house sat in a chair tilted against a wall of the cabin on the shady side of the shack. He was placidly smoking a pipe. His oldest son was plowing in the deadening. A daughter and another son were cutting weeds in the corn patch. Inside the cabin Mrs. Dull could be heard washing and giving orders to another scion called Randy about hanging up the clothes to dry. Four small ragged and barefoot children were playing about the place.

"Chet is a successful father," Andy suggested. "He has raised a large and industrious family. In his old age they will be able to keep him in the idleness to which he is accustomed."

Dull showed no surprise at sight of his visitors. He brought the front legs of the chair to the ground and said "Howdy, genelmen!" without rising. He did not offer the customary invitation to 'light, but they swung from their saddles promptly. They understood that he was giving them the same treatment he had received at Rosemont.

"No use beating about the bush, Chet," Andy said bluntly. "You've heard about what happened to the Gillis family, and we want to talk with you about it."

Chet took a puff at his pipe before he answered. "What did happen to them?" he asked.

"We think Lige has taken them to his camp."

"I'll be doggoned." Chet was a picture of surprised innocence. "Why would he do that?"

"I don't know. Maybe you do." Andy's voice grew

sharper. "What I've got to say is that if he does any harm to them a lot of people around here will think the Ku Klux was only a picnic to what they'll get."

"Whoa!" Larry interrupted. "Let's not go so fast, Andy." He turned to Dull. "My brother is angry about this outrage. So will others be. They are likely to make trouble. Nobody wants that. We come to you to ask you to help us, Mr. Dull."

"How can I help you?" Chet demanded sullenly. "Story I heard was that the Gillis family went a-visitin' somewheres. No use gittin' in a sweat about that. Anyhow, they didn't tell me where they was going."

"They went with Labreu," Larry told him. "We know that."

"You know more abaout it than I do then. Say they did. They prob'ly went peaceable. Lige wouldn't hurt 'em. Why would he?"

"Why did he kill Tim Fallon?" Andy wanted to know stormily.

"Did he? I dunno. You cain't prove it by me. Somebody did." Dull waved this away, as having nothing to do with the business in hand. "If you ask me, you are makin' a lot of talk about nothing. The whole Gillis tribe will show up sound as a dollar when their visit is over."

"We hope so," Larry continued. "But we can't take a chance. We want you to find out from Lige Labreu what he wants. Is he holding them for money? If not, what is his game?"

"I dunno any more'n you do where Lige is," Chet protested.

"If you don't you have ways of finding out," Larry persisted. "It is necessary that you do."

The sly smile of Dull held behind it pleasant thoughts. "I drapped in at Rosemont the other evenin' and offered to try and fix things up between you-all an' Lige. The colonel talked abaout settin' the dogs on me. Seems I was no-'count triflin' trash. I hain't changed none since then. Since I'm dirt under yore feet, why don't you-all go to somebody wuth while?"

Andy turned as red as an angry turkey cock, but Larry's placatory words slipped out before his brother could speak.

"We all make mistakes, Mr. Dull. Just now we can't cherish grievances. What we all want to do is make certain nothing dreadful occurs to that poor woman and her children. You are with us in that, I know."

"Sounds good," Dull sneered. "But right while you air talkin' you folks air fixin' to send a posse out against Lige. And only the other day you jumped my cousin onexpected and whopped him with a whip when he couldn't fight back 'count of yore brother Tom coverin' him with a gun."

"That wasn't the way of it," Andy broke out.

"Never mind, Andy," interrupted Larry. "That is another incident we must forget."

"When I seen the colonel at Rosemont, he was mighty biggity abaout forgettin' bygones." Dull reminded him.

"Will you or won't you go see Lige for us?" demanded Andy peremptorily.

Dull knew he could not refuse. He expected to go on living where he was, and he knew that if he stood out he would be reckoned as an ally of the Labreus and later would be forced to leave. They had let him stay when Lige was driven out before. They would not do it a second time.

"I'll see him for you-all," he gave way sourly. "What you want me to tell him?"

They went over again what was in their minds.

"I dunno where he's at," Chet explained. "Lige is mighty careful not to let anyone know. But I'll git in touch with him. May take me a day or two before one of 'em draps in on me."

That might be too late, but it was the best they could do. They thought Dull was speaking the truth. It would be like Lige not to tell him where his camp site was, since he might be bought or coerced into leading a posse to it as his son had been. The Gobbler naturally would assume that for enough money Chet would betray him, since, of course, every man had his price.

19

AT YANDELL'S STORE in Oldport Mack Gillis was paying for a Winchester rifle and six boxes of cartridges when Major Logan drove up and came in to see the storekeeper. The owner of Hillcrest stopped to speak with Mack. He inquired in his stiff, courteous way for Mrs. Gillis and the children. Mack said they were well, and from the bottom of his heart he hoped that he was speaking the truth. He felt sure that the major had not yet heard of what had occurred to them.

His guilty eyes did not meet those of the planter. He knew that what Logan had seen would later implicate him as an ally of the murderers. He groped for words that would sound natural. The subject that popped into his mind was an unfortunate one.

"I'm glad to see you air better and yore arm is out of a sling," he said.

The major stiffened. His wounded arm was something he did not discuss. It had to do with very personal and private business of his own.

Hurriedly the storekeeper threw in a diversion. "While these Labreus are out I reckon there are others besides Mack who would like to have a nice new rifle like this."

Logan accepted the well-meant suggestion. He knew Mack had not intended to be offensive. Picking up the rifle, he broke it and looked down the barrel. "A good gun," he said. "You're getting it for the Labreus, of course."

The startled gaze of the farmer clung to Logan's face. "Why no, I — I — fact is — "

His denial stuck in the farmer's throat. Perspiration moistened the gold pieces clutched in the tight palm.

Unconscious of the mental disturbance he had caused, Logan pursued the idea. "Glad you are getting a gun like this. Hope you drop one of the ruffians with it."

Gillis drew a breath of relief. Logan had not meant his words as an accusation. A quotation from the Bible flashed through the mind of the harassed man, "The wicked flee when no man pursueth." He must not be so jumpy, or he would give himself away without any need.

"I reckon you're right, Major," he agreed, and handed to Yandell the two gold pieces in payment for what he had bought.

The merchant looked at the coins. They appeared quite new, but the Mint date on them was 1866. He passed one to the major. "Looks as if it had been made this year," he said.

Logan assented. "Someone must have been hoarding it," he guessed. "Had it long, Mack?"

Gillis was caught unprepared. He lied, not convincingly. "Got them from the fellow Jackman in the Richwoods who bought my cows last fall."

Mack thought the stern eyes of the major held a critical doubt. His answer had been a half-second late in coming. In fact the planter was surprised. He considered Gillis above reproach, yet he knew he was lying. The farmer was so poor that he often had to scrape the bottom of the barrel. Like most of the other small landholders in the district he lived on credit until his cotton was ready for the market. That he would have so much money on hand was very improbable. How had he come by it?

That it was none of his business, Logan knew. He handed the coin back to Yandell, settled the small matter that had brought him into the store, and walked out of the building.

Mack got his change and went back to the wagon hitched to a post outside. He was greatly depressed and very much ashamed. Always he had prized the good opinion of Major Logan and Colonel Harville. Ever since the war they had showed themselves friendly. Harville had sold him the farm on easy terms. Now he was ranged against them. His loyalties conflicted, but he felt he had to think first of those dependent upon him.

Beneath the hay in the bed of the wagon he buried the rifle and the ammunition. At the other hardware store in Oldport he bought a second Winchester and several cartons of cartridges. For the third weapon he had to be content with a carbine, since the stock of Winchesters was out in both stores.

When Mack came out to the sidewalk carrying the guns Major Logan chanced to be in talk with a friend on the courthouse steps opposite. The planter stroked his imperial thoughtfully. He did not understand this and found it disturbing. One likely explanation occurred to him. Harville might have sent Gillis to buy the weapons with intent to provide his neighbors with guns to oppose any attacks upon them by the criminal gang. The colonel was both impulsive and fearless. Since the law seemed impotent to deal with the Labreus he might even be expecting to take matters into his own hands. If it had not been for Logan's disinclination to show any interest in his enemy's activities he would have questioned Gillis. This explanation comforted him, since it explained the source of the money and the man's embarrassment. No doubt Harville had told him to buy the guns as secretly as possible without telling why they were needed.

The major would have liked to take part in this clean-up. In the war he had been a good soldier, and he did not like to sit on the sidelines now. But he could not push into anything started by Harville. During the long ride back to Hillcrest he could not shake his annoyance at being excluded. He half decided to head a posse of his own. It could work entirely independently of the one led by Harville.

As he dismounted, his wife met him at the porch, to tell him that Fanny Gillis and her children were in the hands of the Labreus, and that their son Hal had left an hour before to join the hunt for the outlaws. Ed Travis had gone with him.

Perry Logan was taken aback. He had made up his mind too late. But at least he could join the man hunters. He ordered a fresh horse and went into the house to arm himself.

His wife watched his preparations, her eyes worried and anxious. She knew by the rigid set of his facial muscles that nothing she could say would move him. When his mind was made up it was immovable as Bald Knob.

"If the boys have crossed the bayou into the slough you won't be able to find them," she ventured.

"They will have a place appointed for a rendezvous, so that others can join them and bring food," he answered. "This hunt may last a week."

"You won't follow them alone, Perry," she begged. "You wouldn't be so foolish and rash."

"I shall act with judgment, Sallie," he promised, adding with his rare smile, "I put considerable value on my life, since I have a lot to live for." He walked across the room and kissed her.

She held him close for a moment. "Oh, you men! When I married you, it was to send you off to war right away, and now all three of you are in another, and one of you badly wounded already."

With dread she watched his slender, erect figure diminish

in the distance and at last vanish among the white oaks bordering the avenue. He was stiff-willed, and in spite of his cold manner, impulsive when stirred. She knew he held the Labreus in contempt, and she was afraid in his eagerness to join the boys he might set out across the bayou alone.

When Logan rode up to the Harville cotton gin two men were sitting on the loading platform, both of them armed. One was Shep Tolt.

"We're what you might call home guards, Major," explained Jes' Tolable. "No tellin' what these devils will do, so the colonel said for us to stick around here in case they raided this yere side of the bayou."

"Have you seen my boys?" the major asked.

"Yes, seh. They were here quite a while — left with the posse, not ten minutes ago. They were sure rarin' to go. Ed Travis and yore Hal."

"Did you hear what part of the slough they aim to comb first?"

"Yes, seh. They was headin' for the upper end."

"How many in the posse?" Logan inquired.

Jes' Tolable rubbed his unshaven chin in thought. "There was the colonel — fust time he's been in the saddle since — since the accident to his leg. An' his two oldest sons. The youngest one got throwed and hurted jest before they started. Then, o' course, yore boys an' Ed Travis. That makes five. I counted seven. Lemme see. Oh, yes, Abe Colton and Bud Clinton."

"Did they cross the bayou at the bridge?"

"That's right, Major."

The other man spoke up. He was a sandy-haired man

with a long, sallow face. "The colonel fixed it up with Burns to send supplies this evening. He couldn't wait to git a grub outfit ready. Said he would have someone meet the pack train at the hickory slash half a mile above where the old Polk trace runs into the swamp."

"When does the food go in?"

"Not till dark. The colonel didn't want the Labreus jumpin' it."

Logan looked at his watch. It was ten minutes past four. The provisions would not go in for several hours. He did not want to hang around the gin. From the place chosen as the rendezvous he felt sure Harville would work into the slough by way of Moccasin Trace. No other trail would take him there.

He crossed the bridge below Rosemont and followed the canebrake, keeping at first close to the bayou and as far as possible from the swamp. His horse could not push through the thick stand of stalks without the swishing sound betraying its progress, but the keen eyes of the planter searched the terrain carefully as he travelled. One of the outlaws might be lurking here to report to Lige any approach of a posse. That there was some danger in riding this district alone the major knew, but he felt able to look out for himself. In a few minutes he would overtake the posse. It was a defect in his temperament that his contempt for the Labreus made him underestimate their competence.

Cutting across at a right angle, Logan emerged from the canebrake to a slope of blue gums descending to the spongy ground below. A startled pig wallowing in a mud hole scrambled up with a grunt and dashed away through the muscadine vines. On the ridge beyond the hollow was a stand of fine hickories. From the branches above squirrels looked down at the rider curiously. Usually they were wary as trout in a much fished stream, but they seemed to sense that this interloper meant them no harm. The velvet buds of spring had burgeoned into the fuller foliage of summer, but some of the nuts from last year's crop were still scattered on the ground. The rays of the sun tesselated the floor of the grove, relieving the gloom which lay heavy on the dismal marsh in front of him that led into the bottomland of the Cache.

Looking down from the hickory slash, Logan could make out the narrow twisting thread of the Polk corduroy road as it wound deeper into the boggy morass. This, he guessed, was the way that Colonel Harville's posse had taken. Recent hoofprints confirmed the opinion.

A doubt whispered in his mind. It would not be wise to venture into that dark quagmire alone. But Logan was both proud and determined. He could not brook the thought of letting danger hold him back. His place was at the front. The riders could not be far ahead of him.

At times his mount's hoofs sank to the fetlocks in the soft soil. He plunged forward through a tangle of trumpet vines and pawpaw saplings. There was no trail, and the going was heavy. Travel would be easier when he reached the corduroy road.

On the round, rotting poles of the corduroy road the major stopped to breathe his horse. The brown haunches of the animal were wet with sweat, and its belly heaved from the struggle with the suction of the mud. Logan's eyes searched the dirt between the small logs for signs that Harville's posse had passed this way. He swung from the saddle and stooped to make a closer examination.

From behind a dirt hump beside the road, a drawling, derisive voice gave an order. "Fust off, drap that gun, Major."

The muscles tightened around Perry Logan's stomach. He knew that voice, though he had not heard it before for years. Lige Labreu must have been watching him for many minutes while he was crossing the morass. Sure of his kill, the man had waited only to taste more fully the triumph of his victory, to throw fear into the heart of his victim.

20

THE SLENDER BODY of Logan straightened from the crouch, the shotgun still in his hand. His finely chiseled face, cold as granite, did not betray the conviction that the dark shadow of death was hovering over him. It did not show how greatly shocked he was. The outlaw had him covered, of course. He had no chance of escape. But the quick way out would be the easy one, and even after a bullet had torn through him he might have time for one shot.

A ribald laugh sounded as a man's head and heavy shoulders rose from behind a clump of young hackberry bushes. The rifle in his hands pointed directly at the major.

"He ain't drapped that gun, Pappy," the man said. "Time for me to drill him, ain't it?"

"Not yet, Brad." Lige Labreu came out slowly from his cover, ready to shoot instantly. "We ain't aimin' to hurt you any, Major — not if you're anyways reasonable. I got a proposition to make. We'll talk it over nice and friendly, after you have put down the gun."

The impudent, soft slyness of Labreu's voice did not deceive Logan. He knew that behind the shallow, restless eyes was a burning hatred. But with two rifles on him he had not a dead man's chance in a fight. Before he could make a move he would be shot down. It could do no harm to play for time.

"I'll make no bargain with you, Labreu," the planter said bluntly. "You and your whole brood are murdering scoundrels, false as Satan."

"He's askin' for it, Pappy," Brad pleaded. "An' I got a score to settle with him. I ain't forgot the time he and Harville stood by and had a fellow skin my back with a hickory."

"Hold yore horses, Brad," ordered Lige. "I got a use for him alive." He turned to Logan, and his voice held a soft purring threat. "Last call, Major. Throw down that gun naow."

Logan dropped the shotgun.

"That's right sensible," Lige continued. "If you hadn't you would of been deader than a stuck shote by now. There ain't no profit in arguing with two fellows who have the drap on you. Jes' turn raound an' I'll lift that pistol you got in yore hip pocket, Major. That's fine. We-all can take it easy and talk turkey."

"You can't use me to help in any of your devilish schemes," Logan said hardily. "If that's what you are pointing for."

"Nothing like that. You got yore principles like I got mine. I don't figure to be onreasonable. Git the horses, Brad, and we'll be startin'."

"Where you taking me?" the planter asked.

"To our camp. We can talk there nice and comfortable."

Logan knew that the hour of doom was only postponed. They would not take him to their camp without first having made up their minds never to let him get away alive.

As they rode deeper into the swamp the mosquitoes swarmed in denser clouds. The yellow-green sluggish water lay on both sides of the road heavily shaded by the cypress forest. Here and there the ugly knees jutted out of the scum. Big turtles squatted on logs, immovable as the dead timber itself. Occasionally a copperhead slid from the road into the brush. Logan shuddered at the ghastly solitude of death they were penetrating. Presently they left the road and waded up a bayou, circling in and out, crossing small islands, dropping down into the water again, until Logan had lost his sense of direction.

"Every hour you stay here in the swamp makes your ruin more certain, Labreu," he told his captor. "You'll never get away."

"I fetch comfort from the swamp," the outlaw differed. "The Cache is an old friend of mine. You-all never would of cotched me if you hadn't tricked me into trying to burn Harville's store."

The camp of the bandits was on a wooded island. As the three riders sloshed up out of the water to land, Logan was aware that two men with rifles watched their approach, even though Brad Labreu had given warning while a hundred yards distant by hooting twice like an owl.

One of the men was Sim Labreu, the other his brother Craw. Sim showed a double row of bad teeth in a grin. "I see you done cotched a big fish in yore net, Pappy," he exulted.

A gleam of cruelty danced in the cold, shallow eyes of his father. "I didn't exactly cotch him. He bullheaded in, and o' course I couldn't tell him he wasn't welcome. So I let him stay."

"But I don't reckon we'll let him go," Craw jeered. "Not after his high and mighty son shot pore Fin."

Logan looked from one to another with cold contempt. "Too bad he didn't bag the pair of you," he said. "Scum of the earth."

A dull, angry flush suffused the face of the youngest son. "I've a mind to fill you full of lead right damn now," he said, between clenched teeth.

"Don't forget that Major Logan is our guest, boys," Lige said with suave and brutal irony. "We're gonna fix up a li'l agreement, him an' we-'uns."

"No," Logan dissented sharply.

A shutter dropped over the eyes of Lige, a film which left them opaque and bland. "That's what you think naow, Major," he replied, his slitted mouth set in an evil grin. "But I'm a right good persuader. A heap of folks have changed their minds when I put things to them my way."

"It will save you trouble to shoot me now," Logan told

him scornfully. "Why waste time?"

"Sho, Major, I don't mind taking a li'l trouble to git what I want. Let's not be in a hurry. You don't even know what it is I'm gonna ask you." Lige turned to Sim. "Did Gillis git back?"

"An hour ago. With two rifles and a carbine. Cad is holdin' him down at Pit Hollow. He keeps squawkin' about getting his wife and kids back."

"He'll git them, like I promised," Lige said. "The woman is going to tote a letter from the major to his sons."

Logan stood ramrod straight, his steady gaze fixed on Lige. No words came from his close-shut lips.

"Jes' a few lines to tell the boys he's in a tight, and for them to scrape up ten thousand dollars ransom money inside of two days. When we git this the major can ride away peart as a mule that has busted into a corn crib." The bandit's voice was bland and gentle.

Craw opened his mouth to object, but the crafty look his father slid toward him stopped the words. He knew that when Lige was soft and smooth as butter in his talk there was deviltry in the back of his mind.

"Sim, you go bring Miz Gillis and the young 'uns while I fix up the letter with the major," Lige continued. "I told Mack we would look after them as if they were our own kin, and I 'low to keep my word."

From his pocket he took a cheap notebook and the stub of a pencil. These he handed to the major. With the palm of a dirty hand he rubbed his unshaven chin to facilitate thought. "Tell the boys you made a leetle mistake and got cotched by us. Say for them not to worry, 'cause you'll be safe as a nigger at church — if they turn over to me the money on time. You got that down?"

The major's pencil stopped. He waited for the rest of the message his captor was dictating.

"Ten thousand dollars. Not a nickel less."

Logan interrupted. "Do you think I keep ten thousand loose, or even in a bank?" he asked.

"They can borrow it, if they get a move on them. One of them is to come to the old Peters cabin below the ford at eleven o'clock Friday mawnin' and bring the money. He's to come alone. We'-uns will be watching. If anyone is with him — or follows after him — you'll be a gone goose, Logan. Put that down plain."

The pencil in the major's fingers continued to write.

"No monkey tricks," Labreu went on. "Tell him he's not to be armed."

"And that he will be killed, of course," Logan added quietly.

"No, suh," replied the outlaw, affronted. "I'm a square shooter. You both can go off scot-free."

"Do you think they are plumb fools?" Logan inquired. "Or that I am?"

"You did me a heap of meanness onct, Major," the bandit reminded him. "But shucks! In this yere world a fellow cain't nurse a grudge. If yore folks play fair with me I will with them. That's a Christian spirit, hain't it? Oh, another thing to put daown on that paper. Have yore boys tell Colonel Harville to stop pesterin' me with posses. All the good it will git him is to have them shot up like yore boy was. 'Ceppen that next time they will git killed. When we had that last fracas most all we had was six-guns. Now we got new Winchesters."

"So I gather, you dirty scoundrel," retorted Logan bluntly. "You made poor Mack Gillis get them for you to save his wife and children."

"No, sir. Mack volunteered. He hated to see you-all pick on me."

The prisoner did not believe that for a moment. He finished writing and handed the paper to the other man. Lige looked at the scrawl suspiciously. He held it closer and then farther from his eyes as if to see clearer. Logan guessed that he could not read. Without any comment Labreu passed the notebook to his son Crawford. The young man's lips moved as he began to spell out the words to himself slowly.

Sim came over the brow of a low hill, with him Mrs. Gillis and her two children. Logan understood the situation without any explanation. While Mack was getting the rifles for the bandits his family had been brought here as hostages for his good faith.

The woman stared unhappily at the major. She did not know how he had come here, but it was plain he was a prisoner.

Logan said grimly, "There's no fool like an old fool, Mrs. Gillis."

Lige took the notebook from Craw impatiently. "Miz Gillis, read to me what's wrote there."

The woman read the message silently and her startled gaze went to the major for help. If she told Labreu what Logan had written, she was afraid his anger would destroy the planter.

"Read it, Mrs. Gillis," Logan said.

She moistened her dry lips and began.

"I'm a prisoner of that devil Lige Labreu," Fanny Gillis read aloud. "It's my own fault. If this gets to my sons I want them to know there is no use trying to save me. Any offer he makes will be a trap. Don't deal with him. I'm already as good as dead. Go ahead and wipe out the scoundrels. Good-bye."

The message was signed, Perry Logan.

Labreu's lips tightened to a thin, cruel line. His bleak eyes stared at the white, set face of the planter, a red-hot devil of rage burning in them. While his sons broke into savage curses he stood in silence trying to curb the murderous passion aflame in him. Not till his voice was under control did he speak.

"Looks like I'll have to start gobbling right soon," he said, almost in a murmur, his swarthy face turned purple.

"I told you before that there was no use wasting time," the major reminded him.

"He'll sing another tune before we-'uns git through playin' with him," Brad said. "How about startin' in on Mr. Logan?"

The sly craftiness of the old guerrilla asserted itself. "No hurry, boys. We'll take fust things fust." He turned to Mrs. Gillis, a thin, false smile of propitiation on his face. "You see how it is, Fanny. I'm offerin' to forget the past — all the meanness Logan and Harville did to us — but the major here acts like he is God Almighty and won't have it thataway. I'm sending you and the young 'uns back to Mack now. You and Mack go to Harville or to the Logan boys and tell how things are, how Logan butted in and we took him prisoner, and under the circumstances we got to hold him for ransom." He explained the conditions upon which the captive would be released, repeating them so that no mistake could be made.

Fanny Gillis promised to carry the message. She added, anxiously, "I hope you-all won't do Major Logan any harm, Mr. Labreu, while we're gettin' things fixed up."

"We'll treat him nice as we did you and the children, Fanny," the outlaw promised unctuously. "Old Lige ain't half as bad as folks make out. Hit's the old story of giving a dog a bad name. The boys lost their mammy early and they got a rough bark, but underneath they are kind as kittens. Don't you worry none about the major — if his friends think enough of him to raise this money and do exactly like I told you."

Logan said, his slender figure erect and his stern eyes showing no fear, "You can tell my boys that when they hand over this money to these murderers they will be giving the signal for my death — if I am still alive."

The woman and the children were blindfolded before they were helped to the backs of the horses. The last words Mrs. Gillis heard from those remaining in camp was an urgent demand from Brad that to start with they tie up the major to a tree and wear him to a frazzle with a hickory in reprisal for the whipping that had been given Brad years before.

21

WHILE MAXWELL HARVILLE, deputized by the sheriff, was making preparations to ride into the swamp, he was debating with himself about whom to leave in charge of the plantation. He could see that Larry expected to be one of the posse, but he thought the boy ought to stay at home. Larry was not cut out to be a man hunter. Still, he did not want to hurt the feelings of his son.

He tried to make a careless approach to the subject. Lige was smart as a fox, he explained, and while they were in the slough might slip out and burn the house or the gin. Since Larry was the youngest, he was elected to guard the property.

Larry flushed. He guessed his father was not too well satisfied with the reports he had heard about his conduct during the previous incursion into the swamp of the Cache. Since Larry was ashamed of his own softness it was a sore point with him. He would much prefer to stay at the plantation, but that was the very reason why he could not do so. His mind would never be at ease until he had convinced himself that his timidity did not run as far as cowardice.

"I want very much to go, sir," he answered quickly. "It's . . . important to me. Burns can look after the place. And, after all, sir, with that game leg you ought to stay here yourself. We all think so."

"My leg is all right," the colonel answered. "I'm going

this time. That's settled." He knew from Larry's voice and manner that his protest was not perfunctory, any more than it was based on a young man's eagerness for adventure, his resentment at being debarred from a dangerous expedition. It lay deeper than that. Some hint of what was in his son's mind reached him. It might not be fair to try to shield him from peril. A man must run his own risks in life.

"All right, son," he conceded. "You have a right to go if you insist. I'll leave Burns in charge here. Jes' Tolable is holding the fort at the gin."

They were busy saddling when Abe Colton and Bud Clinton reached Rosemont. Before they left the yard Ed Travis joined them, bringing word that the youngest Logan boy was waiting at the bridge.

Harville's party rode down and joined him. There was a short discussion as to the best point of entrance into the slough. Colonel Harville favored the Moccasin Trace. Hal Logan said that since they had to trust to luck, anyhow, and probably wouldn't see any of the outlaws for several days, it did not much matter which way they rode. The trail suggested by the colonel was as likely to be right as any other.

The horses, packed closely near the end of the bridge, shifted positions restlessly, owing to the nervousness of a young bay stallion ridden by Travis. It danced about, went up in the air twice, then made a bolt to get out of the huddle. The animal's weight struck Larry's roan heavily and flung him from the saddle. He went down hard, the side of his head hitting the ground.

Swiftly his brothers dismounted. Tom kept back the milling horses while Andy carried Larry out of the pack and laid him down at the foot of a gum tree. When Larry came back to consciousness his father was bending over him. The others stood around in a semicircle.

"I . . . fell off," he muttered, and looked at the blood-stained handkerchief his father was refolding to get a dry spot.

When he sat up his head swam dizzily. He caught at the colonel's coat sleeve.

They carried him to the house and sent for Dr. Watkins. He dressed the wound and assured the family that Larry ought to be all right in a day or two. If he stayed at home and rested on the sofa it would not be necessary for him to go to bed.

Maxwell did not like to leave him, but Larry laughed at his solicitude. "Mandy will look after me fine," he said. "She took care of me when I had chills and fever long ago."

Reluctantly the colonel set out with the posse.

For Larry the afternoon wore away slowly. He had a headache and felt feverish. Mandy brought him a cool glass of lemonade two or three times. She bathed his hot face with cold water from the well. Presently he drowsed for an hour.

Awakening, he picked up the latest copy of the weekly *St. Louis Globe-Democrat*, the only city paper to which his father subscribed. Browsing through it, his eyes fell on an Indian yarn a reporter had got from a pioneer Texan visiting the city. The old-timer had come from the country west of the Brazos. He had lived there when the

Kiowas and Comanches were raiding the frontier settlements. On one of these expeditions they had captured two young white girls. A neighbor had taken the trail after the marauders, had followed them for a week, and had at last come on their camp when the savages were less vigilant than usual on account of a great feast they had just held. He had slipped into the camp and freed the girls. For many days he had fed and cheered them, and at last had brought them safely back home.

He looked up from the paper to see that Burns was helping Mandy get the food for the posse to the porch.

In spite of the scolding of the old colored woman he went to the porch to see the two pack mules loaded with supplies for his father's posse. Three armed men were to guard them to the rendezvous in the brake near the old Polk road.

Before the party started a wagon creaked into the yard. In it were Mack Gillis and his family. The others stared at them.

"Lige turned you-all loose," Burns said.

"Yes." Mack did not want to discuss that now, though he knew he would have to tell the story later to the colonel. "I got bad news. Major Logan got cotched by the Labreus."

This was a disturbing development. Larry asked, "How do you know?"

"He sent a message by Fanny. She and the children were in his camp. He made them go and stay there. Looks like Lige aims to do turrible things to the major."

"What was the message?"

Even as Larry asked the question his heart sank. He knew what tortures the Labreus were capable of inflicting.

"He swears he'll turn the major loose if one of the Logan boys takes ten thousand dollars to the old Peters cabin below the ford at eleven o'clock Friday mawnin'. He is to go alone or the major will be killed right then."

"Good Lawd!" one of the pack train guards groaned. "He's shore got the dead wood on the Logans."

"The Gobbler will kill off the major sure enough if he don't get the money," another said.

"He'll probably kill him whether he gets it or not," Burns said. "Lige hates him and he won't miss a chance like this."

"How does Lige figure the Logans kin raise ten thousand dollars by Friday with everybody pore as church mice since the damned carpetbaggers robbed us?" a packer wanted to know.

Burns agreed that it would be very difficult. Though some of the planters had estates with good bottomland, almost none of them had much ready money. Last season had been a bad cotton year with prices low, and it had taken all the plantation owners had in cash to carry their tenants through the winter and spring. Larry knew where the ransom money could be got, but he said nothing about this to the others.

Though the capture of Logan would probably cause Colonel Harville to abandon the present hunt for the outlaws, Burns and Larry decided to let the supplies go forward. Maxwell Harville would have to use his best judgment as to what he had better do. Larry thought he would return to Rosemont unless he had already contacted the Labreus.

To a stable boy Larry gave order that his horse be saddled.

Burns looked at him in surprise. "You cain't ride," he said.

"I'm going to Hillcrest," Larry told him.

"You know what the doctor said. For you to lie down and keep quiet. I'll send a boy with a note to the Logans. Dictate it, and I'll write it for you. You hadn't ought to be up at all."

"I have to go to the Logans myself," Larry insisted.

He spoke with such sharp decision that Burns gave up. All the Harvilles were bullheaded when they made up their minds.

"I can have a boy drive you in the buggy," the overseer suggested.

"No, I'll ride." Larry turned to Mrs. Gillis. "Did you see Major Logan? Or did Lige just tell you the major was his prisoner?"

"I saw him and talked with him. Lige had me read aloud a letter the major had written. I don't reckon Lige can read."

"Who was the letter to?"

"To the Logan boys. Lige told him what to write."

"I see. You have that letter now?"

"No. Lige tore hit up and stomped hit into the ground. Major Logan hadn't writ what he told him to. He said he was gonna be killed anyhow, and for them not to pay ransom. I hated to read it to Lige, but the major told me to go ahead." She explained what Labreu had wanted said and how Logan had defied him. Her voice broke a little when she added that she was feared they were going to be awful mean to the prisoner as soon as she left.

"They don't grow with more cold nerve than Major Logan has got," one of the guards said with approving admiration.

Larry said nothing. As he rode from Rosemont he was very unhappy at the news he was carrying to the women at Hillcrest. He meant to cover up his worst fears, but no matter how he dressed up the evil tidings he knew it would be a blow to Mrs. Logan and her daughter.

The road ran through a slash of hickories to a stretch of dense underbrush pushing close to the wagon tracks. It flashed into Larry's mind that this would be a choice spot for a bushwhacker to fire from cover. His eyes swept to right and left over the bushes. The grip on the rifle lying across the saddle tightened.

There was a rustle among the vines and a man stepped from them to the road. He was carrying a muzzle-loading squirrel rifle. The man was Curt Moss. His big, shapeless figure shuffled across the road. Evidently he had not heard the rider, for when he looked up there was a startled surprise on the big dish face. Larry had halted the horse, and the Winchester was in both of his hands now, but still resting on the saddle seat.

Moss stopped at the edge of the road, then started to pass into the brush.

"Just a moment, Mr. Moss," Larry said. "If you are taking a short cut you can travel easier where the brush isn't so thick. Better move down the road to more open country."

Larry had seen a sudden crafty gleam light up the man's face. He might be wrong, but he was afraid that as soon as Moss was in the cover of thick brush the fellow meant to shoot him out of the saddle.

Irritated at this order, Moss broke out angrily. "What's eatin' you? I ain't ever done you any harm, but if you keep on ridin' me I shorely will."

"I'm not going to hurt you," Larry said. "But just now we're not taking any chances with Lige Labreu's kin."

Moss grumbled, but did as he was told. They came to a small prairie. When they had reached center of it Larry released his prisoner.

"You'll be sorry for this," Moss threatened.

Larry did not answer. He was glad he had dipped over the edge of the prairie into a wooded hollow beyond. The road brought him up a long slope to the private avenue leading into the Logan place.

A colored maid came to the door and invited him to come in while she called Mrs. Logan. Larry thought he had better wait on the piazza. It was Diane who presently came to the door.

She said: "Won't you come in, Mr. Harville? Mother is upstairs with Rod, but will be down in a minute."

"It's pleasant here," he answered. "Perhaps I had better not come in."

Her eyes were resting on the bandage round his head. "You've been hurt," she exclaimed.

"Fell off a horse," Harville explained.

A smile rippled over her face. "For a man devoted to peace you seem to get into a lot of trouble. The last time I saw you somebody had been using your face as a target for his fists. You are as bad as my brothers."

"How is Rod doing?"

"He is in a vile temper because he can't ride in the posse with father and Hal. That means he is getting better."

Larry had not answered her smile. The bad news of which he was the bearer filled his mind. He had intended to wait until her mother came to tell it, but now he blurted it out.

"Miss Logan, I've got to hurt you dreadfully. Your father has been taken prisoner by — "

The girl went white to the lips. She leaned against the door jamb to steady herself. "Is he — alive?" she asked, the last words in a whisper.

"Yes. Labreu has sent a message. He wants ransom money."

Mrs. Logan came down the hanging stairway to the porch. Diane walked swiftly to her mother and put an arm around her waist. "Oh, Mother! Mr. Harville brings terrible news. The Labreus have taken Father prisoner."

Larry thought that Sallie Logan was going to faint, but she steadied herself by clutching the back of a chair. Her grip was so tight that the finger bones stood out like small white knobs.

"Will you . . . tell me about it . . . please?" she said.

He repeated the story Mrs. Gillis had brought, putting as hopeful a view on the situation as he could. There were some gaps in his version. He did not mention that Major

Logan had advised against paying the ransom money as he would be killed anyhow. Since the planter was still alive there was a chance he might be saved, though Larry could not see how, and he felt it would be better for Diane and her mother to hope as long as it was possible.

"When we give them ten thousand dollars they will free my husband?" Mrs. Logan asked.

"That's what Labreu says." Larry added that he had kept his word about letting Mrs. Gillis and the children go after Mack had finished his errand for them.

"You know about that, then," Sallie Logan said. "Lige held Mack's family prisoner until he returned from Oldport with some rifles and ammunition. My husband saw Mack buy the guns. He thought Mack was buying them for your father until he learned about Fanny Gillis being a prisoner."

"That explains a lot we did not understand," Larry said. "On the whole it is encouraging. He knew Mack was one of the posse fighting against him, but let him go."

"Yes," Mrs. Logan agreed. But all three of them knew that Mack and Major Logan had different values in this equation. One was a small factor, the other important. Ever since Lige Labreu had been driven out he had carried a fierce hatred against Perry Logan.

Diane turned to her mother, worry in her face. "How can we get the money? Father hasn't that much in the bank, has he?"

"He hasn't five hundred dollars," Sallie answered. "We'll have to borrow from friends — if any of them have it."

That was the rub. None of the neighboring planters

would have it. She would have to go to Brandon and see what she could do there — and there was such little time.

Larry told them hesitantly what was in his mind. He begged them not to reject it without consideration. A bachelor uncle of his in England had died recently and left him a part of his estate. Just now he had twenty thousand dollars lying idle in a Little Rock bank. "We all have to work together against these scoundrels," he added quickly. "They are our common enemies. This will be my contribution to the cause."

Sallie Logan thought this very generous of the son of their enemy, but she was loath to accept the offer. She knew her husband would not like to be ransomed with Harville money. That she was grateful she made clear, but if there was any other way of getting the money she would prefer to take it.

Larry flung into words impulsively the feeling that had been so much in his mind since coming home. He spoke to the mother, but the appeal was directed even more to Diane. This family feud was all wrong. Of course he had been away and not mixed up in it, but for that reason he could see more clearly the folly of it. In the early days, long before the war, their families had been friends. If they would all throw away their stiff-necked pride they might still be.

"Does Colonel Harville feel that way?" asked Mrs. Logan, a touch of irony in her gentle voice. She felt very much as Larry did, but loyalty to her husband kept her from saying so.

"I think he does, but his pride won't let him say so,"

Larry answered. "This trouble with the Labreus is driving us together. Your son is riding beside my brothers at this moment, going into danger to stamp out a nest of murderers. I'm sure you don't like this Logan-Harville feud and will try to stop it."

She agreed, but added a proviso. "I stand with Major Logan in whatever he thinks best."

"He must know the feud is dead," Larry insisted. "Hal saved my life. None of us would hurt him or any of his family. Why can't we all be reasonable and drop a silly quarrel that has no right to exist?"

"I can," Diane broke out unexpectedly. "I hate the feud. It is wrong. Unless we are all insane we'll drop it. Let's take Mr. Harville's offer of the money. It's the only way we can raise it in time. What Father would think does not matter. We have to save his life."

The mother looked at the flushed eager girl. "You are quite right, Diane. I am going to accept this generous offer, Mr. Harville."

"If you can lend me one of your boys to carry a telegram to Big Hollow, I'll get in touch with my lawyer at once," Larry said.

The shining eyes of Diane told him how pleased she was. No doubt the Capulet-Montague feud at Verona several hundred years ago had seemed to her very romantic, but brought down to date with her own family involved, it was a nuisance and an ever-present threat. So much Larry guessed. But he did not know how much more intolerable the quarrel had become to her since his return from England.

Nor did he know how deeply Sallie Logan shared his hope for a termination of the feud. Many an hour she had worried for fear her husband or one of her boys would be killed by the Harvilles. That would never occur now, she felt sure. Perhaps the coming of this boy was a sign sent in answer to prayer, a promise that all the clouds in her troubled sky would be swept away and give place to sunshine.

22

AS LARRY TURNED the head of his horse toward Rosemont he felt a little weak physically, but his spirit was buoyed up by a renewal of hope. The Logan-Harville feud was dead. There might never be any real friendship between the families, but there would be no more warfare. There must be some way of getting the major back alive. The story he had read in the *Globe-Democrat* kept running through his mind. But the rescuer there had been a frontier scout skilled in that type of sleuthing. If he were here now, or someone like him —

It was at that moment Larry had his crazy idea. But he had no time to develop it. A rifle cracked. His horse staggered. Its front knees buckled. Larry felt himself flying from the saddle. He landed in a huddle, the Winchester four feet in front of him. His mind worked in swift flashes.

The falling darkness had saved him so far. He must find

cover in the brush. But on which side of the road? He did not know, for on one side of it his ambusher lay crouched.

He reclaimed the rifle and plunged into the bushes. A bullet whipped past his shoulder as he stumbled into a hollow left by the roots of a down tree. His body landed on a squirming mass of flesh. Flying arms and legs struck out at him. The rush to escape had plumped him into the pit where the bushwhacker had stationed himself.

Larry and his opponent were at too close quarters to use their rifles. Each dropped his weapon, realizing that this was a two-handed rough-and-tumble with his life at stake. They clung to each other desperately, rolling over and over. By the fading light Larry recognized his opponent —Curt Moss. Of the two, Moss was the heavier and the stronger, Larry the more lithe and active.

By sheer power Moss swung on top, but before he could spread his legs and get set the younger man had tilted him over. They were both breathing hard, but Moss was getting the air into his lungs by gasping gulps. He had let himself take on too much blubber for violent exercise. His thumbs felt for Larry's eyes and jabbed into them. To protect himself Larry buried his face in the man's chest and got a finger grip on the fat throat.

Moss heaved himself free, and both scrambled to their feet. Into his enemy's belly Larry sent a hard, short armjolt that made Moss grunt. Another crashed to the chin. The big man knew he could not stand off and trade blows. He tried to close, and a second right to the vulnerable belly drove him back.

He had taken enough, and in his mind was a growing fear of the end. Bolting from the hole, Moss tore through the brush and dropped into another depression thirty yards away. He stopped only because the sound of a rifle warned him that in the open stretch just ahead he would make too good a mark.

The man had left his rifle in the windfall hole, but Larry had caught a glimpse of the revolver at his hip. It would be dangerous to follow him. If one approached the hollow where he found refuge he could shoot from cover.

There was nothing to do but wait. Neither man could leave his shelter without being seen. Larry did not know enough about a .45 to be sure whether it would carry with accuracy the distance between them. It was better to stick to his protection until he had a chance to slip away.

As the minutes dragged away Larry's nerves were taut as fiddle strings. He could not be quite sure that his enemy had not crept out of his hole and was making a circle to get at him from the rear. More than once he half decided to make a run for it, but he fought the urge down. He must stick it out and not break under the strain. His stomach tightened and screwed into a hard knot.

The moon came up and lit the scene with a silvery glow. Larry raised his head cautiously and a bullet whipped past him. It scattered dirt from the up-ended root behind him. He ducked, not answering the shot. But presently it occurred to him that it might be well to let Moss know he was on the lookout. He fired into the air.

It was three or four minutes later that the silence was shattered by a shout of fear.

"Goddlemighty, who's there?" a voice screamed.

Larry rose to his knees. He had to find out what was occurring.

Moss had leaped from cover. He stood for an instant, uncertain which way to run. At sight of Larry his revolver flamed twice. Larry fired. The man stood in the moonlight, his big body swaying a little, then pitched heavily to the ground.

A voice from the brush called, "You all right, Mr. Larry?"

Harville called back, "Yes. That you, Jes' Tolable?"

"Shore is." Tolt stepped into the open and looked down at the prone figure. "Dead as a stuck shote," he said.

"I had to do it," Larry said, his body shaking from a nervous reaction. "He shot at me from ambush. Missed me and killed my horse."

"No regrets about him," Tolt said coolly. "He was a triflin', no-account scoundrel. You sure plugged him good."

"He was firing at me when I hit him," Larry explained.

"So I noticed." Tolt laughed. "I let him hear me coming a-purpose. He got goosey and started to light out. I reckon he figured you was barrin' the way. You'd ought to be right glad you got him, Mr. Larry. Evah since you whopped him he's been ready to waylay you."

Though Larry knew that was true, he was unhappy at what he had done. He did not see how he could have helped killing Moss, after humiliating him at the time of the fight. But death is so final. He was shocked at this tragic result.

Tolt realized how unstrung the young man was and refrained from looking at him. He busied himself gathering the weapons of the bushwhacker and helping Larry strip the saddle from the dead horse. Bridle and saddle they hid in the brush, to be collected later. All the time he kept up a line of cheerful chatter. Moss had been at the gin during the afternoon and had made some inquiries of a Negro boy as to Larry's movements. He had given the boy a dime, a highly suspicious donation, since Curt Moss was notoriously stingy. Tolt had it in his mind to warn Larry, and when later in the day he heard that young Harville had been riding down the road alone it worried him. The chances were ten to one the two men would not meet, or if they did it would probably be under circumstances which would make trouble unlikely. But he could not get the fear out of his mind, and after supper had forked his mule to go meet the boy.

As he jogged down the road there came to Tolt the sound of a distant rifle shot. This made him uneasy, since it was getting too dark for a hunter to see squirrels or turkeys. A few minutes later he caught sight of Larry's dead horse lying in the dusty road. He pulled up and dismounted, then soft-footed forward. His sharp ears caught a faint stir in the bushes, and he had crept toward the sound. The rest Larry knew.

Tolt insisted on Larry riding while he walked beside him and talked. There was comfort in the man's slurring drawl. Behind the words was the implication that a villain who had tried to murder and had fallen victim to his own plot was responsible for his own death. By the time they reached the first Rosemont fence Larry's thoughts were back again on the wild idea he had conceived for rescuing Major Logan. His partner in the enterprise was to be Shep Tolt.

He drew up at the fence and interrupted Shep's monologue. In a few sentences he outlined what he had in mind.

Shep shook his head. "You're plumb crazy," he said. "Cain't be done."

Larry went into more detail. The outlaw camp must be within reasonable distance of the old Peters cabin below the ford, since that was the place appointed for the payment of the ransom money. A Negro had seen Dull crossing the ford on horseback late at night. Prodded by Colonel Harville, the sheriff had gone to the old Peters clearing and found evidence that men had been there not only once but two or three times very recently. Evidently it was a contact point between the outlaws and their spy.

Shep agreed that Larry's deduction was probably correct.

"How many places are there in the slough, close to the cabin, that are suitable for a camp?" Larry asked.

That would depend on how near, Shep replied. It was right boggy down at that end of the swamp. The best spot would be Spook Point. On the little island there was a spring and grass for the horses, and it was so well concealed that nobody knew how to reach it.

"Then we can depend on it," Larry said, "that's where they are. When you say nobody knows, you don't include Jes' Tolable."

Shep looked at his companion with curious, appraising eyes. This nice-looking boy, who had gone shuddery because he had rubbed out a scalawag trying to murder him, was asking Shep to take the damnedest crazy risk with him. It didn't make good sense.

"Say I mebbe could git you to their camp," he demurred. "Dad burn it, we wouldn't last no longer than a snowball in hell. Hit might be all right if I could take a mess of gunmen there, exceptin' that they would shore hear us coming when we splashed through the water."

"And that they would kill Major Logan before we got there." Larry shook his head. "Two of us could get there without being heard. A lot of corn whisky is going to their camp. They will sleep soundly at night. You can stay back with the horses while I slip over to the island and release Major Logan. I don't say it can be done, but I'm going to try. The ransom offer doesn't mean safety for him. He'll be killed as soon as they get the money."

Tolt rumpled his hair, a puzzled frown on his homely face. "You're the doggondest fellow ever I seed. Yore pappy was shootin' up the major the other day. Now you're 'lowing to bust into the gates of hell and come out a-draggin' the old boy with you."

"With your help," Larry added.

"Dad-gum it, I reckon I'll go," Tolt complained ruefully. "I'm always gettin' drug into some crazy thing or other. You'd think at my age I would of learned some sense." He stopped, struck by another thought. "What's yore pappy going to say about this?"

"He isn't going to know anything about it until we've brought back the major," Larry told him.

"Yeah, an' if you git killed I got to come back and git

skinned alive when I tell him."

"I don't expect to get killed."

Larry told him the story of the Texas young fellow who had followed the raiding Comanches for weeks, stolen into their camp, and rescued the two young girls who were prisoners. "They claim you can cut a trail like an Indian and crawl through brush without making a sound," young Harville concluded. "I'm going to find out whether you can live up to your reputation."

They reached Rosemont just as Colonel Harville's posse was getting back.

23

COLONEL HARVILLE HAD a much less exciting story to tell than Larry. His posse had plowed through swamps and made no contact with the outlaws. It had come home as soon as the news of Perry Logan's capture had reached the men at the rendezvous. The tale told by Jes' Tolable and Larry shocked the planter, though he was deeply grateful for the escape of his son. He wasted no pity on the fate of Curt Moss. The fellow had set a cowardly trap and himself become the victim of it. That was according to Scriptural prophecy. But it was an appalling thought that except for the semi-darkness the ambusher's first shot would probably have been fatal.

Maxwell Harville relieved his disturbed mind by scolding Larry. "The doctor said for you to stay home. You could have sent a boy with a note to Mrs. Logan, but you have to go traipsing off yourself. Even so, if you were so hell bent on going, you might have stopped at the gin and Jes' Tolable would have ridden with you. It was God's mercy you weren't killed. I never saw such a boy for runnin' into trouble, and all the time you're talkin' about peace and law for the rest of us."

His son explained that he had wanted to persuade Mrs. Logan to accept the loan of the ransom money. He admitted he had been careless in going alone. Larry was very tired, and it was with a white-faced smile he promised that next time he went to the Logans he would take Jes' Tolable as a guard.

By this time the colonel's exasperation had blown away. He said, gently, "Son, you better go right to bed. You look limp as a dishrag."

To his own surprise Larry slept soundly all night. When he awoke in the middle of the forenoon he felt quite well. Mandy had a hot breakfast waiting for him. He ate heartily, rather astonished at his swift recovery. His father hung around him, amusingly like a hen clucking over its chicks just saved from a hawk, Larry thought.

After consideration Larry had made a change in his plan for the rescue of Major Logan. He talked it over with Shep Tolt, who agreed with him that they ought to include Hal Logan in the adventure. He had a right to share in it, and Larry knew that if they left him out he would be furious later.

As soon as dinner was over Larry joined Shep at the gin, and the two rode to Hillcrest.

"I promised Father I would take you with me next time I called on the Logans, but I don't think he'll feel you are a safe guard when he hears of our little expedition tonight," Larry said with a chuckle.

Hal was at the stable saddling a horse as they rode up the avenue. He turned the animal over to a stableboy and joined them. Young Logan had heard the story of the shooting of Curt Moss, and they talked of it for a minute or two. He wanted to tell Harville he was grateful for his offer of the ransom money, but he found it difficult to begin. When he blurted out his thanks Larry waved them aside.

The money was not doing him any good in the bank, he said. He was glad to let them have it. But he and Jes' Tolable had another plan they wanted to talk over with Hal. It might not succeed, but he thought it would be worth trying. In a few sentences he sketched his idea.

Hal jumped at it, as a hungry trout does at bait. His reckless and impatient nature rebelled at doing nothing active while his father was in danger. Even if they failed, it would be better to try.

Shep made it clear that he could not promise to find the camp of the outlaws. But taking the evidence they had, the logical place for it was an island an old hermit had once named Spook Point. He gave his reasons. Outside of the outlaws, he was probably the only man in the district who had ever been there. On it the fugitives could find fresh water and feed for their horses. The distance from it to the Peters cabin was not more than a couple of miles.

Hal felt sure Shep was right. "When do we start?" he asked.

Not till long after dark, Shep told him. He impressed on young Logan the need of caution. "This is Injun stuff, Mr. Hal," he said. "We cain't ram-stam in an' bull this through. If you got any such notion I'm not doing business with you. We have to slip up to the camp mighty careful. Mebbe we'll have to lie in the brush for hours. Both of you boys will have to take orders from me because you-all got no experience in this here kind of work and I have."

"That's all right with me," Hal promised.

"So you think now," Shep answered dryly. "But when you git kinda excited about being near yore pappy, how do I know you won't git crazy?"

"It wouldn't make sense for me to start a fight, Jes' Tolable," Hal said. "They would shoot Father right off."

"What they would do exac'ly. You remember that when you air a-lying in the brush close to the camp."

Hal was in a mood to promise anything. He realized that without Tolt they could do nothing. The man was risking his life to help save the major. Moreover, he was a first-class woodsman and hunter, having done little else but fish and hunt for the most part of his life.

Larry added his pledge to do as he was told. If they were to do anything rash they might spoil their chance of rescuing the prisoner, he admitted.

They made their arrangements to meet at Big Hollow about eleven o'clock that night. That they were going on rather a forlorn hope all of them knew. But it seemed about the only chance to save Major Logan. Not one of them believed that after he had been paid the ransom money Lige Labreu would return the planter to them alive.

24

CHET DULL ADVANCED through the deadening at the Peters cabin with two rifles trained on him.

He protested irritably. "I done told you who I was, Lige. What's the sense in keeping them guns p'inted at me? One of them might go off."

"So it might," the Gobbler agreed. "Jest a military precaution, Chet. Some ornery cuss might be followin' you."

"Don't you think I've got plain horse sense? Nobody could follow me without my knowing it."

"Tha's right. *Without you knowin' it.* And if you knew it o' course you wouldn't come." Lige showed his teeth in a sarcastic grin. "Chet wouldn't throw daown his kinfolks, even if he was offered a heap of money. Not good old Chet."

Brad added a word. "He wouldn't if he is allowin' to live long."

Dull threw out his hands in a hopeless gesture. "I'll be doggoned if hit ain't plumb discouraging. A man does everything in the world for you when you-all air in a tight spot, and all he gits for it is mistrust."

"You got five hundred dollars of old Flynn's buried money," Lige reminded him. "Don't forget that. Well, what's new?"

"Newest thing is that Larry Harville killed Curt Moss last night. Curt laid for him in the bushes. It was kinda dark, and he missed his shot. Young Harville went after him and got him."

Lige said, "I'll be durned," and tacked on as a rider that Curt always had been a bungler.

Dull told them of the visit to him earlier in the day of Larry and his brother Andy. They had been concerned for the safety of the Gillis family, and had wanted him to negotiate with the Labreus. But since then, of course, Mrs. Gillis and the children had come home and reported Major Logan's capture.

"Have you heard tell what they aim to do about that?" Lige asked.

"I haven't seen ary one of them since. Colonel Harville was in the slough with a posse lookin' for you-all, but soon as he got word about Logan he turned back and come home. Daown at the store there was talk that Larry Harville was left a fortune by an English uncle an' that he has done sent to Little Rock for enough to ransom Logan. They say the Logan family air mighty anxious about the old man."

Again the face of Lige was lit by an ugly, sinister grin. "You kin report to them that the major is doing as well as kin be expected under the circumstances. He ain't what you could call right comfortable, seeing that his back was skinned good yesterday with a hickory. Brad laid the bud on. Logan and Harville gave him a whoppin' onct, so Brad figured turn about was fair play. Any time Harville wants to come an' git his it will be all right with Brad."

"If they come through with this ransom money do you aim to turn Logan loose?" Chet asked.

"Don't you reckon we had better cross that bridge when we come to it, Chet?" his cousin drawled.

"Logan ain't expecting to see his dear family again," Brad

mentioned. "He shore is a game old coot — cusses us out plenty when he takes the trouble to talk with us. I 'low to break him daown yet. I got another hickory limb ready for him tomorrow."

"Have you heard anything abaout how the roads south are guarded?" Lige asked. "Or whether any U.S. deputies are expected to join in the hunt for us?"

"They claim all the roads are watched, but I reckon you could bust through at night, onless you-all had bad luck. There is some talk of gov'ment men coming yere, but I dunno how true it is."

The Labreus rode back to their camp, carrying with them another gallon of the corn whisky with which Dull supplied them. The outlaw gang emptied the jug in the course of the evening, after which they followed Brad's suggestion that they go devil their prisoner. Major Logan was bound hand and foot. A rawhide rope fastened him to a small hickory tree.

The drunken men gathered around the prostrate planter.

"How is yore good health this evenin', Major?" Brad asked mockingly.

Logan looked up at him in contemptuous silence. Brad kicked him twice in the ribs.

"When I ask you a question you talk nice," he snarled.

One of the gang, a man they called Cad Miller, suggested that Brad's cat had stolen the major's tongue. He liked his pun so well that he repeated the key word, to make sure the others got it. "Cat. See the p'int, boys. The cat with nine tails, only this yere one of Brad's didn't have but one tail."

"Mebbe I'd better give him another dose right now and learn him to be more polite," Brad said, and again kicked the victim in the side. "Bet yore boots I could make him holler quit this time."

Lige interfered. "That'll be enough, Brad. You leave the major alone with his happy dreams. Tomorrow we might let him taste the bud again. I'll see about that."

Logan was in his late fifties and Lige did not know how much he could stand. When the ransom money was brought he wanted to be able to show the major alive if his son demanded to see him before giving up the money. It might be better to have him well enough to walk on his own feet. You never could tell what break of circumstances might arise. It was a pleasure to him to watch his enemy suffer, but a fellow ought not to indulge himself at the expense of profitable business. No use in stopping Logan's clock as long as holding him gave them the whip hand.

"You air too softhearted, Pappy," Brad complained. "You pamper yore enemies too much when you git them in a cleft stick. Old Maledon [1] wasn't fixin' for to hang you nice and gentle last Friday. I say, tit for tat. Logan an' his friends were 'lowin' to kill us off."

"Leave it to old Lige," his father said. "I'll tell you-all when to start workin' on Logan. I don't reckon he'll write home about what a nice time he's having."

They made sure the knots were tight before leaving the prisoner. Cad Miller was detailed to guard him, though there was not the least chance of his being able to free him-

[1] Maledon was the official executioner of Judge Parker's Fort Smith court.

self. The outlaw brought him a small pail of water from the spring and held it to his mouth while he drank. At the request of the bound man, Miller flung what was left of the water over his fevered face. The guard was not by nature cruel, and he had an unvoiced admiration for the stoicism with which the planter had taken his punishment. He arranged a bit of mosquito netting over the major's hat to protect him from the buzzing pests that swarmed around them.

Logan lay on his side to avoid the pressure of the ground on his torn and bloodstained back. He did not sleep. Though the pain from the flogging was not so acute as it had been, every move he made was a torment. He did not know whether the kicks from Brad Labreu's heavy boots had broken his ribs. It did not matter much. There was no hope in him. Lige wanted him alive for a time. As a prisoner he could be used profitably for trading purposes. But the Gobbler would never let him get out of his hands while he was still living.

Miller leaned against a tree trunk, the hat pulled down over his eyes. That Lige expected him to stay awake he knew. But Cad thought there was no sense in this. Gradually his body slumped lower. His eyes drooped shut, opened again, and closed. Several times he shook himself awake from a light doze, but always his head fell forward and his lids shuttered. Like the others, he had been drinking heavily. He snuggled down, gave up resistance, and presently began to snore.

25

BEFORE TEN O'CLOCK the lights were all out at Rosemont. Larry lay on the bed in his room, waiting until he felt reasonably sure that the others were asleep. He had changed to his working clothes. Earlier in the evening he had borrowed from his brother Tom, without asking permission, the revolver he kept in a drawer of his bureau. Tom would not be likely to miss it, and if there should be a fight in the swamp it might come in handy.

At ten-twenty Larry rose and tiptoed out to the gallery, carrying his riding boots in one hand and the Winchester in the other. On the porch steps he sat down and pulled on his boots. Ten minutes later he had saddled a small wiry bay horse and was on the Big Hollow road.

In the daytime it had seemed a feasible adventure to ride through the swamp at night and catch the outlaws napping, but the outlook appeared very different now. A field of girdled trees bordered the road beyond the Gillis place, and in the moonlight the deadening looked like some graveyard of the Titans, an eerie spot uncanny when one's imagination was active. Larry felt the scampering of tiny cold feet up and down his back. It was madness to think that they could invade the camp of these murderous devils and come back alive. He wanted to pull up, to turn around and go back home. But he had gone too far to desert. The knowledge that two men were joining him at Big Hollow held him to his purpose.

Shep Tolt and Hal Logan were waiting for him behind Holcomb's store. Answering his greeting, Shep mentioned that he was Jes' Tolable. They took the ferry, to cut off several miles of travel. Cully Sanderson, the ferryman, was a friend of Tolt. He could be depended upon to keep his mouth shut.

Sanderson was inclined to grumble at being aroused from sleep in the middle of the night, but his resentment died away after a whispered talk with Tolt. He had not known how important this night ride was. He still was puzzled at its object, nor could he guess who was expected to fill the saddle of the riderless horse Hal Logan was leading. But Tolt impressed on him that they might be coming back in a great hurry to get across the bayou. The ferryman promised to be waiting for them on the near side when they arrived. If this was a raiding expedition to pick off a Labreu or two while the outlaws were asleep, it met with the approval of Cully Sanderson.

They passed through an oak lead to the lower ground where scattered sassafras and willow trees grew on knolls rising above the more spongy marsh. Occasionally there were buckeyes and sycamores. By this time they were on the old rotten corduroy road, and Tolt was watching for the three persimmon trees that marked the point of departure from it.

The croaking of frogs filled the night. As they advanced deeper into the swamp the surroundings grew more dismal. Mosquitoes buzzed about their heads incessantly. They splashed through the yellow-green water of slimy pools or through ooze into which the horses' hoofs sank to the fetlocks.

Tolt stopped several times to orient himself. They had left the three persimmon trees behind them and were following no trail. But their guide was a natural-born woodsman. He had been once to Spook Point and had instinctively memorized a dozen landmarks on the way. A scalybark hickory tree. A twisted gum that had been struck by lightning. Four cypress trees in a row. Before he reached these guideposts he told his companions what to look for, and though he twice went wrong and had to turn back, he always found at last the beacons that stood out in his mental map.

Larry did not see how he could find his way in this morass which looked to him all alike. He marveled at Tolt's ability to hold a course in such a jungle.

"You're a wonder, Jes' Tolable," he applauded.

Tolt grinned. "What I thought abaout you the other day, Mr. Larry, when the colonel showed me one of yore school books. It was a furrin book, with hen tracks for letters. Seems some fellow was a-beggin' pardon in the book for something or other. Yore pappy said it was Greek an' you could read it."

Larry was puzzled. Somebody begging pardon. Then it jumped to his mind—*Plato's Apology*. "He wasn't exactly begging pardon. But I get your point. You read this swamp as I do a page of the *Apology*, except that you do it far better, since I can just stumble through by using a dictionary. But both of us had to train ourselves to the particular kind of reading before us."

Again Tolt had stopped. He scratched his head, grinning ruefully. "I got to spell this yere bit of readin' out, looks like," he said. "An' I hain't got no dictionary neither."

"Jes' Tolable will work it out," Hal told Larry.

Their guide told them to stay where they were while he did some exploring. He had to find a cypress tree on which he had slashed a blaze, he said. It had to be near this spot, but he was not sure in what direction. He appeared in a thicket of trumpet vines. They could hear the sound of his horse moving in the brush, after which there was silence except for the humming of the mosquito swarms. Presently a distant blood-chilling scream lifted into the air. Larry turned, white-faced, to his companion.

Hal laughed. "Only a painter."

"It sounded like a woman."

Young Logan nodded. "Nothing sounds more fearsome than a painter's cry," he admitted.

Tolt returned, from a different direction than the one in which he had started. "I done found my tree," he said proudly.

As they drew nearer to the camp Tolt enjoined silence. He was careful to avoid brush as much as possible, so that the rustling of bushes might not be heard. It was possible, though not likely, that some one of the outlaws might be returning from Big Hollow even this late at night. The only chance of rescuing Major Logan was by remaining undiscovered.

"All right, Jes' Tolable," Hal said impatiently. "Let's get going."

Shep Tolt rubbed his bristly chin and looked at Logan dubiously. "I got to talk straight to you, Mr. Hal," he said. "We ain't a-going to make it if you git fussed an' in a hurry. All of us are puttin' our lives in the pot, as the old sayin' is, to holp save the major. We have to cotch these fellows asleep. No matter how long we have to wait. Like I said before, we cain't bust in an' take yore pappy from this yere gang."

"You don't need to keep saying that," Hal cut back sharply. "I know it."

Tolt was an easygoing soul. He did not like to ruffle this young fire-eater. But he did not want his eagerness to destroy them all. "You got to act it well as know it. Mebbe we made a mistake in askin' you to join us."

Hal flared up. "Cut out the talk," he said curtly. "I told you I'd let you handle this. Which way do we go?"

The rather slack jaw of their guide tightened. "I hain't sure but what I'm a-goin' home right naow. I'd go a considerable way to git yore father outa the hands of these devils, but I don't aim to invite them to kill me off."

"Losing yore nerve, Jes' Tolable?" Hal asked acidly.

"Might be thataway," Tolt replied quietly. "What sticks out like a nigger's sore thumb is that you 'n me cain't work together."

"Then show me the camp and let me handle it," young Logan said huffily.

Larry tried to pour oil on the ruffled waters. He said gently, "Don't you think, Hal, that we have to do this under Shep's direction?"

"I've kept telling him he was running it," Hal snapped. "What more does he want?"

"I want this to go off smooth and slick," Tolt answered amiably. "If we're gonna fuss about it, we better go home an' quit."

Hal shut his mouth to keep back a sharp response. He did not speak until he had fought down his temper. That Tolt was right he realized. "I was wrong," he said. "I'll take any orders you give, Jes' Tolable."

"Tha's the way to talk, Mr. Hal," the older man said. "I ain't jes' being bossy. But you might say it's neck meat or nothing with us. Here's my idea of this. We'll tie up the horses back quite a way from the camp and wade up to the island afoot. I'll leave you boys in the brush and look things over. Mebbe I'll be away quite a spell if any of the cusses are a-stirrin'. Then we'll move up closeter. Mr. Larry will creep up an' cut loose the major whilst we-'uns cover him in case he is seen."

"Why Larry?" objected Hal. "He's my father."

Tolt did not give his real reason, which was that Larry would not try to hurry the job, that he was more patient and dependable, had none of the explosive daring that might lead him to underestimate danger. Moreover, the guide wanted Hal with him, to watch over and restrain him if necessary.

"We want experienced men to protect yore father and the fellow who is freeing him." Tolt smiled apologetically at Harville. "Mr. Larry is a leetle new to trouble, so I 'lowed to give him a job where he won't need a gun — if any of us do."

"That's fine," Larry said, his throat tightening a bit. This was specious reasoning Tolt had given. The post of danger was in the heart of the camp, a few feet from the sleeping outlaws. He knew he had been chosen because the older man had been afraid to leave Hal alone. He felt shaky. If seen, he would go out in a blast of guns.

Hal gave way, rather resentfully. He felt that it was his own fault he was being held in the background.

They sloshed through more water and tied their mounts on a small wooded knoll to some saplings. Dimly they could make out a shadowy shore beyond them. This was Spook Point, Tolt assured them. He added that he hoped the camp was there and that the outlaws were so doggoned sound asleep that nothing would waken them.

They waded toward the island, Tolt leading the way. Their weapons they held above their heads. Each step had to be taken with the greatest care, since the bottom was slippery and full of holes. If one of them floundered and splashed it might ruin everything. At the deepest point the water reached to their hips.

Tolt stepped out of the stagnant pool, taking care not to make the least sound. The others followed. A fringe of pawpaws and muscadine vines bordered the bank. They stopped to listen. Only the frog chorus and the perpetual hum of mosquitoes broke the silence. Shep Tolt made signs that he was going to creep forward and investigate.

He left his rifle in the bushes. Larry noticed how cautiously the man moved. Wherever possible, he went through breaks in the screen of bushes, avoiding interlacing branches so that there would be no snapping or crackling. If he had to push aside a limb, it was done so gently that there was no rumor of a sound.

Though he could not have been away many minutes, it seemed to his companions that hours had passed before he rejoined them.

"The camp is just over the rise," he reported. "They're lying round a campfire. A wet log is smoking, I reckon to drive away the skeeters. On the yon side of the fire, fifteen — twenty steps back, there was two fellows alone. I couldn't tell who they was, but I reckon it was the major and some fellow guarding him. They were both lying daown near the foot of a tree." He turned to Hal. "Likely yore pappy is tied up an' either chained or roped to that there tree. If he's chained there ain't a thing we can do, but if hit's a rope a fellow could cut it."

"Too bad the major is on the other side of the campfire," Larry whispered. "I'll have to go right past the camp."

"No," Tolt said. "We'll take to the water agin and move along the shore till we've passed it. You want to be awful careful how you move, boys. Some of them was right restless, 'count of the skeeters. If they cotched us in the water, it would be like shootin' ducks on a pond for them."

They stepped back into the scum-covered water and moved in single file close to the bank. Once Tolt stopped for a five minutes that threatened to last forever. He had heard the sound of voices around the campfire scarcely forty feet from them. The murmur of them died away, but Shep stayed motionlessly in his tracks so long that Larry wanted to scream. At last he soft-footed forward once more.

From a small backwater inlet they crept ashore and drew up behind a clump of blackberry bushes. The moonlit camp could be seen quite clearly. There was no stir or sound from it. Two of the men lay about a dozen yards from the others, not more than forty paces from the watchers. One of these must be the major.

Tolt murmured in Harville's ear. "Keep off to the left and move mighty careful. Their guns will be right beside them. If one of 'em wakes jes' lie still. We'll have him covered." He took from Larry the Winchester he carried and handed him his sharp hunting knife. "You don't have to say a word to Major Logan. If he ain't ironed cut him loose and come back still as a fox. 'Course if he's chained you come back alone."

Larry nodded. His throat was tight and his nerves tense. His body was so frozen that he did not think he could start on the short perilous journey. But to his surprise the moment he inched forward the strain relaxed. His mind sloughed the fear and concentrated on the task.

He crept out from the protection of the blackberry bushes on all fours carrying the knife between his teeth. There was an urge in him to hurry, to get it over with as soon as possible. But he knew that might be fatal. Any small stir might wake up a restless sleeper. He wanted desperately to rescue the prisoner unnoticed. Otherwise there would be a battle in which very likely several would be killed.

As Tolt had advised, he bore to the left, creeping up a hump in the ground toward the hickory trees where the captive and his guard lay. One of the outlaws grunted and turned over, so that he faced the major. Larry lay almost breathless, his body pressed close to the soil. If the fellow opened his eyes he could not miss seeing him. Presently the man's respiration became regular again.

The guard was lying with arms stretched out, his chest

rising and falling stertorously. A gun was attached to a belt fastened around his waist. Larry would have liked to slip it from the holster, but did not dare.

Perry Logan woke out of a troubled doze and looked at the white face moving closer to him in the moonlight. Larry put a finger to his lips in warning. The major stared, unbelieving.

What Logan saw was incredible. He had counted himself already a dead man, and unless his eyes were playing tricks a friendly enemy had come to this hell hole to help him. If miracles still occurred this must be one.

Already Larry was sawing at the rope which bound the feet of the prisoner. After this had been severed he cut the one tying the wrists. It took him a little longer to work through the rawhide thong fastening Logan to the hickory.

The major was too stiff to rise. Larry helped him to his feet. He stood there clinging to Harville, with no power of motion in the rigid legs. Larry bent down and massaged the calves and thighs, working the circulation back into them, while the major rested a hand on his back for support.

There was no use trying to creep back to the blackberry bushes. The released man had to regain the use of his legs or he would be helpless. Presently they took a step forward, Larry's arm around the waist of the planter. Logan winced at the pressure on his lacerated back, but set his teeth to stand the pain. He tottered uncertainly, helpless as a child learning to walk.

As they took that slow jerky walk Larry was too busy helping the older man keep on his feet to look over his shoulder, but the fear was in him that a bullet might at any moment crash into his back.

Logan became with each step more master of his legs. They would have reached the bushes safely if his weight had not come on a small smooth branch that turned under his foot. He went down heavily, the stick cracking sharply.

Hal leaped out of the bushes. He and Larry dragged the major into cover. But the mischief was done. One of the outlaws had jumped to his feet, rifle in hand. He fired toward the shaking blackberry clump into which the figures were vanishing.

Tolt's muzzle-loader flung a bullet into the man's belly and he keeled over. The other outlaws were taken at disadvantage. They jumped up, startled and unsure, not knowing who or where the enemy was. Bullets poured at them from the bushes. Another man was hit and cried out. Larry thought it was Craw Labreu.

"Let's git outa here," Sim cried, and broke for the shelter of the trees.

The other outlaws followed at his heels. It was in their minds that they had been trapped and might be wiped out.

Hal snapped an order to his companions. "Get father to the horses before they come back. I'll stay here and keep firing till you're across the slough, then I'll join you."

With Tolt on one side of him and Larry on the other, each supporting him just below the armpit, Logan waded through the water. They heard the booming of Hal's rifle and twice at least an answering shot. They were in the shadow of a cypress at the edge of the far bank when there came to them the sound of horses splashing into the slough. They caught sight of riders crossing a hundred yards below them. Larry counted six horsemen, one leaning forward and clinging to the horn of his saddle. That must be the wounded man Craw, the fellow Hal had hit. The outlaws were breaking camp in a panic. They had probably left a dead man there. One worry jumped to young Harville's mind. The fleeing badmen would pass close to the knoll where the mounts of the rescuers were tied. If they caught sight of them they would know from how small a force they were running. They might return, or at least take the saddled horses with them.

His two assistants were helping Perry Logan out of the water when Hal joined them at the knoll. The four horses were still tied to the saplings where they had been left an hour earlier.

They listened, to make sure the Labreus were not coming back. The sounds of their retreat had long since died away.

"They done got a bellyful, I 'low," Tolt said jubilantly. "I been promisin' myself to git one of the cusses, an' I shorely did tonight."

Hal produced a bottle of whisky and gave it first to his father and then to Larry. Both of them were shaking with the cold from the wet clothes that clung to them. They were abstainers, but both took a deep drink. Tonight this was a much-needed medicine. Jes' Tolable said, "Here's howdy, genelmen!" and tilted the bottle high. Young Logan helped himself to two swallows.

With some difficulty they lifted the planter to the saddle. He was an ill man, suffering a great deal of pain on account of the motion of the horse, but he shut his teeth and made no complaint. Whatever he had to endure would be nothing comparable to whar had been in store for him if he had not been rescued from the hands of Gobbler Lige. He was an inordinately proud man. It would hurt his vanity to have it known that he had been brutally kicked, but he would be unhappy all his life if it were known that he had been stripped and horsewhipped like some scamp caught stealing a pig.

26

THE RIDE BACK to the ferry was intolerably long both to the major and to Larry. Young Harville was not entirely recovered from the accident, and he had set his body too hard a task. He was so completely exhausted that he slumped in the saddle and his shoulders sagged.

Hal noticed how he was shaking. "You're chillin'," he said.

That he was having a chill, Larry admitted, but there was nothing to do about that now.

"We'll feed you quinine, boy, when we get you to Hillcrest," he promised.

Cully Sanderson was waiting for them at the bayou and he ferried them across. Tolt gave him a sketchy account of their adventure. The ferryman had seen nothing of the outlaws. They had probably recovered from their fright, slipped back to find the camp deserted, and were busy moving it to another place. Jes' Tolable was of opinion that they would not remain in the district much longer if

Craw Labreu was able to travel, but would try to slip through the patrolled road leading to Texas. The Gobbler must know that all the settlers in the neighborhood would be rising against his gang.

When they reached Big Hollow Hal proposed that his father stay with Dr. Watkins. The major would not consent. He wanted to get home where guards could be set and all of them safeguarded. Watkins agreed to go with them to Hillcrest and stay a day or two, since just now he had no serious cases. The doctor had a more personal reason for going. Lige Labreu might pick him up again to treat his wounded son Craw, and this time he might not get back alive.

Watkins hitched up his buggy and Perry Logan was helped into it, after which the small cavalcade continued to Hillcrest.

Larry stopped at the side of the road leading to Hillcrest and said something about going home accompanied by Tolt. Hal overrode the suggestion with such abrupt decision there could be no doubt of his sincerity.

"You're white as a sheet," he said. "A fool could see you're sick. You're going to stay right here till you're well. Mother will see one of the girls nurses you, and she'll boss the job herself. Jes' Tolable is going to stay with us too. We might need that darned old muzzle loader of his again. Early in the mo'ning I'll send a boy to tell Colonel Harville you are here."

He did not want to be any trouble, Larry said.

"It would be too doggoned bad if we put ourselves out a mite for you," Hal broke out, with obvious sarcasm.

"You come along, fellow. We'll let you know when you've worn out yore welcome."

Within five minutes of their arrival everybody at Hillcrest was awake and busy. In the kitchen the cook was making coffee and rolling out a batch of biscuits. Upstairs the maids prepared beds for the guests. Mrs. Logan helped Hal put her husband to bed, and later gave him coffee and a dish of floating island. He declined the hot biscuits and bacon she offered. Though concerned at the major's condition, Sallie Logan was radiant with happiness at the unexpected safe return of the head of the house.

While the others were making preparations to take care of the arrivals and Jes' Tolable was still at the stable seeing the animals were fed, Larry saw Diane alone for one brief minute.

She came into the parlor where he was waiting, her eyes eager and shining with the deepened color of strong emotion. She said, in a low-pitched, husky voice, "Hal has told us everything you have done."

Larry was embarrassed, yet delighted at the warmth of her gratitude. "I got the idea we might rescue your father in the night, so I told Hal and he said he would try it," he explained. "It was Jes' Tolable who really did it all. He guessed right about the camp, and guided us there and planned what to do. I just went along."

"You just went along," she echoed, fond scorn in her voice. "All you did was — everything. You organized this rescue. You crept out and freed father while these murderers were lying all around. Before that you saved me from that wild animal, and lent us the ransom money. You have broken up this silly, terrible family feud. Is all that nothing?" She finished with a sob choking her throat.

He said, a smile on his white, tired face, "It's a lot if it has made us friends." His grimy hands went out and took her small ones in his. "I want to talk about that . . . some day."

Larry was covered with filth and mud to the waist. His hands and face were bramble-scratched. There was a dirty bandage around his head. But to this girl who could not keep the love light out of her eyes no man had ever looked so beautiful.

A colored girl walked into the room with some quinine capsules and a glass of water on a platter. "Doctor Watkins says for you-all to take two of these naow," she told the guest. "Soon as you have drunk some coffee and et some food I'm to show you where you sleeps at. Doctor 'lows he will be in to see you soon as he has got Major Logan fixed up good."

Though Larry was very tired, he did not enjoy looking so much worse than any tramp he had ever seen. He asked Diane to have the boy Hal was sending to Colonel Harville in the morning bring back some decent clothes for him.

Twenty minutes later he was in bed wearing one of Rod's nightshirts. The chill was over, and he was burning with fever. Dr. Watkins came in and gave instructions to the middle-aged colored man who had valeted Larry while he was bathing and making ready for bed. There was not much to be done except see the patient had plenty of quinine and was kept comfortable. Watkins left him a sleeping powder in case he needed it, with a promise to look in next morning.

Larry did not find it easy to sleep. His mind was full of what he had seen and done in the past few hours, of the perilous adventure and its happy finale. He fell asleep at last dreaming of the girl.

27

GOBBLER LIGE HAD MADE a mistake, though he did not intend to admit it. The bitter reproaches of Brad and the others were justified. He ought to have rubbed out Perry Logan instead of holding him for ransom. His inordinate love of money had betrayed him. They had stayed too long in the Cache bottom. By this time they ought to have been well on their way to Texas.

Now he was in a tight. They had lost one of their men, a desperado they had picked up at Fort Smith after breaking jail. That could not be helped. It was an incident of their way of life. Men who lived outside the law could expect to die young. What worried Lige was the condition of his son Craw. He was hurt too badly to travel. It stood out like a jagged flash of lightning on a dark night that the net was closing in on them. They had to get away now — before daybreak — or it might be too late. His men were getting panicky and were blaming him. The only haven they could see was Texas. If he did not take them there at once they would bolt.

They had stopped in an oak slash to bandage Craw's wound. He had been shot in the chest and could go no farther, though he kept protesting that if they would fix him up and stop the bleeding he could make it all right. The man was desperately afraid they would leave him here alone — to die in the swamp or to be taken to the gallows at Fort Smith. He knew that the ruling thought in each of their minds was how best to save himself.

"We'll take you to Doc Watkins, son, and have him fix you up nice," Lige said, after they had done the best they could for him. "Don't you git scared. Yore old pappy will see you through."

They lifted Craw to a saddle and headed for the bayou. Since they had to get away secretly they could not take the ferry but had to follow the longer route by the ford.

Brad dropped back from the lead to talk with his father. "If we take Craw to Watkins, the doc will spread the word soon as we've gone and they'll be on our tails quicker than scat," he said. "We won't have a dead man's chance. They'll telegraph ahead that we're coming."

The bleak eyes of Gobbler Lige looked into those of his son. They were blank and expressionless, with something in them remote and inhuman. He said, gently, "We ain't a-goin' to Doc Watkins."

Brad looked away. He did not ask what Lige meant. He did not want to know. A shiver ran up and down his spine.

"I'd better git back in the lead," he said, "seeing as I know the way to the ford and Sim don't."

"Don't wait for me and Craw when you git to the ford," Lige ordered. "And after you git across turn south."

"You mean — not to take the road for Big Hollow?"

"I said go south. I'll be with you right soon."

The eyes of the son dropped. "Whatever you say," he mumbled.

Lige fell in beside the wounded man. "How you makin' it, son?" he asked.

Craw clung to the saddle horn with both hands. There were beads of moisture on his clammy forehead. "How much further is it?" he gasped.

"Not far now to the ford, and only a little ways from there."

"You-all won't leave me, will you?" Craw pleaded.

"Long as you're alive I'll stay right with you. I'm gonna give you a rest at the ford and let the others ride on so as the doc will be dressed and ready for you."

"He'll fix me up so I can go on with you, won't he?"

"Bet yore boots. We'll take him with us to look after you."

Lige supported the wavering body of his son. "Jes' a li'l bit further, Craw. We kin see the bayou now through the trees."

When they reached the ford the others were no longer in sight.

"If I was to rest mebbe you could bring the doc to me," Craw said feebly.

"A good idea, son. Stick it another minute till we git acrost. You're gonna have a long rest."

When they reached the deepest part of the ford Lige let his horse drop back till its head nosed the flank of the other animal. The crash of his revolver whipped across the bayou. For a moment the grip of Craw's fingers on the saddle horn held the body balanced. As they relaxed it plunged head first into the sluggish water.

Lige did not throw back his head and gobble. He looked down into the dark waters that covered his son, shocked at the terrible finality of what he had just done. A sense of impending doom shuttled through his mind.

Before Craw's startled horse could reach dry land he caught the bridle. His weight on the near stirrup, he unsaddled the animal. Blanket and saddle he dropped into the bayou, then slipped the bridle from the gelding's head. Swinging the rein, he struck the freed horse a sharp blow with the bit. It splashed forward, scrambled up the bank, and disappeared in the brush. The bridle Labreu flung into the stream.

A quarter of an hour later he caught up with the rest of the party.

Sim asked, "Where's Craw?"

The others had stopped when Lige galloped up and grouped around. Their eyes all centered on their leader.

"I've got bad news, boys," Lige said. "He fell off'n his horse and got drowned. I couldn't make out to save him."

None of them said anything. The clothes of Lige were not wet. He had not been in the water. They remembered the sound of a shot that had drifted faintly to them.

Lige continued, bravely cheerful. "I've lost my youngest boy, but I can see it's for the best. He was a mighty sick man — shot through the lungs. He couldn't of lived long. But long enough to be dragged to Fort Smith and hanged, dying though he was. And that ain't all. He knew our plans — to cut across the Choctaw Nation and head for the

Brazos. They would of deviled them outa the pore boy shore as sin. He died nice and easy. We got to know it's a heap better for him to be through his misery."

Brad said hoarsely, "I reckon you're right." He swung his horse round and started down the road.

They traveled all night, and when daylight broke tied up in the brush on the banks of the White River. They had no food with them and dared not go scouting for any at the farmhouses in the vicinity. Their hope of safety lay in getting across the state without being discovered. During the day they grumbled and cursed at their luck, blaming one another and particularly Lige for having led them into this section. Yet they were careful not to make their complaints too violent and too personal, for they had a deep-seated fear of their leader. None of them wanted him gobbling over his body. That he had killed Craw they felt sure. Privately they agreed that it had been wise and a kindness to the wounded outlaw. But hard though they were, the thought of a father destroying his own son shocked them.

The fugitives slept a good deal during the day. They took turns in staying awake to watch the horses and guard against the approach of enemies.

A towheaded boy out hunting stumbled on their camp. He stopped at the edge of the small clearing, startled at the sight of so many armed men sleeping. His instinct warned him of danger and he back-tracked softly unobserved. He hurried home to tell his father what he had seen.

The farmer did not pay much heed to his son's story, but a few hours later a passing neighbor stopped to tell him that word had come by telegraph for law officers to be on the lookout for the Labreu gang. The men notified the sheriff of the county that there were campers in the brake by the river, and a posse was quickly organized.

To the outlaws the attack came as a complete surprise. Before they could reach cover one of them was killed and another shot in the leg. The wounded man was Sim Labreu. Before he could crawl to his horse he was captured. His father and brother, with Cad Miller, managed to mount and break through the trap. They galloped away wildly, following the same road they had taken in the night. But this time they were riding north. In a cornfield they found a hiding place till dark.

It was clear to the bandits that at present they must give up the attempt to reach Texas. They were too hot to try so long a journey. In every county they crossed, officers would be waiting for them. Lige could think of one spot where nobody would be looking for them. That was in the Cache slough. They had last been seen thirty miles away from it. Since they had been driven out of it, with the loss of three men in all, their hunters would not think them fools enough to return. If they could get back unobserved they would be safe for a few days. They had left plenty of food at Spook Point. Once there, they could pick it up and move to another camp. In the event they were discovered and the hunt got too hot they could cross the bayou and hole up at the deserted Flynn place. The house had the reputation of being haunted and most of the natives, both white and colored, avoided it as they would the plague.

When night fell they took the road again, traveling fast as they could safely drive their mounts. By-passing Big Hollow, they made a wide circuit around the village. Unseen by anyone, they forded the bayou and rode into the swamp. The moon was high when they reached their old camping ground at Spook Point.

Brad swung from the saddle, stiff from the long ride. His stomach was flat as an empty mail sack. "Food first off," he said. "I'm so dad-gummed hungry I could eat a polecat."

Lige still sat his horse, narrowed eyes sweeping the site of the camp they had left twenty-four hours earlier. There were several things wrong about the setup. They had left a dead man lying beside the fire. His body was gone. There had been sacks of provisions hanging from the limbs of trees and cooking equipment on the ground. The sacks were nowhere to be seen. Neither were the Dutch oven, the fryingpan, the coffeepot. The rifle and money belt of the dead man had been taken. Somebody had been here and made a thorough clean-up.

28

ANDY CAME DOWN to the breakfast table with news. "Larry is not in his room. He must have gone out."

"Queer," Tom said, buttering a hot biscuit. "My six-shooter has gone."

Their father was startled. It flashed into his mind that the blow on the boy's head might have been more severe than Dr. Watkins had thought. It might have disturbed his thought processes.

"Did any of you hear him get up?" the colonel asked.

None of them had. This was a little odd. They were country people, and they rose at dawn. The youngest brother, used to more urban habits, was always the last to appear in the morning.

"Did he say anything about going hunting?" the planter inquired.

Tom shook his head. An idea struck him "Tell you what. He doesn't know anything about shooting with a revolver. I was showing him couple of days ago how to hold and aim one. He's out practicing. When Larry came here he was what out west they call a sure enough tenderfoot, but I'll say for him he learns fast."

Maxwell Harville was not quite satisfied with this explanation, but he went on with his breakfast Five minutes later Mandy appeared with another plate of hot biscuits and the information that Mr. Hal Logan and Jes' Tolable were outside and wanted to see the colonel. The planter put down his napkin and walked out to the porch.

"I have come to tell you, sir, that yore son Larry is at Hillcrest," Hal said.

"What is he doing there?" the colonel asked, astonished. "And why didn't he come himself?"

"He's runnin' a fever, but Dr. Watkins says he'll be all right in a day or two. Right now he is in bed."

"Sick in bed? I don't understand. Why at Hillcrest?

Why not at home, if he's going to be sick anywhere? He isn't out of his head, is he?"

"No, sir." Hal's eyes warmed. His impulsive enthusiasm broke through the calm with which he had set himself to tell the news. "Fact is, Larry Harville is the gamest man in Arkansas today — and about the best. That boy went into the Cache slough last night, right spang into the Labreu camp, and brought my father home alive."

The colonel was astounded. This was beyond belief. "But — could he? First thing, he didn't know where the camp is. Second — "

Maxwell Harville's words failed him. There were so many other impossibilities flooding to his mind, barriers to an acceptance of this story.

"Jes' Tolable guessed where the camp would be," Hal explained. "And he sure is a wonder. They took me along on account of it being my father who was a prisoner."

Andy and Tom had come to the porch and were listening.

"You're tellin' us that the three of you went in and brought back Major Logan?" Tom cried.

"That's what," Tolt said, grinning. He was very proud of what they had done and did not object to sunning himself in the general applause.

"Larry was wounded," his father said quickly.

"No, sir. He's all right, except for chillin' from wading in the slough so much." On Hal's face there was a thin momentary smile. "The Labreus are toting all the bullets that hit their mark. Jes' Tolable killed one fellow, and another was wounded."

"How in time did you do it?" Andy asked.

"We slipped up on them while they were asleep. Jes' Tolable and I covered Larry while he crawled into the camp and cut loose my father. Hell broke loose when my father stumbled and fell. One fellow heard him and jumped up shooting. Jes' Tolable drilled him. The others panicked and lit out. Then we came home. Larry was all in, so he stayed at Hillcrest. If he feels thataway, he'll be welcome all the rest of his life as a guest."

The Harvilles had never heard anything as amazing as this. They asked questions until the whole history of the night was before them. Tom and Andy felt defrauded that they had not shared in the adventure, but they realized that it would have been unwise to take a larger group to the camp. It would have greatly lessened the chance of a surprise.

A few minutes later word reached Rosemont from Cantrell that the Labreu gang had been seen by a farmer riding south between two and three o'clock in the morning. The man had been up looking after a cow that had just calved when he recognized the Gobbler in the moonlight at the head of the party.

Colonel Harville deputed his two sons and Tolt to go to Spook Point and bring out the dead man. Maxwell himself joined Hal and rode with him to Hillcrest. It was a strange sensation to be riding up the avenue to the house of his enemy beside the young man who had emptied his revolver at Andy on the courthouse square at Brandon. Yet in spite of his embarrassment he knew that the feud was forever dead and was deeply glad of it. His son Larry had killed it.

Mrs. Logan met him in the parlor and showed no evidence in her manner that the situation was awkward. She was pleasantly friendly, and when she spoke of what Larry had done there were tears in her eyes. She led him upstairs to the room where his son was lying.

"We have quite a hospital," Mrs. Logan said happily. She felt it was a small price to pay for having all her worries swept away at once. "But Rod is hobbling around already. Dr. Watkins says Larry will be well in a few days. And all my husband needs is a long rest and good nursing. These terrible men treated him very badly." She went into no particulars of what they had done.

Harville said he hoped to see the major as soon as he felt well enough. After all that had occurred it would not be possible to harbor any more ill-feeling. He was willing to be a good neighbor on any terms that her husband proposed.

When his father came into the room alone Larry was finishing breakfast in bed. Maxwell Harville could not keep out of his face the emotion that flooded up in him.

"You might have got killed, you crazy boy," he said reproachfully. "I never heard of a madder business than that of last night."

"Or of one that came out better," Larry added smiling at him.

"Thanks to the good Lord." The colonel knew that he owed his son an apology for the thoughts he had concerning his pluck. But he was not going to make it. Some things were better unsaid. The boy had come through fine. Which was all that mattered. Larry would understand without a lot of words.

"You'll be glad to know that we are shet of the Labreus,"

he said. "The whole caboodle of them — all that are left — rode south last night. Headed for Texas I reckon. One of these days the rangers there will clean them up." He looked down at his son a gleam of mirth in his eyes. "They're paid to run down scalawags. You cain't do it all, boy — you and Hal and Jes' Tolable. Unless you want to traipse to Texas for another fling at them."

Larry laughed. "Not I. Not ever again. I've had enough — too much. I won't complain if I never see a gun any more."

"That's fine." His father looked around the pleasant bedroom with approval. "Any complaint with the way the Logans are treating you?"

"Not yet. Are you taking me home now?"

"Mrs. Logan says no. You're to stay here till you are well. I gather you are their wounded hero."

Larry raised an imploring hand. "Please. I can get along fine without that kind of talk."

Maxwell had been sure his boy would take it that way. A right-thinking man could be happy because in time of peril he had shown valor, but unless he was a coxcomb any reference to what he had done must embarrass him. He could not help knowing that in the background shadowing all bravery there is fear, without which there cannot be courage, and that in the case of an imaginative man the borderline between the two may be very close.

Downstairs the colonel met on the porch the two Logan women and Rod. The latter had just limped out, supported by a colored man, and was resting on two pillowed chairs.

He said, "I hope you won't mind my not rising, Colonel

Harville, account of this doggoned shoulder that still troubles me some."

"I hope it's doing well," Harville said.

"Fine." Rod laughed, taking the bull by the horns. "Looks like I won't have any Harvilles using me for a target either from now on. That boy of yores is a sure enough feud buster."

"Your brother Hal did his full share," the colonel mentioned. He added, in a burst of confession, "Fact is, I never did have my heart in it."

Rod was amused. He was a blunt man who usually said what he thought. "For a man whose heart wasn't in it you were shootin' mighty straight on the courthouse square that day," he said.

His mother was shocked. "Rod!" she reproved.

Maxwell Harville was smiling broadly. "That's all right, Mrs. Logan. We'll never get anywhere if we hush-hush this. Best way is to speak right out. I'm not sensitive about this any longer. I did wrong. Your son Hal and my boy Larry, with the help of these confounded Labreus, have brought me to my senses. Looking back on it now, I cain't see why I ever was such a fool."

Diane said, in her low throaty voice, "I think we're all very happy that it is over."

"All will now be quiet along the Potomac," Rod said. "We won't even have the Labreus to practice on."

Mrs. Logan shuddered. "I hope I never hear of them again."

"You'll hear of them, Mother," Rod predicted. "Gobbler Lige will be news until he has been killed." He added, vindictively, "I'd like another crack at him, for what he did to father."

"He and his gang will probably reach Texas, by lying up days and traveling nights," Harville hazarded. "But I don't think they will last long there. Like you, Mrs. Logan, I don't want to have any more truck with them."

Hal came out of the house with a message from his father. If he was surprised to see Colonel Harville he gave no sign of it.

"I read the other day that there is nothing new in life," Hal said. "The fellow that wrote it is daffy. When you and I shake hands that is new, Colonel."

"All one happy family," Rod murmured sardonically.

"Don't pay any attention to him, Colonel," Mrs. Logan said. "He is just as pleased as the rest of us, but doesn't like to admit it."

"That's right," Rod said. "I'll be joining the church at the next revival."

"I wish you meant it," Sallie Logan told him.

Hal gave his message. "Father isn't very fit just now, Colonel, but he asked me to tell you that with yore permission he will call on you in a few days."

Maxwell Harville's face lit up. He said there was nothing he would like more.

29

CHET DULL WAS SLEEPING the placid sleep of the righteous when he was awakened by the sound of a hoot owl. He did not come to full consciousness but remained in that nebulous land where one floats pleasantly on dreamy currents. The owl was persistent, and Chet reluctantly became aware that he was being signaled. This depressed him, for he knew who must be outside. He had thought he was through with the Labreus, and here they were back again. Whatever brought them, he knew that their return was bad news for Chet Dull.

He rose quietly from bed and pulled on the trousers lying beside it. For a moment he considered taking a pistol with him, but he gave up the idea. It would not do him any good. If the outlaws meant him any harm, which they probably did not, he would never get a chance to use it.

As he opened the door and slipped out, the hoot of the owl came again. It was from a clump of scaly-bark hickory trees in front of the cabin about fifty yards distant. Chet walked forward barefoot, his trousers held up by one suspender. He did not enjoy that walk. In the moonlight he was too easy a mark. When he reached the grove he breathed more freely.

Lige Labreu's voice was harsh and bitter. "What the hell kept you so long?" it demanded.

"I was asleep — woke up kinda slow," Chet explained. "What's wrong, Lige? Thought you would be sixty miles from here."

"Don't ask questions!" the Gobbler snarled. "We want grub — plenty of it — quick."

"Sure," wheedled Chet. "Whatever you say, Lige. You want me to bring it out? Or will you come in? Sue will fix you-all something hot if you want it thataway."

"Bring us first off what you have cooked. We're starved. And don't tell her who we are. Understand?"

Chet understood too well, though as yet he had no information as to what had occurred. Lige was in a vile temper, and when in that bilious mood he was always dangerous. As Dull shuffled back to the house, his mind was busy trying to figure out what had brought the outlaws back. He had heard that Craw was wounded, but that left two still missing. Of course they might be somewhere in the brush.

While Dull was packing into a basket cold biscuits, a slab of salt side meat, some corn bread and sweet potatoes, his wife's querulous voice inquired what was the matter. He shushed her.

"Don't wake the kids, old woman, and don't ask no questions. Git up and find that sack of peaches the young 'uns picked yesterday."

"Hit's them Labreus again," she charged, her heart heavy with dread. "I thought we were shet of them for good."

His harsh whisper warned her. "You don't know nothing. You ain't seen 'em or heerd of 'em. No matter who asks you."

Dull had made of her a household drudge, but he was her husband, the father of her children. Though she knew he was worthless, he was her man and she still clung to him. Fearfully, she watched him go out with the laden basket.

Except the peaches, there was nothing in it but leftovers. Lige was so unpredictable. At sight of the food remnants he might fly into a passion and . . .

Even to herself she did not complete the thought. Ever since the return of the Labreus after their escape from prison she had been badly worried. She knew her husband was trafficking with the outlaws. One day she had nailed down a loose plank in the floor. Next time she swept, the plank was loose again. Moved by curiosity and suspicion, she had investigated and found in the recess below a small sack filled with gold pieces. When she had tried to discuss this with Chet he had roughly told her to mind her own business.

But she could tell that he was disturbed in mind. Often he did not sleep well and was unusually irritable. She had lived with him too long not to know that he was afraid, both of Lige and of the men hunting him.

Chet explained to the fugitives that these scraps were all they happened to have cooked, but his old woman would fix them up with hot coffee, fresh biscuits, and ham and eggs if Lige would say the word. Brad thought that would be a good idea, but his father vetoed it. He did not want anybody except Dull to know of their return. In the morning Dull could buy supplies for them at the store, and after dark deliver them at the old Peters clearing. They would take with them now a Dutch oven, a fryingpan, and a coffeepot. He must make up some story for his wife about their disappearance. For one day, Lige said, he and the others could make out on squirrels they shot in the woods. He warned Chet not to act so as to stir up suspicion when he was buying the stuff, and to make sure nobody was following him when he crossed the ford to reach the Peters cabin. He was to come on horseback and not bring a wagon.

He would be mighty careful, Chet promised.

"You'd better," Lige threatened. "I hate to have to gobble over you, Chet. Nobody has seen us yit, so we'll know if any posse comes a-huntin' us that you must of talked."

As soon as the fugitives had ridden away Sue Dull drew her husband out of the house for a talk. They sat on a bench, lowering their voices almost to a whisper.

"I'm skeered, Chet," she said. "So air you. Do we have to do what Lige Labreu says? One o' these days they'll git him, and if we're mixed up with him they'll git you too." Bitterly, she added: "An' like as not Lige will git skeered you're betrayin' him and shoot you daown fust."

Dull was tired of carrying the burden alone. He threw up his hands and admitted he was just as much afraid as she. But what could he do?

He could skip out and go visit his brother at Pine Bluff for a couple of weeks, she said.

"An' if I did I wouldn't put it past Lige to burn this house daown with you an' the young 'uns in it," he answered hopelessly.

She murmured, her fear-haunted eyes on his, "You could tell Colonel Harville where at Lige is roostin'."

"I cain't tell what I don't know."

"You've fixed to meet up with him somewheres."

He retorted irritably, "Lige ain't nobody's fool. I couldn't git to him lessen I came alone. Soon as he found I was being followed I would be the fust one killed."

"Still, if you was to go to Colonel Harville and tell him — "

"Git that outa yore haid," he told her roughly. "Fust off, Harville has got no use for me. He told me that plain. Anyhow, what could he do? He hasn't had a hell of a lot of luck tryin' to hunt Lige daown. Would you expect him to put a regiment round our place to keep Lige from doing us a meanness?"

He rode over her suggestion more harshly because he had himself been dallying with the same thought. He had discarded it because the danger was too great. Lige was wary as a fox. He was not going to let himself be trapped by Dull as a decoy. If his suspicious mind found any basis for the belief that his cousin was betraying him he would rub out his spy at once. Moreover, Chet had no confidence that Colonel Harville would put himself out to protect him. He would use him, if he could, to get the Labreus, but it probably would not worry him much if in the process Dull came to grief.

30

AS TOM HARVILLE WALKED into the store he passed Mrs. Dull going out with a basket of groceries. Jud Holcomb beckoned him into his office.

"Something kinda queer," he said. "Chet was in an hour ago and bought quite a bill of goods. He got both coffee and sugar. Now Mrs. Dull gets another pound of Arbuckle and some sugar."

"Maybe Chet didn't go straight home and his wife doesn't know what he bought," Tom suggested.

"He headed for home," the storekeeper objected.

"Is it important?" Harville asked.

"I dunno. Probably not." Jud fired an apparently irrelevant question at the young man. "Where at is the Labreu gang?"

"I can tell you about some of them," Tom replied. "Hal Logan killed one and Jes' Tolable another. Craw's body was fished out of the ford this mo'ning with a bullet hole in the back of his head. Another of them was shot yesterday down on the White River and Sim Labreu was captured. That answer yore question?"

"I'm talkin' about the others."

"My guess is that Lige and what's left of his gang are holed up like foxes hoping to make a break to get away at night."

"Sure enough. But where?"

"You think they are near here and that Chet was buying for them?"

"I dunno. Might be. What else would explain the Dulls buying coffee and sugar twice the same day?"

Jud might be right, Harville thought. The outlaws had been surprised on the White River, and those who had reached their horses had lit out fast. They had headed toward Big Hollow, but had left the road at some unknown point. There was a chance that they might have slipped back to it during the night. But would not that be madness after having lost five of the gang already on account of having come to the Cache? Still, Lige did not have much choice. Posses were closing in on him from all sides. He might figure on taking refuge in the bottomlands for a day or two and then cutting across country to the Mississippi in the hope of getting a boat down to New Orleans.

"I'd better look into this, Jud," Tom decided.

He walked out of the store and glanced down the street. Mrs. Dull was still in sight several hundred yards distant. Tom untied his horse and swung to the saddle. Presently he drew up beside her and dismounted.

"Like to talk with you, Mrs. Dull," he said.

She looked at him sharply without stopping. "What you want to talk about?"

He walked beside her, leading his horse. "Let me carry the basket," he suggested.

"I'll carry it." She guessed what he had in mind and was both suspicious and frightened.

"It's very dangerous to have anything to do with the Labreus," he said, his voice gentle and friendly.

"Then you had better let them alone," she said stiffly.

"I mean it is dangerous to befriend them," he explained. "They are desperate criminals and are going to be destroyed. It would be a pity if any harm came to decent people on account of them."

"Are we decent folks?" she asked bitterly. "That ain't what Colonel Harville told Chet when he talked of settin' yore dogs on him."

"Father was annoyed because of the insulting proposal Lige Labreu sent him by Chet. This is too serious for us to hold grudges now. If Chet is taking food to these men he is likely to get into trouble."

"Who said he was taking food to them?" she demanded.

"I hope he isn't." Tom felt he could not let this drop without making her understand how serious the consequences might be. "It has struck twelve for the Labreus, Mrs. Dull. They are a bad, murderous lot. If it had not been for Hal Logan they would have tortured and killed my brother Larry. If it had not been for Larry, Major Logan would have been dead before now. Gobbler Lige is a terrible man."

"You don't need to tell me how bad he is," she cried, with weak violence. "I know. I'm skeered to death of him."

Tom's eyes rested on the gaunt, poorly nourished woman. A faint flush had whipped into her sallow cheeks. He had never given her a second look before, but he realized now with surprise that she must have been pretty once. Maybe she had not always worn draggled clothes that hung on her like a sack.

Until this moment he had not considered her point of view. It would not have been important to him, since one has to contact unhappiness closely to sympathize with it. He saw she was living in fear. Dread was riding her thin shoulders heavily. She knew her husband was involved in helping the outlaws and that a sword was hanging over his red head. Tom guessed she was less afraid of the law than of Lige. The man was forcing Chet to help him just as he had compelled Mack Gillis, by holding a pistol at his heart. She knew of the sudden rages that swept the Gobbler. When Chet ceased to be of use, or if he fell under suspicion, he might be rubbed out ruthlessly. Just as Labreu's own son Craw had been. She did not have proof any more than

Tom did that Lige had fired the shot that killed Craw. But some one of the gang had done it, and surely not without orders from his father.

"If you are afraid of Lige hadn't you better join us, Mrs. Dull?" Tom said. "We'll look after you."

She shook her head. "You cain't. No use talkin', Mr. Tom. I'd rather you left me. If he heard of us being alone here he would git mad."

There was no use saying any more. The fear of Labreu was too deeply grounded in her. He had found out what he had come to learn. The outlaws were back in the Cache swamp.

"If you change your mind, come to us," he told her. "We'll do anything we can to help you. And if you give us information that will trap him, we'll remember it afterward."

"I got nothing to tell you," she answered. "I dunno where Lige is. Neither does Chet."

Her voice sounded stubborn, as if she felt she had talked too much.

Tom swung to the saddle and rode back to the store. Hal Logan was tying his horse to a post.

"Heard about the Labreu gang?" Hal asked. "About how they got jumped on the White River and one of them was killed?"

Tom nodded. "I've got later news even than that. Lige and what's left of the band are back in the Cache bottom."

Hal stared at him. "What makes you think so? Why would they come back again after the bad luck they had here?"

"Where could they go and be less looked for?" Tom

added briefly his reasons for thinking they were in the swamp.

"Looks like you and I are going to get another crack at them," Hal said, accepting Harville's reasoning.

"What we have to do first is check up on Dull. If this food is for the Gobbler he will have to deliver it somewhere."

They agreed that Dull would not move until after dark. He might have the wagon at home now or it might be hidden in the brush. The immediate job was to find him, then follow the wagon. Both of which had to be done without arousing suspicion.

Tom reported to his father what he had learned and the deductions he had made. The colonel neither accepted nor rejected his conclusions, but he agreed that they should be tested. At work of this sort he did not know anybody likely to do better than Shep Tolt. A messenger found him down by the bridge attending to his trotline and brought him to Rosemont.

31

COLONEL HARVILLE PUFFED at his pipe thoughtfully. He was not satisfied with the plan Tom had outlined.

"It's too simple, son," he objected. "I know Lige. He's as much fox as wolf. The old devil has his back to the wall. You can be sure he doesn't trust Chet any farther than he could throw a two-year-old by the tail. He has got to use him, but he is worrying for fear Chet will lead us to him. So he'll have a man watching the bayou to make sure nobody is following him."

Andy had an inspiration. "We don't need to follow Chet. What's the matter with us lying down in the wagon until we get to the meeting place?"

"There isn't going to be any wagon," Maxwell Harville said. "If Lige is in the swamp — and I'm inclined to think he is — his orders to Chet were to bring the food on horseback. I'd bet a bale of cotton against two bits that the old scoundrel thought of that before you did, Andy, and checked against it."

"Then what are we to do?" Tom wanted to know.

"Do like the Yanks did in the war. They cut us off from our supplies. We were starving. We had no horses to haul our cannon and mighty little ammunition. That whipped us."

"Lige has guns and horses. If Chet takes him in food — "

The colonel interrupted Tom. "You've put yore finger on the nub of it, son. Chet must not take him food. It's up to us to see he doesn't. Get him and bring him here."

"Mrs. Dull may have scared him, so that he has gone into hiding," Andy suggested. "After hearing about her talk with Tom he would know we would do something about it."

"Our job is to find him," his father said. "Before it gets dark. If we don't we must have men stationed at all the points where he could cross the bayou. I'll attend to that. You boys and Jes' Tolable run him down before he starts if you can."

"We'd better get going," Andy said. "It will be dark in another hour and a half."

Tom did not quite like this Fabian policy. He was afraid the outlaws would slip away from them. He hung back to ask another question. "Say we do starve them out. What's to hinder them from leaving by the other side of the swamp and not this way?"

"They would have to cross the whole state. Lige learned his lesson on the White River. He'll try to cut northwest through the unsettled country to the Tennessee line and from there to the river. If they can reach the Mississippi they will probably separate."

Shep Tolt agreed with the colonel. If they could break clean for thirty or forty miles, the outlaws would have a good chance to reach the river and escape. Once out of Arkansas they would not be likely to run into a posse any direction they turned.

Hal joined the riders at Big Hollow. Nobody in the village had seen anything of Dull since he had left with the provisions. When the four horsemen reached the Dull clearing the children told them that their father had left an hour earlier. They did not know where he had gone. The wagon was in the yard, but the food had been removed from it.

Mrs. Dull offered no more information than the children. "Oh, it's you again," she said to Tom, and set her mouth obstinately.

That she was worried the hunters could see, but she had evidently been told to say nothing.

"I see he took with him the food he bought," Tom said.

"What food?" she said sullenly. "If you-all had all these hungry mouths to fill you would know why he has to buy grub."

Shep rested his weight on the right stirrup and offered friendly advice in a slow drawl. "Now you got to be reasonable, Sue. Chet is in a tight. He cain't git that stuff to Lige. The bayou is being watched at all the crossings. If he hain't careful he'll be killed off. We got the dead wood on what's left of the Labreus. This yere country is gonna stomp them out like they were rattlesnakes. You kin still save Chet. Mebbe tomorrow hit will be too late."

Her face worked piteously. She did not need to be convinced of what Shep had just said. She knew it to be true.

"Lige will do us a turrible meanness if Chet don't—don't—"

"He won't git the chance. We'll move you-all up to that empty cabin on the colonel's plantation ontil we have got the Labreus. Lige won't know you are there, an' if he did he wouldn't dass come near."

She broke down, and between her sobs told them that Chet might be in the hickory slash below the Gillis place, if they hurried and reached him before he started.

Andy promised to send two colored boys with a wagon to move her and the children this evening. She could start packing up the beds, cooking utensils, and food.

It was already twilight. Soon darkness would cover the land. They rode at a canter, to reach Chet while he was still in the slash.

"He will prob'ly be waitin' daown in the gully under the chinquapin tree," Tolt said. "We'll tie back a ways and slip forward, coming at him from both sides of the gully."

"Fine, if one of the Labreus isn't there with him," Hal said dryly.

"I don't reckon any of them will be on this side of the bayou in the daytime," Tolt said. "That wouldn't be smart, 'count of someone mebbe seeing him."

After tying their horses the party divided, Tolt and Andy approaching the gully from the far side and the others from the near.

Chet was taken completely by surprise. He was lying on a grassy spot fifteen or twenty yards from the tree when Shep Tolt's drawling advice startled him.

"Take it easy, Chet. We got the dead wood on you. Reach for yore gun, an' you'll be toting half a pint of lead, by gravy."

Dull leaped to his feet. He made a gesture to draw and thought better of it. His dismayed glance jumped from one bank to the other. He knew he was caught.

"That ain't no way for to talk, Jes' Tolable," he protested, a whine already creeping into his voice. "Hit ain't friendly."

Andy moved down to join the man and disarmed him. "Don't try to pull any guff on us, Chet," he warned. "Yore game is up. We know who was to get the grub on that loaded horse."

The trapped man did not waste an instant changing fronts. "Lordy, boys, I'm shore glad you got here in time. I been sweatin' blood on account of Lige. He done told me he 'lowed to gobble over me if I didn't holp him. I would of come to you-all, but I knowed he would take hit out on the woman an' young 'uns."

"I don't suppose he paid you two bits," Hal jeered.

Again Chet made a swift decision. There was no use denying what they could prove. "Yes, sir, he did. Fact is, if I hadn't tooken the money he would of suspected me right off. Every time I see him I'm skeered he'll kill me."

"Where do you meet him?" Hal demanded.

"Daown at the old Peters deadenin'. I hain't seen him but three times."

"At what hour were you to show up with the food tonight?"

"Soon as it got real dark."

"One of the gang will be watching the bayou at the place where you were to cross," Tom said.

"Tha's right, Mr. Tom. Lige don't leave no loopholes."

"Why don't we go and comb the scoundrels out?" Hal asked impatiently. "There are only three of them."

"They wouldn't be there, no matter how careful you-all crept up on them," Chet said. "Lige won't be at the cabin but back in the canebrake somewheres. Soon as he suspicioned everything wasn't right they would skedaddle."

Jes' Tolable agreed. They would be wasting their time on a wild goose chase.

They took Chet with them to Hillcrest and locked him up in a cabin that had formerly been in the slave quarters. The major thought it best to have him guarded until the Labreus had been captured. Perry Logan was sitting on the porch with the other two convalescents, Rod and Larry. Tom and Andy did not stay more than a few minutes. They had to make arrangements for bringing the Dull family to Rosemont.

Larry asked the major a question. "The Labreus will

have to get food, sir. What will they do?"

"I'm wondering about that," Logan answered. "They will raid some place, of course. But where?"

"They have to get out of the swamp at once, before posses cover every outlet," Larry said. "Tonight they will make a try, don't you think, sir?"

"Probably."

"Lige will want food for several days, since it won't do for him to be seen at any farmhouse between here and the line. The best place to be sure of getting plenty is at Holcomb's store. Nobody sleeps there at night. It would be easy to break in."

The major looked at him with sharp approval. "Young man, you have a head on you. Of course, that is what he will do — and soon."

"If you think so, we had better be ready for them," Hal said. "Colonel Harville has guards all along the bayou. There aren't many available men left."

Larry said, "Count me one."

Mrs. Logan had just come out to the porch. "You're not well enough to go."

"I'm all right," Larry said. "Thanks to your kind care of me."

"I'm going," Rod mentioned. "I can ride a horse well as anybody."

"Now Rod," his mother chided, and knew protest was no use. Her sons were like that. Perhaps all men were. When it came to action they went their own way. She suspected that even Larry, gentle and considerate though he was, would do as he thought best, once his mind was made up.

Sallie Logan had become very good friends with the young man. Her sharp eyes had discovered that her daughter was in love with him and that he was not indifferent to Diane. She was pleased. It was her opinion that Larry would make an excellent husband. From the viewpoint of a rather poverty-stricken South he was quite well off. He had the pleasant manners of the English, had traveled widely, and was well educated. What was of more importance, he had character. All the Harvilles had that, but in this youngest son it expressed itself with charming modesty. With a girl like Diane his consideration for others and his generosity of mind would count greatly. She realized that Major Logan — and probably Colonel Harville too — would feel such a marriage unsuitable in view of the past. There would be initial embarrassments. But both of them, she felt sure, would accommodate themselves to it in time. Her sons liked Larry, though they had not ever thought of him as a possible brother-in-law. She had watched their opinion of him change. At first they had been scornful of his timidity. He had no zest for danger and was all for peace. But they had come to respect him, because when the pressure was on he would take any chance necessary.

When they went into the house Diane was at the piano. Hal helped the major take the stairs to his room and Sallie Logan followed. Rod went to the stable to order his horse saddled. Larry walked into the parlor.

Diane was singing the song "County Guy," from Scott's *Quentin Durward*, and she did not notice the entrance of the young man. Her voice had not been given much training, but she sang with sweetness and feeling.

"Ah, County Guy, the hour is nigh,
The sun has left the lea,
The orange flower perfumes the bower,
The breeze is on the sea."

Larry knew she was more romantic than he. It was in the blood of Southern girls brought up in the semi-feudal tradition of plantation life, and it had been encouraged by the attitude of the men, who put their women in a rarefied atmosphere apart from the realities of life. Though Larry was no poser and had very little in him of the Byronic hero or the cavalier of Scott, he was not above dramatizing himself to suit her fancies. He moved forward quietly.

"The lark, his lay who trill'd all day,
Sits hushed his partner nigh;
Breeze, bird, and flower, confess the hour,
But where is County Guy?"

Her voice died away. She sat still, her fingers on the keys, her eyes fixed on some imaginary scene far away. Larry put an arm around her shoulders and she looked up, startled at his presence.

This was the time and the place, he thought. The song, a very popular one just then, was familiar to him. He sang the last stanza, revised to suit the occasion.

"The star of Love, all stars above,
Now reigns o'er earth and sky;
For high and low the influence know—
And here is County Guy."

Color flooded her cheeks. She felt very shy, self-conscious, and at the same time tremulously happy.

Larry lifted her from the piano stool and took her in his arms.

32

LIGE LABREU AND CAD MILLER lay in the canebrake behind the Peters clearing. Chet ought to have shown up hours ago. They needed food, and their tempers were on edge.

"Looks like Chet has done thrown us down," Cad complained. "I'm so doggoned hungry my belly button and my backbone ain't more than three inches apart." He added, irritably, "You don't reckon they could of got Brad."

"Brad is all right," his father said, slapping a mosquito that had lit on his cheek. "He's hidden daown clost to the ford. Long as there is a chanct Chet will come Brad has to stay there to check up."

"I always did think Chet was a slippery cuss," Cad said.

The steel-trap mouth of Lige tightened. A red-hot devil of malice burned in his eyes. "If he's sold us daown the river I'll shore pump lead into him. He never did have the nerve of a rabbit."

"I ce'tainly made a hell of a mistake when I threw in with you-all at Fort Smith. If I'd stayed in jail old Judge Parker couldn't of give me more than five years. But I had to bust out with you like a dawggoned fool." Cad spoke with bitter hopelessness. He believed he was near the end of his trail. Everything had gone wrong with them ever since they had reached the Cache bottom.

It was well past midnight when Brad joined them. He had seen nothing of Chet or of anybody else.

"We cain't stay here and starve," Lige decided. "It's neck meat or nothing with us. We'll make a break right now to get away."

"How about grub?" Brad asked.

"We'll hold up Holcomb's store on the way and pick up enough food to last us till we reach the river," his father said. "If we're lucky we'll make it fine."

"And if we're not we'll turn up our toes to the daisies," Cad grumbled.

The hunted men struck the bayou first at what was known as the lower ford. Before the horses had waded in twenty yards a bullet flung up a spurt of water just ahead of Lige. A second rifle joined the attack. Lige swung his horse round and made for the sand pit he had just left. The other two splashed back after him hurriedly while the guns roared again from the opposite bank. The outlaws found shelter in the canebrake.

"If it hadn't been dark they would of got one of us shorely," Brad said angrily. "They act like we're a bunch of wolves."

Lige knew that all the fords and the bridge were guarded, but his hunters could not have gathered men enough to line the bayou. The scudding clouds above were heavy. They would have to pick a place where they would be least expected and swim across.

They rode up along the bayou and stopped at a deep wide stretch with a steep bank on the farther side. The horses would have to swim almost the entire distance. If there were guards stationed at this point they had not a chance to get over alive. Even if it were not protected they would have some trouble getting the horses up the bluff.

Lige waited till the moon was completely obscured. Large gum trees lined both banks and threw shadows over the water.

"Let's go," Lige growled, and put his mount to the sloping bank.

"To hell, I reckon," Miller said, with an uneasy laugh.

Unmolested, the horses swam across. They fumbled along the shore to find a spot where the bank was not too steep to climb. Lige's mule clambered up. The others joined him.

Cad and Brad tore down a fence, and they moved along the rows of a cornfield to the woods beyond. They crossed a road into the brush and cut over rough prairie and hickory slashes till they reached the outskirts of the village. By way of a pasture they came to a lane leading to the business street.

The outlaws saw no sign of life when they rode into Big Hollow. They did not know that a pair of eyes were watching them intently around the corner of a house across the street from Holcomb's store. Not a light showed in the village. To make as little noise as possible the fugitives walked their horses down the dusty street. They dismounted and tied at a hitch rack behind the store.

Lige peered through a window into the dark interior.

Apparently the place was deserted as he had expected. Jud Holcomb lived in a frame house two hundred yards distant. With the butt of his revolver Lige tapped gently on a pane and broke the glass. He reached in and undid the latch. Very quietly he raised the frame and eased himself over the sill. His son followed him. The Gobbler struck a match and looked around. It was a general store in which everything was sold from molasses to horse collars. For many years he had not been in the building. The match flickered out.

"Stay where you are at," he told his son. "I'll unbolt the back door fust off. We might have to light out in a hurry."

He soft-footed through the darkness to the door and opened it. "Everything all right?" he asked Miller.

"So far," Cad answered. "But I'm sure goosey. Sooner we git outa here the better pleased I'll be."

"We won't be long," Lige promised.

He moved back between the counters trying to locate the food he wanted.

"Grub is over here," Brad said in a whisper.

Miller tiptoed into the building. "There's a lamp on the wall here. How about lightin' it?"

"Someone might see it and git to wonderin'," Brad said. He struck a match. "Cut off a slab of that cheese, Cad."

"And then git back to the horses," Lige ordered.

Miller sawed off a hunk of cheese in the darkness from a whole one resting on a wooden support. He had not finished when Brad stumbled over a keg of eight-penny nails and overturned it. The contents poured over the floor in a noisy stream.

"Goddlemighty, what's the matter?" Miller cried, his nerves jumpy.

Lige ripped out a savage oath. "You trying to wake the dead, Brad?" he snarled.

"I cain't see in the dark," Brad flung back at him angrily. He had barked his shins and they hurt.

Apparently he had awakened somebody. They heard sounds from the floor above and presently footsteps. Holcomb appeared at the head of the stairway running to the second story. He was in his nightshirt and barefoot, but he held a revolver in his hand.

"Get out of my store," he ordered.

Brad fired and Holcomb clutched at the railing to steady himself. The sound of his weapon came almost like an echo of the first shot. Young Labreu staggered against the counter. A bullet had ploughed through his jaw.

Holcomb's knees buckled and he pitched forward. He half slid, half rolled down the treads. Supported by the counter, Brad fired at the body of the storekeeper as it bounced down.

"Stop shooting, you dawggoned idjit," Lige growled. "You'll have the whole country here." He lit a small wall lamp. "Bring that gunny sack, Brad. We got to git a move on."

Staring at Brad, Miller cried, "Lawdy, he plugged you."

Lige was reaching for a sack of coffee. He swung round and saw blood streaming from his son's face.

"Git grub into the sack, Cad," he ordered. "I'll look after Brad."

He took the bandanna from his neck and tied up the

broken jaw, while Miller stuffed into the sack coffee, flour, beans, and a ham. From a show case near the front of the store Cad took several sacks of smoking and plugs of chewing tobacco.

"Let's go," Lige snapped.

They hurried from the building, to face a staggering surprise. Their horses were gone.

Lige ran forward to the road. At the end of the street, two hundred yards away, Lige caught a glimpse of them just turning off the road. They were out of sight before he could even fire a shot.

"Go git 'em, Cad," Lige cried. "Without 'em we're gone."

Miller started on the run.

A light came on in a house set behind the main street. Excited voices reached the outlaws. A bullet whistled past them and buried itself in the log wall of the store. They drew back along the shadowed wall to the rear of the building.

"What's keepin' Cad?" Brad asked fretfully. "If he don't git here soon — "

Two shots, one just after the other, boomed down the street cañon. They heard the slap of running feet. Cad's anxious voice cried, "Where at are you-all?"

Lige answered, not too loudly, and Miller joined them.

"Didn't even see the horses," he gasped. "Fellows with them must of lit out on the run. This town is on the shoot. We gotta git out quick."

Already Lige was wading across an empty lot covered with dog-fennel. The others followed. They climbed a stake-and-rider worm fence into a cotton field and ran crouching between two rows. On the yonder side of it was a small stream on the banks of which pecan trees were growing. Already Brad found traveling difficult. He began to lag.

His father dropped back to hearten him. "We're gonna hole up at the Flynn place," he said. "Nobody ever goes there. Hit's supposed to be haunted. We kin lie up there till you're strong enough to travel. We'll rustle up some horses."

Brad said "Fine," but the word came from a man empty of hope. They were afoot, and the whole country was roused against them. He recalled with a shudder what his father had done to Craw.

They had escaped without pursuit. Nobody had seen which way they had come. Lige held the party at the brook long enough to wash and dress as best he could the wound.

"They trapped us," Miller said morosely. "They must of figured we would try to git food at the store. If I had my sights on yore cousin Chet I shore would drill him."

Lige promised that they would be all right at the Flynn place. Nobody would think of looking for them there.

33

AS LARRY RODE beside the Logan boys to Big Hollow his mind was full of the girl he had left behind. She had promised to marry him if he could get her father's consent.

Just now he was filled with the faith that would move mountains, but he did not feel too sure that Perry Logan would see this his way. He was a stiff-necked old fellow, and he might take a lot of persuading.

Nearly all the men of the village had been drafted into service by Colonel Harville and were guarding the crossings of the bayou. The three young men found Holcomb at home. He was glad to learn from them that they intended to spend the night at Big Hollow. While he did not really expect a visit from the Labreus, it was possible they might slip past the cordon of watchers and come this way.

The idea of Larry that Lige might burglarize his store to get some food came to the merchant with a shock. But when he considered it this seemed reasonable, providing the outlaws could get this far. He decided to spend the night on a cot he sometimes used when he worked late figuring accounts. It was upstairs, on the second floor. If the Gobbler tried to break in he could fire down at the bandits from one of the windows.

Larry advised him very strongly to do nothing of the kind. The outlaws were desperate men, with their backs to the wall. Holcomb had better stay out of it and let younger men do the job. But the merchant was stubborn. It was his store. He was not going to let a bunch of scurvy cutthroats rob it without lifting a hand. Under persuasion he promised to keep from sight until those outside could take a hand.

"We're taking a long shot anyhow," Hal said, dismissing the matter. "Chances are that Lige won't ever show up in Big Hollow."

The young men made the office of Dr. Watkins their headquarters for the night. The doctor himself was out helping guard the ford.

They scouted the village and the roads leading to it, sometimes in a group and again individually. Rod found that he had overestimated his strength and retired to the darkness of the office until such time as he might be needed. Occasionally the others returned to him and reported no enemy activity as yet. The hours dragged monotonously and the heat of their enthusiasm died. What had at first appealed to them as a promising adventure was turning into a bore. But none of them suggested giving up the watch.

When the two younger men wandered down the main street for the twentieth time Larry's watch told him it was two o'clock. He was pretty well fagged and he sat down to rest on a bench in front of a cobbler's shop opposite the Holcomb store.

Hal grinned at him. "Take it easy, boy," he said. "Looks like I won't need any help to tackle all the Labreus that show up tonight."

"Too bad my poor guessing has robbed us all of a night's sleep," Larry replied.

"You didn't rob me of any," Hal answered. "If I weren't here I would be covering the bayou with the others. Anyhow, a fellow can't be right all the time. You hit a pretty good average." He waved a hand and wandered down the road.

Left to himself, Larry leaned back and let his thoughts drift to his sweetheart. Presently he fell into a light doze. From this he came awake with a jerk. The sound of horses' hoofs reached him. Jumping up, he slipped behind the shop and peered around the corner. Three horsemen emerged from the darkness. There was not light enough for recognition. They might be some of his father's men on patrol, or they might be the outlaws. The riders left the road and passed behind the Holcomb store. From the faint sounds that drifted to him he judged they were tying their mounts at the rack.

He waited, uncertain what was best to do. A voice might tell him who they were. Intently, he listened. He heard something like the tinkle of falling glass.

Larry decided to find Hal. With that in mind he soft-footed down the alley. After covering fifty yards he stopped. Why not cross the street, slip back in the shadow of the buildings, and see what he could find out before reporting to young Logan? Very likely these men were not desperadoes but friends.

The moon was under a cloud as he tiptoed through the dust to the opposite pavement. He passed between two buildings and came into the open lots behind them. While he was edging toward the store close to the walls, he thought, I'm being a fool again. His throat was as dry as if coated with lime. His hands were clammy.

From the shadow of the nearest store he looked across a vacant lot to Holcomb's. Three horses were hitched at a rack. No, one of them was a mule. Lige Labreu rode a mule. A window in the side of the building was broken. Through it he saw a match flicker. It lit for a second the face of a man — a crafty, evil face. An icy rope tied the watcher's stomach into a knot. Those inside were the Labreu gang.

At precisely that instant a dangerous suggestion flitted through his mind. If he could steal their mounts the bandits would be afoot and helpless. He rejected it violently. What he must do was escape and tell the Logan boys of his discovery. If he fooled around here he would be trapped.

Larry drew back — and stopped. The whisper was in his brain again. The hitch rack was not more than twenty yards. The animals would be tied by slipknots to ensure haste in leaving. In five seconds he could gather the reins, mount, and be off. *If he were not instead lying dead in the dust.*

He told himself he was crazy. If he tried it he would need both hands and would have to leave his rifle here. He put the gun down very gently and found his legs were too shaky to carry him forward. He drew a deep breath. Power flowed back into his body. A second later he was tugging at the nearest rein. He ducked under the animal's head and freed the mule. The third knot stuck. He had the other two reins in his left hand and he had to work the knot out of the leather.

His feet were just settling into the stirrups when there came a crash from inside the building that almost unnerved him. He thought at first that he had been shot. The horse he was riding went into the air. The other reins were straining his wrist and arm socket. Fortunately the animals plunged forward together.

Two guns sounded, almost at the same time. Another roared. He looked back, and was amazed to see nobody. They were not shooting at him.

Gradually he gained some control over the animals. He guided them across an empty lot and into the road. Somebody called to him to stop. It was Hal. He shouted an answer, but could not check the led horses. Over his shoulder he cried to Logan to look out for the Labreus.

Larry swung off the road to the left into a lane. The galloping horses slowed to a canter and then to a trot. The thought was urgent in the boy's mind that he must get back to help the Logans. The brothers were cut off from each other, with the outlaws between them. To him came the whine of a rifle shot, and a few moments later two more. His friends might be in desperate need of him. He must get rid of the animals and return to them.

The lane ran into a road on the other side of which was an enclosed space. He caught a glimpse of white markers and knew this was the Big Hollow graveyard. The gate was open. He passed through it, dismounted, and freed the mule and one horse. After closing the gate he pulled himself to the saddle of the third mount and headed for the village.

He had reached the first scattered houses before he remembered that he was not armed. Abruptly he jerked the horse to a halt and left it in the nearest yard. Cautiously he cut across a vacant lot toward the Holcomb store. No doubt his rifle would still be lying where he had left it. There had been no shooting since he had left the graveyard. Very likely the Labreus were already getting away as fast as they could. But he could not tell in what direction and he might run into them.

By way of the cobbler's shop he arrived at the main street. There were lights in the store. He heard Rod's troubled voice and made out the words.

"We'll have to send for Dr. Watkins. Anybody know where he is posted?"

An old man's voice answered. "I reckon you'll find him at the ford. I heerd him an' Colonel Harville talkin'."

Larry walked into the store.

Hal cried, "Golly, I'm glad to see you. I thought maybe — " He did not finish the sentence.

"What did you do with their horses?" Rod asked, looking up from the wounded man whose thigh he was bandaging.

"Left two of them in the graveyard, the other at Pappy Lemon's place," Larry told him. "What about the Labreus? They got away, I suppose."

"Without their horses," Rod said. "Boy, you've done a good night's work. We'll soon run them down."

"They shot Jud Holcomb." Larry's gaze fastened on the unconscious man. "Is he — will he — ?"

"They hit him in the leg. He ought to make it, but we've got to get the doctor in a hurry."

"I'll go," Hal said. Grimly he pointed out to Larry bloodstains on the counter and drops on the floor.

"Jud must have hit one of them."

The store was filling up with old men, women, and boys. Larry reclaimed his rifle and Rod posted him in the street. Logan gave his own rifle to a seventeen-year-old boy and stationed him behind the store. There was one chance in a thousand the outlaws might return.

34

THE OUTLAWS REACHED the haunted house weary, depressed, and angry at one another. Lige Labreu was bitter at Cad Miller for not having guarded the horses better. He blamed Brad for stumbling over the nail keg and waking the storekeeper. Both of the younger men felt the Gobbler had brought the party to disaster by directing the flight to the Cache bottom instead of straight to Texas.

Brad was too ill and exhausted from loss of blood to have much energy left for recrimination, but the tempers of his father and Miller were worn to a razor edge, ready to cut loose at a word. Neither trusted the other at all.

It was while they were wolfing down a hastily prepared breakfast that Lige let slip the explosive word. He snarled an order to Miller to pass the coffee, tacking on an insulting phrase.

Cad shoved the pot at Labreu so suddenly that the hot liquid splashed over the older man's hand. In a fury Lige jumped to his feet, but before he could draw a revolver from its holster Miller's .45 had him covered. They glared at each other, their cold hard eyes clashing. Neither of them spoke. The Gobbler knew that in all his turbulent, treacherous life he had never been nearer death. Miller had given plenty of proof that he was a ruthless killer. A crook of his finger would be enough.

Brad flung out a biting protest. "Harville will like it fine if you fools do his job for him," he cried.

Lige talked for his life, suavely, in a wheedling voice.

"Brad is right, Cad. I reckon I'm a bit jumpy, what with him being wounded and all. We been always good friends, you an' me. No sense in us fussin', jest on account of being in a kinda jam. We got to hang together, no two ways about that."

It was running through his mind that he would have to deal with Miller soon, but not now. In a day or two he would shoot him in the back when he was not looking.

Cad knew that Brad was right. They might have to fight their way out of this, and two men were better than one. He laughed sourly, his mind seizing on a word Lige had used.

"They ain't a-going to give us a chance to hang together. What they aim to do is shoot us down like a pair of painters soon as they find us. Onless you use a heap more sense than you been showing. Far as gettin' sore at you goes, I don't 'low to take orders from you or anybody else. Lay off'n me, if you know what's good for you."

The gargoyle grin on the face of Lige was false as Satan. "After all we been through together, Cad, you an' me don't want to have any trouble. It wouldn't make sense. We got to be reasonable. Fust thing is to rustle some horses before it gits too light. Then we'll lie holed up here till night and burn the wind outa this neck of the woods. That's how it shapes up to me."

Miller grumbled that he was not looking for any more trouble. He had plenty on his lap right now. It was jim-dandy to talk about getting horses, but he would like to know where.

He pushed the revolver back into the holster, but kept his icy agate eyes on Labreu.

"There's a fellow named Bronson raises a li'l cotton and corn on a clearing about a mile from here," Lige said. "He's got to have horses or mules. 'Course they will be work stock, but we cain't be choosy right now. What say we mosey daown and borrow what he has got?"

Light was beginning to break in the eastern sky when they started. Their way led them close to the walnut tree where Lige, fifteen years before, had hanged Flynn and left his body dangling in the air. Labreu was a thick-skinned ruffian with little imagination, but he felt a cold shiver run down his spine. For a moment he thought he actually saw there the twitching body of the carpetbagger, a triumphant grin on the sly, sardonic face. Flynn was getting his revenge at last on the Labreu gang, even if it was too late to do him any good. Except Lige, all of those who had tortured him were dead, and the race of the Gobbler was running out. One of his sons was dead, another lying wounded in the haunted house, and the third on the way back to Fort Smith to be hanged. A score of hunters were closing in on Lige himself for the kill.

He pushed the dread to the back of his mind and began to talk of the good times they would all have with the girls of New Orleans. Miller looked at him, contempt and hatred in the smoky eyes. He guessed that Labreu was whistling over his own grave to keep up his courage.

In the corral behind the Bronson barn they found a swaybacked mare and a bony white mule of uncertain age. After a swift glance sizing them both up, Miller said bluntly that he would take the mule.

"Anything you say, Cad," Lige agreed. When the time of final decision came he was not going to do his arguing with words. "We'll git another horse somewheres tonight after we have started."

In one of the stalls of the barn a cow was tied. The outlaws found only one saddle, one with a broken stirrup leather tied together by a string. Cad put it on the mule. His companion's narrowed eyes glittered, but he made no objection.

"I kin fix some gunny sacks into a saddle for Brad," he said, and picked up three to take with them.

A boy's voice sounded. He was coming to the barn from the house through the dog-fennels, a milking pail in his hand, and he sang a ballad that just then was having a great vogue in the South:

"*Jesse had a wife. She's a lady all her life,*
And the children they were brave;
But the dirty little cowards who shot Johnny Howard,
They have laid Jesse James in his grave."

Lige drew his .45 and crouched. From his throat came a snarling sound that was a threat. Miller stood at his right, half a step behind him.

"Put back that gun," the younger man ordered. "You ain't a-going to kill the boy an' rub out our last chance."

The Gobbler choked back his fury. He had no choice but to obey. In swinging round to fire at Miller he would lose a half second or more, and during that short space of time the other could pump two bullets into his heart.

"If we leave him here he'll rouse his pappy an' they'll guess where we're at," Lige whispered angrily.

"We'll take him with us and turn him loose later," Miller

snapped. "Shet yore mouth. Here he is."

The boy's song stopped abruptly. He stared, open-mouthed, at the two men in the shadows of the stalls.

"Take it easy, bub," warned Miller. "We don't 'low to hurt you none, if you keep quiet. The idee is that we're borrowin' these two sacks of bone till we kin find something better to ride."

The youngster still goggled at them, his startled eyes big as walnuts. He was a barefoot, freckle-faced lad of about fourteen, thin and sallow. The Adam's apple in his throat jerked up and down in alarm.

"But — you — you— "

"You done guessed it right, son," Miller nodded. "This yere friendly gent with me is Lige Labreu. We got to take you with us for a spell, but you act nice an' everything will be jest fine."

The boy began to cry.

"I'd better pistol-whip him," Lige murmured.

"You won't touch him," Miller retorted roughly. "The boy is my rabbit foot."

"If you take the mule Pappy cain't cultivate the corn," whimpered the boy.

"Don't worry none about that," Miller comforted. "He kin do it tomorrow after you have brought the mule back to him."

"Shore enough," Lige added, with his evil grin.

Miller had lived too long with Labreu not to know that this feigned submissive agreement was dangerous. The man was waiting for an opportunity. Until the moment when they separated forever Miller did not intend to stop watching him for a single second. The younger man meant to see the boy was released safely. Though he was never to know it, that care for the lad's life saved his own.

The boy sat behind him as they rode back to the haunted house. His teeth were chattering with fear, but he had a queer sense of comfort in Miller's presence. The man had not let Labreu hit him with the pistol. He had promised that he would not be harmed. Bobby Bronson, riding with his arms around the thick body of the outlaw, felt sure of his goodwill. Of the man astride the sway-back mare he was desperately afraid. All his life the name of Lige Labreu had been a word to terrify naughty children. Nothing stood between him and the Gobbler's violence except the friendliness of the sturdy scoundrel who was protecting him.

They rode single file through a grove of saplings, Labreu leading the way. He would rather have been in the rear, but he was building up a pretence of restored amity. Miller drew up to him when they emerged into a few acres of prairie ground. Lige pulled up the mare and turned to speak. The sky fell in on him. He found himself sinking through space.

"You — killed him," the boy gasped.

"Not Lige," Miller said, looking down at the lax body his rifle barrel had knocked from the mare. "But he'll be dead long enough for us to git away. He was 'lowing to kill us both off, boy. Only I was the fustest to cut loose."

He headed into the brush and rode steadily for half an hour before he stopped.

"Git off," he told the boy.

Bobby slid to the ground. He began to cry. "Don't shoot me, mister," he pleaded.

"Stop bawlin'," the bandit ordered impatiently. "Didn't I done tell you I wouldn't hurt you? Git this right, kid. I saved yore life. Lige was bound and determined to finish you off."

"Yes, sir," the boy agreed. "I'm a heap obliged."

"Mebbe you are. I dunno." Miller looked at him, face hard and set. "You kin run home to yore folks. Turn about is fair play, ain't it? If you want to help me escape you got a chance. Don't tell about me. Jes' say you slipped away from Lige when he wasn't lookin'. 'Course you know now he's holed up at the haunted house. You must of guessed that. Act like all three of us are there. By the time they have got Lige I'll be a long way on my road."

Bobby promised. He wanted to say something about the mule but the outlaw forestalled him.

"I'll turn this critter loose soon as I git a remount," he said. "About tomorrow hit will be home again."

"Yes, sir." Bobby could not find words to express what he wanted to say. He repeated himself. "I'm a heap obliged. I—I hope you git away all right."

"I hope so too." Miller laughed grimly without mirth. "Mebbe I'm a fool for letting you go, but—"

He waved a hand quickly. "On yore way, boy."

The outlaw rode into the brush. Bobby never saw him again. Neither did anybody else in that district. He must have reached the river safely. Probably he boarded a boat going down to New Orleans, and from that town pushed westward to Texas.

Years later a man who had been a witness against Miller at his preliminary hearing in Judge Parker's court met a cowboy in a saloon at Lampasas. They came face to face and stood staring at each other.

" 'Lo, Cad," the witness said. "Glad to meet you. Hope you don't hold any grudge because — "

The cowboy interrupted him sharply. "My name's Ed Hunter. I never saw you before."

Abruptly the man in chaps wheeled from the bar, strode out of the building, and walked to the hitch rack outside. A moment later he was galloping out of town.

35

WHEN BILL BRONSON caught sight of his son on the path leading to the house his anxiety flashed to anger.

"Where in billy-be-damn you been?" he demanded. "I'm gonna wear you to a frazzle for this monkey trick."

The boy began to cry. "I been with — with Lige Labreu," he sobbed. "They come here to git the stock an' took me with them."

The father's face was a picture of amazement. Of his son's story the most astonishing feature was that Bobby had escaped while Lige and one of his men were having a fight.

Inside of an hour armed men began to converge toward the haunted house. They did not go too near. Shots from inside warned them that the bandits were on the alert.

Colonel Harville took charge of the attackers. His sons

Andy and Tom were with him. As more men kept reaching the scene he put a tight cordon around the house. Larry and the Logan boys did not share in the fight. They were all sound asleep at Hillcrest making up for the wakeful night at Big Hollow. Larry never regretted this, but when Rod and Hal learned they had missed the wind-up they were considerably annoyed.

Harville knew he could storm the Flynn house by sheer numbers, but he wanted to avoid casualties on his side. The house was on a wooded knoll, the timber on one side running down to the lower land to the left. Sharpshooters worked their way up through the grove to within seventy yards of the house. From here they made a dash to the dilapidated barn. By means of crevices in the logs they could see through the empty oblongs where the windows had once been. Jes' Tolable's muzzle loader commanded the stairway leading to the second story.

Desultory firing continued all morning. At times the crackle of rifles was close as that of a bunch of firecrackers; again there were periods when there would be only one or two explosions in a quarter of an hour. It was midafternoon that Shep Tolt's long rifle sent a bullet tearing through the body of a man trying to slip down from the upper story. The fellow plunged over the railing into the stair well like a swimmer diving into a pool. Brad hit the floor already dead.

Occasionally a shot from the house gave warning that at least one defender was in action.

Tom proposed to his father that they charge the house. "There cain't be more than one or two alive after the way we've peppered the house," he said. "An' if he can stall us off till dark he may slip away. Or both of them, if there are still two."

"Not yet," his father said. "I've got another plan for smoking him out."

He had sent for a wagonload of hay. When it came the horses were unhitched and men pushed the wagon up to the summit of the knoll. Screened by the hay, they moved it down a slope through the grove toward the house. As a diversion four or five riflemen poured a furious fire into the building from the other sides.

Andy set fire to the hay. Those behind the wagon set it rolling down the incline. When it bumped into the wall the hay was already a mass of flames. The men ran for the cover of the nearest trees.

The flames licked at the dry walls and crept up to the roof. The roar of them increased as the fire leaped forward along the walls and the roof.

From the back door of the house a dip led to a gully which ran down into a deserted field. Tom guessed that it was here any of the gang still living would make the try to escape. Behind some blackberry bushes he and Mack Gillis crouched, their eyes fixed on the blazing house. If anybody was to come out of it alive he would have to move soon.

A man, bent low, ran out of the back door and made for the gully.

"Hit's the Gobbler," Gillis cried.

At least a half a dozen rifles must have been turned on him as he crossed the yard into the ditch, but none of them scored a hit. It was a dog-leg gully, and for a minute the men behind the blackberry bushes lost sight of him. He came into view at the apex of the angle, still running hard.

Tom shouted to him. "Hands up, Labreu. You're through."

The hunted man stopped. Harville was standing up, waist-high above the bushes. Still panting deeply, Lige threw his gun into position and fired. The bullet from Tom's Winchester ripped into his heart. They found the outlaw lying face down, the fingers of one hand clutching at the red soil of the eroded gully.

Shep Tolt was among the first to reach Harville and Gillis. He looked grimly down at the lax, prone body.

"He'll never gobble again," Shep said. "No regrets, I reckon."

Days later, in the cold ashes of the burnt house, only one body was found. There had been three of the bandits. One of them must have escaped. What had become of him remained a mystery until Bobby Bronson broke down and told his father the true story of his escape.

36

SALLIE LOGAN SAID to her husband, "I think you are going to have a caller this evening."

Major Logan was in the garden with his wife. He was carrying a basket for her while she clipped roses for the house. Her manner suggested to him that this news was more important than it sounded.

"You don't mean Colonel Harville?" he said.

"I mean his son Larry."

"He went home only two days ago," the major said.

"Two days are a long time at his age sometimes," she answered, smiling.

"What are you trying to tell me?" he asked.

"Something I think you already know, that he is in love with our daughter."

"I was afraid of that and I don't like it," he replied, after a silence. "How does Diane feel?"

"She is head over heels in love with him. There is nothing we can do about it, Perry. We may as well accept it."

Logan explained that he had nothing against the young man as an individual. On the contrary, he thought him a fine young fellow. But — he was a Harville. After more than a generation of bad feeling between the families so close a tie would be unnatural. He was afraid it would only bring unhappiness. Personally he was under very great obligations to the boy, both on Diane's account and on his own. He must acknowledge that, even though he opposed his suit.

He was surprised at the firmness of his wife's stand. Usually she took her lead from him, but he could see she had not the least intention of doing so now. She had always been against the feud, she told him in a torrent of words. It was wrong and it was silly. Larry had come from England and proved it to them. All the younger generation were ready to forget the enmity. Indeed, they had already done so. If any unhappiness arose on account of it, this would spring from the stiff foolish pride of their elders. She for one would not join in this.

Logan knew when he was beaten, and at last he realized his wife was right.

"Is this young man going to ask me tonight for our daughter's hand?" he asked.

"I think so. I had to prepare you."

There flashed to his mind a picture of the moment when in the outlaws' camp, lying there bound with torture and death ahead of him, he had caught sight of Larry's face. It swept away the frozen resentment of all the years.

"If you and Diane wish it that way I shall give my consent," he promised. "The truth is that I like him and approve of him. What Maxwell Harville's attitude will be I don't know."

She laughed happily. "Leave the colonel to me and Diane. We'll manage him."

When Larry came, the major was sitting on the porch. Fireflies in the garden lit the darkness of the velvet night. Diane was in the parlor playing the piano.

Larry said what he had come to say diffidently but firmly. To his surprise Major Logan was friendly and cordial.

"I think you must have told Diane of your feeling toward her," he said with one of his rare smiles. "She is in the parlor. Perhaps you had better tell her again."

Larry walked into the parlor — into a world that for a moment at least was flooded with music.